The Castration

by

William A. Carey and St. John Barrett

PublishAmerica

Baltimore

First printing

ISBN: 1-59129-394-4
PUBLISHED BY PUBLISHAMERICA BOOK PUBLISHERS
www.publishamerica.com
Baltimore

Printed in the United States of America

CHAPTER 1

D ay dawned clear and cold. The steps to the courthouse had been swept of last evening's dusting of snow, and a group of heavily bundled venire men stood in front of the outer brass doors. Those who lived outside the city and had not arrived in Portland the day before had risen long before dawn to drive icy roads from nearby farms and towns. Publicity of the impending trial had also brought a collection of would-be spectators, now talking in hushed tones below the courthouse steps.

When a deputy U.S. Marshall swung the heavy outer doors of the courthouse open at 8:00 a.m., the waiting venire men gratefully filed into the warm entrance hall and then to seats in an adjacent room where they would wait to be called into the courtroom itself. By then hundreds of near-frozen but hopeful spectators remained outside for their turn, fifty at a time, for admission to the spectator section of the courtroom.

At 9:00 a.m. a deputy marshal unlocked the oaken door to the courtroom, and the first fifty spectators filed in. The dignity of the courtroom was itself, without judge or bailiff, sufficient to hush its viewers. Built at the turn of the century, in a style that would not be duplicated today, it was carpeted in deep green throughout with dark wood paneling from floor to the twenty foot ceiling. The ceiling itself was crisscrossed by dark beams forming a series of squares, the surface of each painted red with gold leaf edging and bearing a green medallion at its center. The rail separating the public from the rest of the courtroom was of the same dark wood as the side panels. Beyond the rail stood two large, heavy oak tables for counsel, each surrounded by nine arm chairs with additional chairs pulled alongside the table furthest from the jury box to accommodate the surplus of attorneys and defendants who would be appearing in the case. The judge's bench was elevated some three feet above the level of the floor, with the clerk's enclosed desk in front, the witness box on the judge's right, the bailiff's table on his left, and the jury box, with seats for twelve jurors and two alternates, on his further right. On the bailiff's left was a side door through which prisoners could be brought and taken. Opposite was another side door through which the judge could enter and exit and through which the jurors would pass to and from the jury room. Almost against the wall opposite the jury box was a table and chairs for reporters, with additional chairs reserved for them just in front of the rail. A lectern for counsel's use in addressing the court stood directly in front of the clerk's enclosure.

"All rise!" As the sound of shifting feet subsided, the deputy U.S. marshal who served as courtroom bailiff continued intoning the ritual with which he had opened this court for the past sixteen years. "This honorable Court, the United States District Court for the District of Maine, the Honorable John Smith presiding, is now in session. All those having business before this honorable court draw near and be heard. God save the United States and this honorable court."

Judge Smith appeared through the side door in black robe and strode briskly to the bench.

"Good morning, gentlemen."

"Good morning, Your Honor."

"Any preliminary matters? If not, we will proceed to select a jury. Mr. Marshal, you may bring the venire."

The marshal, moving as briskly as had the judge, reopened the door through which Judge Smith had come and shepherded a string of some one hundred venire men to the seats that had been temporarily reserved for them just behind the rail. The judge welcomed them, thanked them for their service, explained the nature of the case, introduced the attorneys for the government, introduced each defendant and his counsel, inquired whether any juror had heard of the case and had any preconceived views on it, and inquired whether any were acquainted with any of the defendants or the lawyers. After excusing several, Judge Smith directed the clerk to draw the names of fourteen of those remaining to be seated in the jury box. The judge then proceeded to ask those in the box a series of questions that had been proposed to him by the attorneys.

"Are any of you of the view that persons of Sicilian extraction are more prone to violent crime than others? If so, raise your hand."

No response.

"Have any of you heard of the Mafia? If so, raise your hand."

All the prospective jurors but three raised their hands, and Judge Smith proceeded to question each separately.

"Mrs. Winters, what have you heard about the Mafia?"

"I've heard the Mafia is based in Sicily and runs a lot of organized crime in this country."

6

"How did you hear this?"

"From television and from newspapers."

"Bearing in mind that some of the defendants are of Italian origin and that the evidence may disclose that some were born in Sicily, would that in any way affect your judgment in this case?"

"No, sir."

"Would you be less inclined to believe a person with a name of Italian derivation simply by reason of his or her name?"

"No, sir."

"Do you have any feelings, either favorable or unfavorable, toward persons of Sicilian ancestry?"

"No, sir."

"Can you render a fair and impartial judgment on the charges against each defendant without regard to his ethnic origin, his business associations, or his family connections?"

"Yes, sir."

Judge Smith turned to another prospective juror who had raised his hand.

"Juror number three, Mr. D'Amico, what have you heard about the Mafia?"

"Pretty much the same. I've heard they're into drug dealing, prostitution, and stuff like that. I've picked it up from the news and also from having been a police officer for three years in Portland."

"Would what you have heard affect your judgment in any way if you are selected as a juror in this case?"

"No, sir, but I would as soon not serve. My wife's family is from Sicily."

"Thank you for your candor."

By the noon recess, Judge Smith had completed his questioning of the initial panel of jurors and had excused three on the ground they did not appear capable of exercising unbiased judgment in a case with overtones of organized crime. Although he had not excused Mr. D'Amico, he excused two others when they responded that pretrial publicity would prevent them from deciding the case solely on the evidence.

Having assured himself that the prospective jurors remaining in the box would be fair and impartial, Judge Smith allowed the attorneys, Page Moore for the government and Abe Priest for the defendants, to direct a limited number of questions to the jurors for the purpose of extracting information that might help them decide whether they would exercise any of their "peremptory" challenges – by which they could excuse a fixed number of jurors without having to state a legal cause.

Both sides were particularly interested in Mr. D'Amico. Page Moore went first.

"Mr. D'Amico, you say that your wife's family is from Sicily. Is any of her immediate family still there?"

"No. Her parents are dead, and her only brother came here when he was a boy."

"What does he do?"

"He's a lawyer in the State's Attorney's office in Rhode Island."

"Do you or your wife still have contacts in Sicily – correspond, that sort of thing?

"No."

"Do you or your wife belong to any organizations in which persons of Italian ancestry are particularly active?"

"No."

"No further questions of this juror." Abe Priest took over.

"Mr. D'Amico, you say you spent three years as a police officer. Did that involve arresting persons for violent crime?"

"Sometimes."

"In your experience, were those persons more apt to have Italian names than Irish, Polish, Spanish, or anything else?"

"No, sir."

"Do you believe persons of Italian ancestry have the same rights in our system of justice as anyone else?"

"Certainly."

"They are presumed innocent until proven guilty?"

"Yes, sir."

"And if, after hearing all the evidence, you have a reasonable doubt about the guilt of any of these defendants you understand it will be your duty to find that defendant not guilty. Is that right?"

"That's right."

"And you'd do it?"

"Yes, sir."

By day's end, the attorneys for both the government and the defendants had exhausted their assigned number of preemptory challenges to the seating of particular jurors, and Judge Smith adjourned the trial until the following morning to permit those jurors selected to settle their affairs at home before being sequestered for what bode to be a lengthy trial.

The morning of the second day was devoted to opening statements to the jury by the attorneys. Although Moore's opening statement on behalf of the government was factual and dispassionate, his simple recitation of what the government would prove held the jurors spell-bound.

Priest's opening statement was more passion than fact. Despite Moore's repeated objection that it was improperly argumentative – and highly prejudicial – Judge Smith allowed defense counsel relatively free rein, and Priest deftly used it to impress the jurors early with the points he wished to make. "This man, Silento, that the government would have you rely on is a liar! When you hear him, ask yourselves: Is he corroborated? The answer will be, 'No!' Ask yourselves: Where are the photographs that the government says these men killed for? Where are they? Where? The government will have no answer. If the government was honest with you, the answer would be that there are no such photographs. There have never been such photographs! So why is Silento doing this? Why? Because his mind, warped by the cancer that is destroying him and maliciously envious of his life-long employers and benefactors, has succumbed to the temptation, cynically proffered by the government, to strike a blow in malice and to live out the rest of his life in the government's care. This man is capable of anything! As the government itself will show, he has deliberately inflicted unspeakable horror on people who have done him no ill, and the perverse falsehood upon which this prosecution rests is the fitting culmination of a life of predation and falsehood. And why are the government prosecutors doing this? Out of blind zeal and arrogance! For a feather in their cap! Believing it is enough to show you ladies and gentlemen that these defendants have roots in Sicily, that they are not ashamed of their Italian names and ancestry, that they have been and are aggressive – perhaps overly aggressive – in their business ventures, the government will ask you to presume from this that they must, as a group, be guilty of the atrocities that Silento attributes to them. But His Honor, Judge Smith, will instruct you at the conclusion of the trial that the government must prove guilt beyond any reasonable doubt and that it must do so on the basis of evidence properly admitted in this case. We will show and you will find that the fantasy of a diseased and vindictive mind – the mind of Dominic Silento – cannot satisfy that burden."

CHAPTER 2

Sicily!
Central jewel of Mare Nostrum!
Land of the olive tree, the orange grove, row upon row of ripening grape;
Land of salty breeze and crystal night;
Land fought over since men have coveted land; disputed by Phoenician, Greek, and Roman; plundered by Saracens; held hostage by Normandy; witness to massacre and enslavement, treason and betrayal; scene of Archimedes senseless murder by Roman legionaires.

But yet a land of music, of laughter, the generous hand; pleasure in color, in good food, in games, in grace of movement, in extravagant gesture.

Giovanni Scalia was inheritor of all of this. Born in 1890 in Monreale, just outside Palermo, he grew up in a churchgoing, sheepherding family along with four older sisters and two brothers. Although their life could be considered, here and now, a life of poverty, they were not deprived. In season there was an abundance of the world's best peaches, pears, grapes, oranges, pomegranates, melons, and vegetables of every sort. Without regard to season, there was meat, fish, dried beans, rice, olives, olive oil, peppers, tomato paste, onions, and – perhaps most importantly – garlic. All for just the planting, tending, and harvesting. A bit of soil, some planning, and much hard work could yield an abundant life. The Scalias' life was abundant.

World War I brought a bonanza. With its violence, disorder, mountains of military supplies, and gullible doughboys, Sicilians like Giovanni thrived – along with ordinary thieves and prostitutes. There was money to be made, and Giovanni made it. He shared in the Allies' glut by whatever means at hand and thanked his patron saint for his beneficence.

The wartime feasting was not without competition, and Giovanni competed as Sicilians had for centuries. He and his family had always known that visible wealth was retained only by force or threat, and it was foolhardy not to use them. To rely on the local polizia, absent personal obligation or bribe, would have brought laughter. So Giovanni deliberately made himself a man to be feared. And feared he was.

It was but a small step, a step easily taken, from using intimidation to protect his property to using intimidation to acquire it. Giovanni took this step without knowing.

Giovanni's eldest son, Natale Salvatore, learned from his father and prospered. And he more than prospered; he became a man of distinction in his community and in his own eyes. He was gray by thirty. At forty, his thick hair was snow white. Early bouts with polio and meningitis had left him with a cane, on which he depended for even the shortest walk, and a quaver in his voice no therapy could remove. But these were his only physical disabilities. This patriarch, now honored as "Don Salvatore," stood ramrod straight, his broad shoulders topping a lean, muscular body.

Salvatore's only grandson, Vito Scalia, was five when his father, Salvatore's only son, was killed in an automobile accident. The next year his mother, Rosa, took him to Monreale to spend the first of many summers with his grandfather. The don's sprawling estate, which included the sheep ranch long in the family, served by now as Palermo's de facto center of government. Apart from being the largest employer in the area, the don was de facto prosecutor, judge, jury, and ombudsman for all wrongs claimed to have been suffered or inflicted by members of his extended family – which included not just relatives, but friends, employees, and business associates. The law was as the don decreed. His justice could be harsh, often tempered with mercy, and always swift. From his judgments there was no appeal.

The don made sure that his grandson had the best of tutors and attended the best of schools. Vito proved to be a good student – attentive, hard working, often a favorite of his teachers. Handsome and athletic, he was also a leader among his peers. And he was his grandfather's hope and treasure.

When it came time for Vito to choose a career, and he said he wanted to help manage the family's businesses, the don decided it would serve both the interest of Vito's education and the future servicing of the family's commercial interests in the United States to send his grandson to Harvard University. And so in September 1970 Vito followed the route from Palermo to Rome to New York to Boston that so many of his countrymen had followed, with mingled fear and high hope.

As he had in his schooling in Italy, Vito did well at Harvard, and, as the end of his last semester approached, he found himself near the top of his class. Then the shocker.

Vito's final grades would determine whether he would graduate summa cum laude with that top sliver of his class so anxiously recruited by corporate America. When he sorted through the day's mail, he saw it: the envelope containing his final grades. He tore it open and breathed a momentary sigh of relief as he read down the list: A, A+, A+, A. Then the jolt. His mind refused to accept what his eyes were telling him: Marketing III . . . C+.

Vito, his thoughts in turmoil, stormed from the door of his apartment and strode toward the old red-brick colonial building that housed the faculty offices. That bitch! No, it must be a mistake, a simple mistake. But how could she have let it slip by? The final exam had consisted of a single question. It required the selection of a hypothetical new product and an explanatory essay describing the steps to be taken in bringing it to market, from inception to placement on store shelves. Vito was confident his product selection had been as ingenious as the invention of panty hose, and that his marketing program had been aggressive and equally imaginative. *Maybe too imaginative for that dumb cunt,* he thought.

Vito didn't wait for the elevator. He sprinted the stairs to the third-floor faculty offices, two steps at a time. Once there, he paused to catch his breath before a door bearing "Susan Greif, Assistant Professor." Scalia knocked, heard a voice, and opened the door.

At a desk facing the door was Susan Greif, Vito's Marketing III instructor. Razor thin, a plain high-necked dress covering her bony frame, she looked at him through thick glasses.

"I see you received your grade."

"I did. There must be a mistake. The grade should be at least an A minus. Certainly no lower than a B plus." He brandished the single sheet of grades like a weapon, abandoning all pretense of civility.

Greif, pulling back, maintained her composure. "There's no mistake, Mr. Scalia. You simply blew it."

"That's crazy! I had it wired. How did I blow it?"

"Mr. Scalia, please lower your voice. Your arrogance is no more acceptable here than in the classroom. But that's beside the point. The marketing program you proposed was too aggressive – almost devious. It put excessive emphasis on the abilities of the promoters and not enough on the quality of the product. And, frankly, some of the promotion schemes smacked of commercial bribery. But most of all –"

"Listen, this is the real world we're talking about. Not a classroom. You don't get your stuff on the shelf, you don't sell squat. I don't care how good the product is."

Greif pursed her lips. "You didn't let me finish. The main problem was that you completely rejected the need for a demographic study or a test-market analysis. Now, the problem with such an approach is that –"

Vito knew that if he didn't take his eyes off that skinny throat, he would soon lose control. His eyes wandered to a neat row of file folders on a shelf behind Greif's head. As he knew, they held the results of over three years of painstaking research for a doctoral thesis she was now about to write. For her, its completion was the door to full professorship and tenure.

"Mr. Scalia, did you hear what I said?"

"No. I was thinking of something else."

"I said that in view of your extraordinary record, I'm willing to submit your exam to the head of the department for his independent review and, perhaps, that of his more senior colleagues."

"You do that, and fast," Vito spat, turning on his heel. *Skinny bitch!*

That evening, Vito dialed the don's personal number in Monreale.

"Nonno, sta Vito. I have a problem, and I need some extra money."

"What is it, my son."

"Remember la donna professore I told you about? She has refused to give me the grade that I earned. She can change it, but needs to know what it can cost her if she doesn't. Nothing else will do."

"What will it cost, my son?"

"I can get a good man to take care of it for ten thousand."

"You will not injure her?"

"No. That is unnecessary. She will understand when she loses some of her property."

"And that will convince her to change your grade?"

"There is no doubt. I know the woman."

The don paused before his final question. "Vito, you are not angry with the woman?"

Vito too paused. "No, I am not angry. I simply need to get my grade."

"You will have the money tomorrow."

The next day, true to her word, Susan Greif submitted Vito's examination paper to her department chairman for his independent review.

A week later, fire gutted the building housing the faculty offices. An assistant professor suffered third-degree burns over half her body in a futile attempt to save the contents of her office. Two weeks later, his final examination having undergone independent review by the department chairman and two full professors, Vito received notice that his grade in Marketing III had been changed to A-. He would graduate summa cum laude.

That evening Vito reported the good news to the don. "Yes, Grandfather, the family honor is restored, and it could not have been done without you. Grazie tante!"

As Vito reassured his grandfather, he felt a tiny seed of fear in the pit of his stomach. He had never deceived his grandfather before – nor feared him.

CHAPTER 3

Maine imposed its hard and rocky traits on those who early settled there. With its shore of granite, its stingy soil, its hard winters leaving but four months for growing, and its stormy sea, only the hardy stayed and, staying, grew more hard.

This was not land for men to fight over. It was the land itself – and the sea – that had to be fought. The plough suddenly stopped by the hidden rock would be laid aside, the rock uncovered, pried loose, and carried or dragged to join other rocks on the field's edge. And then the plough would bite again the sparse soil until next blocked by unyielding granite.

But for those who persevered there was the possibility of wealth. The inexhaustible timber could be fashioned into ships, and with ships the men would fight the sea. The streams could be dammed and the power of their flow harnessed to machines that would make furniture or fabric or shoes.

There was surely no premium for talk. The virtues that spelled success were hard work, persistence, ingenuity. And men did not have to keep locks on their doors. There were no thieves. One could not long survive in this community of survivors by bluster, threat, or deceit. The land and the sea bred men as unforgiving as the land and sea themselves.

But neighbors were neighbors, whether they talked much or little. There was always a helping hand in trouble or in special need.

In time, the beauty of the coast, the woods, the glacially scoured lakes, and the mountains brought to Maine people who had prospered elsewhere and sought either surcease or temporary diversion from their hurlied lives. Beginning around 1870, Maine became a favorite resort for summer vacationists, and camps, summer hotels, and boarding houses began to multiply along its rugged coast and around its pristine lakes. And it was not just those who had prospered elsewhere, and brought their prosperity with them, whom Maine attracted, but also those for whom prosperity – at least mercantile prosperity – meant little. Painters, poets, novelists, and craftsmen of every sort found in Maine both refuge and joy.

Among Maine's latecomers were Tom and Sarah Goden.

* * *

For as long as anyone could remember, the tools of trade around the households of Tom Goden's family in New York had been guns, nightsticks, handcuffs, writs, subpoenas, and legal briefs. Roughly half the male Godens were New York City cops and the other half lawyers; and the female Godens married either cops or lawyers in about the same proportion.

Tom was born into the police side of the family. His father was a hard-working and well-respected captain of police whom many thought could someday become Commissioner. It was soon evident that Tom was exceptionally bright, and it didn't take long for his uncles on the lawyer side to push him toward a legal education. In their minds mundane police work was for the plodder, the unimaginative. Beyond that, it carried physical risk that a good family man might better avoid. So, they urged, take up lawyering. Their blandishments nearly worked. Tom completed two years of law school before realizing his heart lay with police work.

Tom's two-year diversion to legal academe was not wasted. Although his father ingrained in him a respect for law enforcement and its enforcers, two years of schooling deepened his appreciation for the history, structure, and process of the law itself. Thus, from his family's perspective, Tom ended up neither wholly fish nor fowl, but sort of a fish with feathers.

Tom never regretted his police career. In just ten years, hard work and the good-old-boy network earned him lieutenant's bars in the detective division, and word was that if he kept his nose clean he would someday head it. He was thriving by simply doing what he loved doing most, when Sarah entered his life.

Sarah Schubert was a fierce competitor. She graduated near the top of her law school class and was quickly hired by a prestigious Wall Street law factory at one of those obscenely high starting salaries such firms flaunt as a recruiting tool. Why, Sarah wondered, did street-wise clients pay bills they knew reflected this unnecessary largess. She specialized in the defense of white-collar crimes and occasionally some not so white-collar. Like Tom, she was very good at what she did.

Their acquaintance was struck with Tom on the witness stand in the Federal Courthouse at Foley Square, a stone's throw from the Brooklyn Bridge. One of Tom's murder investigations had turned up evidence of interstate extortion in violation of the federal Hobbs Act. He was a key witness for the United States Attorney; Sarah was counsel for the principal defendant. Her cross-examination nearly demolished Tom because he was studying her rather than her questions.

Tom saw two people. The first was a stern woman in wire-rimmed glasses, a severe courtroom suit, white blouse and no jewelry, who could mentally eviscerate a hostile witness.

The other was his own reconstruct. He stripped away the glasses, the suit, and the courtroom persona of the fine-tuned defense machine, starting at the ankles and working up. He liked what he saw – sensational legs, well-rounded but firm hips, flat stomach, and a chest delightfully out of proportion. He gauged that the top of her head was about level with his shoulder. But it was the face and what it promised that pushed him over the brink – perfect creamy-white complexion, lustrous dark-brown hair, and, when relaxed, soft features and gentle, kind eyes that smoked only when kindled. A feeling of contentment spread through him.

"Lieutenant Goden," Sarah asked sharply, "do you have the question in mind?"

"No," he replied, "you'd better have the court reporter read it back."

The trial was long. When it was over, Sarah and Tom began to date. Their marriage two months later came as no small surprise to their friends. Tom's cronies in the department predicted he would be back to his old womanizing within a year, two at most. But it never happened. While neither could have planned it, they were bound as much by their differences as what they held in common. Although they had branched in different directions, each was doing what each loved best and doing it well. The move to Kennebunkport came after six years of happy marriage.

Tom would miss the days of the big cases, the major investigations, but this was now his town – his own little fief. And it was unquestionably a quality-of-life improvement. That Sarah's earnings provided the comfortable house on the river and other of their luxuries was no change from New York. But time had dulled Tom's sensitivity to the disparity in their earnings, and he now accepted with more than grudging grace her support of their life-style. Their life in Maine was near idyllic. It did nothing to prepare them for what was to come.

CHAPTER 4

Don Salvatore stood on the balcony of his villa taking in the warming rays of the morning sun, his spirits high, his mood expansive. Vito had received Harvard's highest honor, and the indulgent grandfather, having rewarded Vito with a summer of skiing in the Chilean Andes, now awaited his arrival to attend the don's annual festa that marked the end of summer and the coming of the harvest. The don walked to the edge of the balcony and called down to his gardener, who was pruning roses. "Guido," he called, "you will bring your family to the festa this evening?"

"Si signore. We will be there – and early!"

"Don't overdo the dancing, Guido. Just because you have a young wife, an old grizzler like you shouldn't try to show the rest of us up."

The gardener put down his shears and stood hands on hip. "Pfft! She makes me young, and those who can't keep up should stay near the punch bowl and not let their jealousy sour the fun of others."

The don beamed. "I'll tell that to those who can't keep up. But how is your little one? Did you take her to il dottore as I told you?"

"Si. He gave her something and the fever has gone."

"Bueno! Take her a rose and say it is from me."

* * *

That evening, when Vito Scalia entered the candle-lit ballroom of the villa, it was already filled with the don's friends and family – and with their friends and family. The crowded dance floor, ringed with tables, was alive to the beat and wail of the band – three electric guitars, saxophone, drums, and an accordion – all Monreale locals, there as much for the party as to perform. The bandstand, overhung with an Italian and an American flag, was at the far end of the basketball-court-size ballroom. On one side, french doors opened to a patio, with steps descending to the garden and the woods beyond.

Vito made his way toward a table near the bandstand, where he had spotted Don Salvatore and Gabriel Buffalino seated with a group of city fathers from Palermo. Pausing every few feet to greet, or acknowledge a greeting from, his many friends, he slowly worked his way down the side of the dance floor. "Vito, what brings you back to Terra Dei?" "Couldn't find a job in the United States?" "The girls don't treat you right over there?" "Sorry to hear you flunked out of that fancy school." "Glad you'll be here for the spring shearing."

Finally at the don's table, Vito embraced his grandfather and squeezed a spare chair into space the don and Gabriel had made for him. Introductions done, Vito suffered patiently the don's proud account of his Harvard achievement, well knowing that what the Palermo heavies would most enjoy the don would leave out. Vito's eyes wandered the dance floor. So many memories! There was Franco, looking not a day older, with the same auburn-haired girl he had pursued so hotly when in school. If looks could tell, he had finally snared her – or her him. And Sebastian! That tank who flattened Vito when he moved to block the goal that spelled defeat for Monreale in the season-ending game four years ago. And there was Dominic Silento, son of the don's gardener and Vito's best friend.

Vito and Dominic had grown up together – exploring the hidden places of the don's estate, swimming forbidden streams, wrestling, quarreling, conspiring. And the glue of childhood friendship had held through young manhood, when Vito played goalie and Dominic fullback on the Monreale soccer team. Dominic, smaller and more wiry than Vito, lacked Vito's good looks. With an underslung lower jaw and a prominent nose, Dominic appeared somewhat as a bird of prey. But his forbidding look belied a sunny disposition and a quick wit. And soccer! Graceful as he was quick, he was the one, with the score tied, who could explode the length of the field for the winning goal. And he had remained Vito's best friend. Dissimilar as mercury and steel, they somehow bonded.

In the four years of Vito's absence, Dominic had come to hold a special place with the don. The don had seen through Dominic's bounce and effervescence to an inner toughness that was being wasted. And so, Dominic entered the service of the don, but not in his father's more gentle footsteps. He did not tend roses; he became the youngest of the don's enforcers, one of his soldati.

Vito watched as Dominic, at the end of the dance, gracefully excused himself from his partner and shouldered his way toward Maria Buffalino, Gabriel's sister. The two Buffalinos, Gabriel and Maria, had been Vito's second best friends. Gabriel had been his companion in more serious undertakings – selecting a necktie, completing a school project, buying a bicycle. Maria was pure spice – teasing, goading, competing in physical games with a zest and skill that only boys should have.

Vito had seen Maria more than once since his return, but had not sought her out as he had Dominic and Gabriel. She had changed. No longer the gadfly, the welcome irritant he had known, she had become in his four years of absence more quiet, more reserved, and perhaps – and here was the rub – more self-assured. She had also bloomed to classic beauty – narrow-waisted, full-breasted, dark-haired. Seeing the outward change, he was vaguely uneasy that a deeper change lay inside.

Vito's eyes had followed Maria as she danced. With obvious pleasure, she glided and twirled effortlessly about the floor, her red and green bolero skirt swinging a half beat behind her feet, her dangling shell earrings in constant agitation. A succession of partners kept her dancing whenever there was music, and she slowed only for occasional warm laughter at a partner's, or her own, misstep.

As Vito watched Maria begin her dance with Dominic, the don's voice intruded.

"Very pretty, isn't she?"

"Yes, she is," Vito replied without expression.

"Well?"

"Well what?"

"Well, why do you sit there like a bump on a log?"

Vito hesitated, then walked onto the floor. Dominic, seeing him coming, smiled and surrendered Maria with a mock bow.

Vito, ignoring the bow, took Maria lightly in his arms. Although the two had been friends since toddling infancy – playing together, walking to school, picnicking, sharing secrets, competing, doing together all that children do easily together – he now felt an unexpected awkwardness. She let him be the first to speak.

"It's been good to see Gabriel again. How is the rest of your family?"

"They are well."

"Don Salvatore has done things in style again."

"Yes, he has."

Vito lapsed into silence. But he danced easily, and Maria followed smoothly. As she began to fit more comfortably into his arms, he could smell the red hibiscus in her hair, the sweet smell of hair itself, and feel her body responding to the rhythm of the band. He began to perspire. Sensing that she must feel his body through their clothing, he pulled slightly away, only to find her pressing more firmly against him. Lifting her head, she looked squarely at him. Then, putting her cheek against his, she brought her lips to his ear. "Vito! What is *that* ?"

Vito's awkwardness dissolved. Taking her hand in mid-dance, he led her through the French doors to the courtyard and the darkness of the garden beyond. With the sound of the band drifting from the open doors on the warm evening breeze, they embraced. As their tongues sought each other, their embrace became frantic, their breathing in gasps, until finally, arms entwined, they half ran to the deeper darkness of the woods beyond.

* * *

More than one pair of eyes had followed Vito and Maria as they left the ballroom. But it was one man, attentive to their every move and gesture, who quietly left by the same French doors through which they had gone. Stopping only to retrieve a flashlight from his parked car, the man followed closely enough to note their progress from the garden to the woods. When they stopped, panting, in the seclusion of the woods, the man crouched behind a large plantain, watching as Maria took the hibiscus from her hair and Vito urgently undid the top button of her blouse. The man, suppressing laughter, awaited the climactic moment. Then, leaping from the shelter of the plantain, he shone his light fully on the naked couple. Before either Vito or Maria could react, he had swept up their strewn clothing and was running through the woods, his laughter drifting back. Maria was first to recover her tongue.

"Who was that?"

"I don't know who the fucker was. But I'll find out – bet on it!"

* * *

The man from behind the plantain had dropped the clothing at the edge of the woods before returning to the ballroom. His laughter again suppressed, but eyes dancing, he watched Maria and Vito return separately an hour later. Enjoying the festivity, he stayed until the band wound down and then returned to his small bachelor apartment in Monreale.

The man had a regular daily routine. After work, he would eat and drink with friends at a small bistro and then negotiate the short distance to his apartment. He didn't break this routine the night before Vito's scheduled departure for New York two days after the don's festa.

On that night, after a bit more wine than usual, he steadied himself with

21

the handrail as he climbed the stairs to his second-floor apartment. He neither saw nor heard the two ski-masked figures enter the building just as he reached the landing. He walked to his door, fumbling with his keys. His fingers found the right one, but he had difficulty with the lock. Finally inserting the key, he sensed a movement behind him. As he turned, he took a blow to the base of his skull.

Regaining consciousness, he found himself stretched on the floor of his apartment, naked, his hands and feet bound by thin wire, his mouth taped. Blood oozed from the bindings. He could glimpse one of the men taking instruments from a worn sheepskin bag. If he could only free his mouth of the tape, he would tell these codardi where his little cash was hidden! Ice water suddenly struck his face. The two men lifted him to his knees before a low coffee table. The items on the table, of a type long familiar to him, struck sudden terror. He shook his head violently from side to side. Madness! Too terrorized to breathe, both an actor and a spectator, he watched in perverse fascination. Moments later, again prone, he heard his own shriek.

The man told no one of the events of that night. He bound his wound, let time do the healing, and kept silent. But time did not heal the inner wound, and that wound would warp his life forever. Although he never learned who the masked men were, he never doubted whose message they carried.

CHAPTER 5

Going north from Boston on U.S. Highway 1, not far into Maine, the shoreline turns from north to east at Wells Beach and continues in that direction past the Kennebunks and the Kennebunk River. The shoreline turns north again at Cape Porpoise. This quirk in geography means that the Kennebunk beaches face south. Because the hot air of summer normally comes as a southerly wind, it is cooled by chill water before reaching the beaches, providing pleasant atmosphere for the summer communities of old New Englanders, artists, and craftspeople – communities that are among the oldest in North America.

One enters the Kennebunk River from the Atlantic. From there the river, rising and falling with a twelve-foot tide, serves as the boundary between Kennebunk on its west and Kennebunkport on its east. Just before entering the river, boaters are treated to a spectacular view of Kennebunkport's Walker Point and the imposing oceanfront home that was the summer residence of the President of the United States.

The river once served as a safe haven for shipbuilders in constructing and launching large seagoing vessels. Today it teems with sail and power boats. For the first mile, it runs north past marinas, old shipyards, lobster-boat moorings, riverfront homes, restaurants, a yacht and tennis club, gift shops, and a monastery. At about the one-mile mark, where the river is barely twenty yards wide, a tiny bridge connects Kennebunk and Kennebunkport. To the right is Dock Square, the commercial hub of Kennebunkport. In summer people gather on the bridge to watch boats slip their moorings and head toward the ocean, while other boats head upriver with water skis to negotiate the challenging slalom-like course the river offers at high tide. Dock Square itself is a compact cluster of shops, restaurants, and inns. In season, it bursts with tourists; off season, it is recaptured by the locals.

Allison's is a restaurant and bar on Dock Square, to which good food and reasonable prices attract the year-around residents. On workdays, Tom Goden regularly went to Allison's for afternoon coffee and for chatter with other customers. During the winter doldrums, he lingered more than in other seasons.

* * *

It was a brisk winter day – the kind of day he particularly liked – when Tom was sitting at his window table in Allison's that afternoon he would long recall. High, thin clouds were beginning to obscure the early afternoon sun and there was a smell of snow in the air. As he finished his first cup of coffee, he saw the limousine move slowly across the bridge and into the square. A car with two men trailed twenty-five yards behind. The limo turned right at Ocean Avenue and headed in the direction of Walker Point, its escort trailing. As he let his eyes follow the vehicles, his mind noted that before the presidential presence they would have seemed strangely out of place, out of time.

* * *

Inside the limousine, one of the three passengers looked up from the dossier and photograph he held to ask, "What got him up here?"

"Claims it's a better life, and he was ready for a move. It wasn't money. His wife was a trial lawyer in the city, but was ready to get out. They vacationed here and got hooked on the place. When he learned the chief's job was open, he applied. He was only thirty."

"Why did the town pick him?"

"The selectmen were impressed by his credentials and hired an outfit in the city to check him out. They liked what they found."

The third man studied Tom's picture again. It showed a smartly uniformed man, well over six feet tall, apparently in prime physical condition, with a pleasant, squarish face, sparkling hazel eyes, and light brown hair long enough to curl at the ears and neck. "Good-looking bastard," he observed. "Does he chase skirts?"

"No, they chase him," replied the first man.

"And?"

"Never strays, as far as we know."

"Why not?"

"Loves his wife."

"That simple?"

"That simple!"

"Why no kids?"

"Two bad miscarriages. The doctor said not to risk a third."

"This scar along his cheekbone looks ugly. How'd he get it?"

"When he was with the New York P.D., a doper went berserk in a crowded store, pulled a blade, and grabbed a clerk. Goden made a move and freed the woman, but got sliced."

The second man leaned forward and addressed the driver. "Slow down by that driveway on your right." Then he turned to the third man. "We're coming up on Goden's house. It's the white frame with black shutters."

The third man made a careful appraisal as the limo slowed to five mph. "Nice. Very nice! Right on the river. A view of the ocean, big lawn, its own pier. Goden can't do all this on his police salary. If he's clean, it must be his wife."

"It is," the second man agreed. "She's a top partner in Clinton & St. John in Portland."

"Amos St. John?"

"Yeah."

The third man frowned. "Why didn't Amos tell us this?"

"Why should he? He probably assumed we already knew from the MARTINDALE listing. I saw her name but it didn't register at the time. You wanna use someone else?"

After a pause, the frown faded. "No, this could work to our advantage."

The limo and the trailing car were approaching Walker Point. Inside the limo, the third man returned the dossier to his briefcase and stretched his arms. "We're almost there."

* * *

It was an hour after the limo and its escort had passed through the square, and Tom Goden, deep in his annual winter doldrums, was nursing his second cup of coffee.

Tom drained his cup and signaled the waitress for his check. She was a bulky veteran who seemed able to float from table to table.

"Here you are, Chief. Feels like it might snow."

"That's the forecast. If we get a good one, maybe it'll give us something to do."

"Things that slow at the station?"

Tom grimaced. "That's the year's understatement!"

She smiled and played along. "Nothing that a good murder or two wouldn't take care of – right?"

"Well, not that drastic, Jean, but it's a tempting thought."

Leaving the restaurant, Tom passed two men on their way in. The three exchanged curt nods, and Tom walked across the square to his squad car. About to pull out, he paused. Something bothered him, but he couldn't say what. Had he left something in Allison's? No. Maybe he'd forgotten something Sarah had asked him to do. In vague frustration, he put the car in gear and headed for the station. Arriving, it dawned on him. It was those two men. He had seen them before. But when and where, he couldn't say. Shaking his head, he cut the engine and went in.

* * *

They were finishing dinner when Sarah broke into his thoughts. "Tom, what are you thinking about so hard?"

"I don't know," he sighed absently, as he tried to keep the last strands of pasta on his fork.

"You don't know what you're thinking about?"

"Don't be sarcastic."

"Aren't we sensitive. It's that time of year again, is it?" There was a trace of mischief in her grin.

"You could say that."

"What's the problem?"

Tom put the fork down and shrugged. "This afternoon I ran into two guys I've been thinking I should recognize. It's been nagging me."

"What did they look like?"

"Big and dark-complected. Camel hair overcoats. It's been awhile, but I've met them before."

"Did they seem to know you?" Sarah rose with the dinner plates and walked to the kitchen. Tom followed.

"I have no idea. We just passed each other as they were going into Allison's. I can't put my finger on it, but there was something about them that seemed out of place."

"Here we go again," Sarah said, almost to herself.

"What's that supposed to mean?" Tom challenged.

"Honey, it means I can hear your so-called instincts grinding."

"They're usually right."

"I won't argue that. You want some coffee?"

He ignored the question. "Why are you laughing?"

26

"I was just thinking that now you have your first project of the year."

"You're right; and I'm gonna milk it for all it's worth, assuming I get the chance."

* * *

Another day passed with no sign of the two men. On the second day, Tom was driving into Dock Square when he saw them walking toward Allison's. Then the men seemed to have second thoughts, turned, and crossed the street. Keeping his eye on them as they entered the Colonial Pharmacy, Tom parked, opened his car door, and then hesitated before getting out. Reaching across the seat to the glove compartment, he removed his camera. He walked to The Copper Candle, a shop diagonally across from the pharmacy.

It was a cold blustery day, and, except for the Copper Candle's owner, David Armstrong, the shop was empty.

"Good morning, Tom, what's with the camera?"

"A little field trip, David." Armstrong was a voracious reader of spy novels, and the eyes sparkled in his round jolly face as he anticipated Tom's request. "Can I get some pictures from this window?"

"Go ahead. Just be careful of those oil lamps. You break'em, you own'em."

Tom knelt on one knee and pulled back a corner of the green cloth serving as a background for the window display. A minute later the two men emerged from the drug store and stood for a moment. They seemed to be looking at his squad car. The camera clicked three times. Then they turned left and walked quickly around the corner of the drug store.

He put the camera under the counter, thinking it was time he introduced himself.

"What the hell's going down?" Armstrong asked.

"I'm about to find out. Probably nothing."

Tom hurried from The Copper Candle to follow the men, but by the time he turned the corner, they were already in their car and soon speeding across the tiny bridge into Kennebunk. Tom saw the car, but it was too far away to read the license plate. Sonofabitch! He ran back to his own car and raced after them. He crossed the bridge and drove up the hill to the traffic light. Here he could turn left, right, or continue straight. He went straight. It was the wrong choice.

The two men were on the Maine Turnpike heading south. The limo was fifty yards ahead. "I'm hungry. We should've had breakfast at that restaurant before we left."

"Too risky! I'm sure that was Goden. They told us to keep a low profile. We don't wanna give that mother the chance to jack us around."

* * *

As soon as the lab had developed the photographs taken by Tom from the window of the Copper Candle, he dispatched duplicate sets of prints to Dan Butkovitch, the pit bull who had been Tom's immediate superior in the New York City Police Department and was now a deputy commissioner, to Vincent Inserra, the special agent in charge of the FBI's Portland office, and to Jerry Borghesani, the commandant of the Maine State Police. He then hand-carried two other sets of the prints to the desks of two officers of his own department, Lieutenant Carl Tito and Sergeant Mike Magruder.

Tito was a twenty-five year veteran of the force; Magruder a relative rookie. Together, they comprised a Mutt and Jeff team. Tito was short, a little paunchy, and had the craggy coast of Maine for a face. Magruder had the scrubbed good looks of a rangy college athlete fresh off the basketball court.

"Carl, here's a set of the pictures. Pass them around and see if they ring a bell with anyone, but it's probably a waste of time. Maybe they flew here. You and Mike check the car rental companies at the airport. Get the rentals for the past two weeks. And wipe that smile off your face."

"Hey, Chief, I wasn't smiling."

"Bullshit! If you weren't, you were getting ready to."

"Anything else?" asked Tito, gamely fighting the laughter threatening to erupt, while sensing that this might be more than make-work.

Tom rubbed his chin and thought for a moment. "Yeah. Those guys were here at least three days. Assume they weren't visiting somebody. Maybe they were getting the feel of the area for some reason. Try turning something up at the real estate agencies."

* * *

Nearly a week passed with no word from New York, the FBI, or the Maine police. The car rental angle yielded nothing. Nor had the real estate search. It was late afternoon, and Tom was debating whether to leave the station early when his intercom buzzed.

28

"Chief, Commissioner Butkovitch is on the line."

"Thanks, Edna, put him through. Dan, I was beginning to think you'd forgotten me. Any luck on the pictures?"

"Yeah. But it wasn't easy. They dropped from sight over ten years ago. You ran into them the year before you jumped ship for Kennefuckport."

Tom frowned. "Very funny! Stop trying to bust my balls."

"Actually, you did us a favor, Tom. It's worth knowing they're around. We might even know who they're working for."

"Dan, for God's sake, stop screwing around and tell me who they are."

Butkovitch roared with delight. "O.K., O.K. The one on the left is Carlo Lumbardino. The other one is Carmine Gambini. When you knew them they were young Sicilianos – outfit enforcers. Like I say, we thought they'd packed it in."

"Jesus Christ!" He closed his eyes and tried to visualize two men he had encountered over twenty years ago during his investigation of a brutal gangland slaying. "Those bastards are vicious. What were they doing around here?"

"Tom, what are you muttering about?"

He scratched his head and then picked up the set of pictures from his desk. "Just thinking. Carlo and Carmine – the happiness twins. They weren't here in the dead of winter for a vacation. My guess is they were with someone I didn't get a look at. You said you might know who they've been working for?"

"Yeah, we do. Remember Tony Rosato?"

Tom thought a moment. "Didn't people say he muscled in on a Pepsi distributorship in Brooklyn?"

"That's right. After you left, he turned to booze. Now he has the biggest discount liquor operation in the city. Every year someone else sells out to him at a bargain price. But no proof there's muscle. You know the drill. Anyway, the 'happiness twins', as you call them, we're pretty sure they're on Rosato's payroll."

"Dan, do me a favor. Send me his picture and whatever up-to-date material you have on him and his gunzles."

"I'll do it."

29

CHAPTER 6

Memorial Day weekend marks the unofficial start of Kennebunkport's summer season. Summer homes and inns are opened; tourists begin to return; and pleasure-boat traffic on the Kennebunk River increases. The 1992 weekend was cool but sunny. The president was at Walker Point. Next door, Vito and Maria Scalia watched a fifty-foot schooner under full sail beat its way past the five-acre estate they had purchased for their home 19 years before. They were in the den putting finishing touches on the invitation list for their daughter Camilla's wedding.

The large den stood in contrast to the soft, tasteful elegance of the rest of the ten-bedroom white Colonial. Occupying the left corner of the house facing the ocean, it was Vito's creation, his control central, his turf. Its walls were glass – floor-to-ceiling windows on two sides and mirrored walls on the others. Chromium leather-slung chairs complimented an enormous glass-topped chromium desk and matching conference table, each bearing a telephone console.

Maria was sipping coffee. Her red housecoat, cinched at the waist, clung to her body. Her black hair and a touch of makeup made her picture-ready. A recent photograph of Camilla on the desk would have led one to believe the two dark-eyed beauties were sisters.

"I talked to Grandfather yesterday," said Vito. "He still plans to come. Says the wedding of his great granddaughter is something he can't miss."

"How old is Don Salvatore?" Maria mused, her eyes still on the invitation list.

"Seventy-five, but you'd never know it. The man is amazing. Amazing! He hasn't lost a step."

Maria looked up. "Do you still think it's wise having your business friends? Gabriel doesn't think so. I don't either. What if some cop like Goden recognizes them?"

Vito frowned. "Maria, we've been over that. They're family as well as customers. I've told grandfather and he approves. Besides, they won't go to the church. They'll only be here at the house for the reception. The Fourth of July weekend is such a mob scene that they'll go completely unnoticed. I guarantee it!"

"What are the logistics?" she asked, in a tone that could have played well in the military.

"Simple. On Thursday, Grandfather flies into Kennedy. He'll stay with Gabriel, along with the two who are coming with him. Gabriel will drive them here Friday and they'll stay with us until Tuesday or Wednesday. The others will fly into Boston on Thursday and Friday, and drive separate cars here on Saturday. Nobody will be flying into Portland and nobody will be arriving together."

"So you've proved my point. You invite them to our daughter's wedding because they're family and then tell them to sneak their way in. Some family!"

"Those are precautions. Nothing more. It's the only way I could get Gabriel off my back. At times, your brother can be a very big pain in the ass. So can you."

"One of the guests might know them," Maria persisted, ignoring the gibe.

"Not a chance. And even if someone did, so what? These are legitimate businessmen." Vito, in crisp jeans and a burgundy windbreaker, was bent over tying his Topsiders, impatient to get to the boat.

"They say so now, but they haven't always been."

He snapped straight in his chair. "You just don't get it, do you? This is our home and our daughter. I invite who I goddamn well please. Anyone tries to interfere with our privacy, they answer to me. Is that clear?"

"Vito, lower your voice and stop glaring. Someday that temper is going to piss off the wrong people."

Her husband stormed from the room, and Maria was left aimlessly leafing through the invitation list. Each name deepened her sense of foreboding. *Why,* she asked herself, *should the mother of the bride have to dread a wedding?*

* * *

On July 3rd a long black limousine passed through the gates of the Scalia residence, pulled around the circular driveway, and stopped. The doors opened and three men emerged. Gabriel Buffalino bear-hugged his sister. Then he and Vito embraced briefly. The other two men helped a fourth man from the car and unloaded the luggage. One of them said something to the driver and the limousine sped from the grounds. Vito rushed forward and held the older man in a much longer embrace. Then he kissed him on both cheeks.

"Grandfather, welcome to our home. You do us great honor."

Maria followed suit. "Don Salvatore, you look so well! I pray you had a good trip. Come, we have lunch waiting. But first, a little wine perhaps – a toast to your safe arrival."

"Ah, Maria, you look lovely, my child. I am ready for the wine." Then Don Salvatore, with a sudden thrust, playfully rapped Vito's rump with his cane.

Vito turned to the two other men who had arrived with the don and extended his hand. "Dominic, Carmine, long time no see."

Maria, her attention on Don Salvatore, had barely noticed the presence of the other men. Now, walking toward the house, she heard her husband's greeting and, turning, recognized a familiar figure coming toward her. "Dominic Silento!" she exclaimed.

Dominic, smiling broadly, walked to where she stood. Embracing her, he pulled back and held her at arm's length. "Hello, Maria. It's been a long time. You haven't changed – beautiful as ever."

Maria hugged him again, turning to Vito as she did. "Why didn't you tell me Dominic was coming?" Without waiting for an answer, she took his arm. "Come, Dominic. We have some catching up to do."

Later that afternoon, after his guests had settled in their rooms and changed to more comfortable clothing, Vito led the visitors outside to enjoy the view of Walker Point and the mouth of the river. Breathing in the crisp Maine air, they traversed some thirty yards of gently sloping lawn to a group of a dozen white-painted chairs set on the emerald of the manicured grass. About twenty feet further, the lawn ended with a row of small granite blocks separating it from the steeper, brushy embankment down to the narrow, rock-strewn beach.

Don Salvatore chose a wooden Adirondack chair directly facing the water and, with the head of his cane grasped in both hands, sat firmly on the chair's front edge, defying its design for those who would rather half-recline. Gabriel, Dominic, and the rest sank into other chairs, which were clustered for easy conversation.

The don, having waved away the white-jacketed attendant taking drink orders, intently scanned his surroundings. Although many trees familiar in Sicily were unrepresented here – the olive, orange, almond, plantain, essentially all the deciduous fruits other than the apple – he noted many old friends – above all the pines, but also hemlock, chestnut, cypress, and spruce. He watched, bemused, as a lumbering crow sought to perch on the swaying tip of a hemlock. "Foolish bird! You know enough not to try a landing there!"

32

But what most held the don's attention was the water – the sea and the river and the junction of the sea with the river. Neither of these was the crystalline blue of Sicilian coastal water, but they were more active, more alive – the flow of the tides, the brownish water of the river thrusting into the bluer sea and then, seemingly spent, being thrust back. And the water traffic! No mere lazing of sail on blue, but the thrusting power boats pushing first against the river's current and then returning against the tidal surge. These, and more, the don watched.

But finally, his attention turned again to the trees. He knew that the many hues of green would in little more than two months become a miracle of color unknown in Sicily. The picture calendars mailed to him by Maria showed scenes he could scarce believe – the brilliant red, orange and gold of the maple, the oak, the birch. To many of these trees he could attach names from the shape of their leaf or the tone of their bark, to many he could not. If only he could sit on the edge of this funny chair until the colors came! But he would be back – not for the long spell of snow and ice, but for that short burst of color.

Vito, sitting next to the don, could no longer resist his question. "Well, nonno, what do you think?"

"Bueno! Bellisimo! Il Presidente has chosen well, and you have done well to follow him! There is no more beautiful scene in Sicily. Surely, your family will flourish – not just in goods, but in grace and beauty."

Vito, fulfilled, turned his attention to other of his guests. "Dominic, why haven't you come here sooner? Surely there is no business of the don sufficiently important to keep you from a visit."

Dominic's response, his gaze steady, seemed somewhat stilted.

"Vito, each of us has his own path. If they join, so much the better. But if they don't, we must go our own way. I have gone mine."

"Well, let's at least have a glass of wine together while we can. Saluto!"

Replacing his glass on the right tablearm of his chair, Vito reached beneath the chair with his left hand, retrieving a soccer ball from the grassy surface, and began lightly passing it back and forth between his hands. Soon, he was on his feet lightly tapping the ball from toe to toe, to knee, to head, to ankle, and back to toe.

Maria, next to Dominic, suddenly warned, "Vito, watch your glass!" Momentarily distracted, Vito allowed the ball to roll several feet down the slope. In a flash, Dominic was on the ball, dribbling it away from Vito. Vito, with a roar, went after him, and, just as he reached the thief, Dominic neatly

33

sidestepped while maintaining possession of the ball. Maria shrieked with delight, leaped from her chair, and joined Dominic in a game of keep-away, completely frustrating the slower, if more determined, Vito.

Vito was already slowing when Dominic, himself visibly fatigued, stumbled to the turf. Maria, concerned for her friend, threw up her right arm, made a whistle of her fingers, and blew a shrill time out. "Game's over! Monreale the winner, two to one! Refreshments for all players will be served in the clubhouse." With the don leading a burst of applause, she threw an arm around Dominic and, waiving Vito to follow, led her husband and friend to the entrance of the recreation room.

Having taken control as referee, Maria now slipped behind the bar and took over as barkeep. "What'll it be?" she bantered, filling three tall glasses with ice as Dominic and Vito eased themselves onto bar stools. Vito bantered back, "One Monreale blaster for me, and a pink lady for my friend." As he said this, Vito lightly put an arm on Dominic's shoulder. A shudder ran through Dominic's body. Maria looked toward Dominic for his order, but Dominic did not respond. Then, looking steadily at a row of bottles over Maria's head, he said in a low, even voice, "Take your hand off my shoulder and don't ever touch me again."

No one spoke. Vito, looking at Dominic, slowly lifted his arm. Dominic did not shift his gaze.

"Well, you guys are a strange group! And I don't care what you ordered, you're getting what I serve you!" Maria opened a bottle and filled each of their glasses. The three tried for several minutes to resurrect a conversation, then fled to the shelter of the other company on the lawn.

* * *

That night, as Vito and Maria prepared for bed, Maria recalled the scene at the bar. "Do you have any idea what was wrong with Dominic?"

"None whatever. I can't believe his fall could have been that embarrassing."

"Have you ever seen him react like that before?"

"Never. We've had some hairy times, but I've never seen him like that."

Neither pursued it further, and Maria put the incident from her mind. But Vito remembered. He now knew, for the first time, that Dominic could be dangerous – not just to the don's enemies, but to the family. He also knew, with equal certainty, that the don would not believe it.

CHAPTER 7

Samson Smythe was born and raised in Cicero, Illinois. It was a community of precisely square street blocks, small houses, and immaculately maintained yards. Cicero bordered Chicago's west side and two thoroughbred race tracks, Sportmans Park and Hawthorne. Chicago – the city of the broad shoulders, Carl Sanburg, Vachel Lindsay, Clarence Darrow, Al Capone, Paul "The Waiter" Ricca, and Tony "Big Tuna" Accardo – was thick in his blood.

When he was fifteen, Smythe landed a part-time job in the mail room of the *Chicago Tribune*, the city's largest newspaper. The paper was his first and, as years passed, his only employer. From his first day at work, he craved printer's ink and fantasized about the time when he would have his own column. He had one by the time he was twenty-five, and by the time he was thirty-five, he enjoyed a national reputation as a crime reporter. His stories were syndicated in many of the country's major newspapers. Organized crime was his specialty; its members were his targets.

On Tuesday, June 30, Samson Smythe, his wife Tricia, and their daughter Jan, were seated on the large screened porch of their house on Greenwood Avenue in Evanston, Illinois, a half-mile from the campus of Northwestern University, where Jan would enter her senior year in the fall. She had just returned from a week-long trip to San Francisco, where she had stayed at the home of a classmate, and was telling her parents the highlights of her visit.

"Marge has a friend, Gina something. It'll come to me in a minute. Oh, I remember, Gina Magaddino. Anyway, Gina had a party at her parents' house on Russian Hill and invited us. What a place! I mean, talk about money. Her father has some kind of import-export business. Nice people."

"Sounds like you had a good time, dear," said Tricia.

"I did. San Francisco is a neat place. Anything exciting happen while I was gone?"

"Not much," Samson replied. "That militant gay group – Act Up – is marching in the Fourth of July parade and that has everyone bitching."

"They're doing the same thing in Kennebunkport because the president's going to be there," Jan said.

"Where did you hear that?" Tricia asked.

"Gina Magaddino told us. She's a bridesmaid at a wedding in Kennebunkport on Saturday. She's going with her parents and they're planning to spend a week or two. I'd like to see the place. You see it on TV all the time, and it looks glorious."

Her father was suddenly attentive. "Who's getting married?"

"Camilla Scalia. Her father owns some big investment business. They live on the ocean near the president. The reception's going to be at their house."

Samson strode to the kitchen and returned with an open can of beer, his mind processing what he had just heard. But his memory bank surfaced no data on either a West-Coast Magaddino or an East-Coast Scalia. Maybe he had become a victim of his own media, and the sudden association of two Italian names was sufficient to get his antennas tingling. He recalled that Antonio Magaddino had been identified as a participant in the notorious Apalachin, New York gathering of November 14, 1957. But that was ancient history and Antonio had been from Niagara Falls. Still, the name evoked an echo. When he got to the office tomorrow morning, he'd call Hundley.

"Samson, I'm talking to you. Are you sure you won't go with me to visit mother? Jan will be away and you'll be alone for the Fourth of July weekend."

"Tricia, we've been over that."

"Come on, Mother, give Dad a break. You know he plans to go sailing. I mean, who wants to spend time in Kansas City in the summer if they don't have to."

Samson smiled gratefully at his daughter. "Thanks, honey, you hit the nail on the head."

When Smythe arrived at his office early Wednesday morning, he promptly called Dick Hundley, whom he had known since Hundley's days as Chicago's police commisioner and from whom his considerable knowledge of organized crime was largely developed.

Over the years, Hundley had become one of the country's leading authorities on the Mafia, a secret organization with roots in Sicily. It was the ultimate governing body of the organized crime cartels operating throughout the United States, concerning which he was no less an expert. Hundley, fifteen years the older of the two, became Smythe's mentor, and eventually his inseparable friend.

When Hundley's wife of forty years died and a year later he reached mandatory retirement, he sold his Chicago home and purchased a winterized bungalow in northern Wisconsin, where he pursued his two remaining interests

– fishing and research into the structure and operation of the Mafia and organized crime.

Smythe was only an occasional visitor, but the two men talked by phone two or three times a week. Although separated by distance, Hundley remained, as he had been, Smythe's most knowledgeable and valued professional resource.

On this call, his friend's tone was abrupt. "Samson, this will have to be quick. I'm flying to Atlanta to see my daughter and I'm behind schedule. You caught me going out the door."

"Just one question, Dick. San Francisco, Magaddino, does that ring a bell?"

There was a moment's pause. "It does if you're talking about Patsy Magaddino."

"He's in the import-export business."

"He's the one. A nephew of the Apalachin Magaddino, Antonio. Patsy's big, real big! He's clean now, but he's a Mafioso. No question about it. He swings with some very respectable people. Has for years. But before that he ran the waterfront out there. The union didn't mean shit. If you wanted your goods moved, you dealt with Patsy and his people. It was only a matter of time before he owned half the businesses on the dock. Listen, Samson, gotta run. Be gone for a couple of weeks. I'll call when I get back."

Well, well, isn't that interesting! thought Smythe, hanging up the receiver now buzzing his hand. He propped his feet on the desk and mulled over what he had just learned.

Smythe spent the remainder of the day composing an unrelated story for the Sunday edition, dropped by his favorite restaurant for drinks and dinner, and reached home by 10:00 p.m. After a stop in the kitchen, he turned on the TV and plopped into his recliner. The evening news was showing footage of Kennebunkport, Walker Point, and the scenic oceanfront as backdrops for a clip about the president's weekend visit.

Damn, that looks pretty, Smythe thought, as his mind turned again to Magaddino and the upcoming Scalia wedding on Saturday. It was probably just a coincidence. After all, Hundley had said that Magaddino was now respectable. There was nothing to suggest that this Scalia knew anything about his distant past. *Shit! I couldn't place him, and I've been at this for years. But, Jesus, what if it's an outfit wedding reception right down the street from the President of the United States? Even if it's a hundred-to-one shot, can I afford to miss it?*

Smythe's mind composed a headline: "Mob Daughter Ties Knot In President's Backyard." Nope, not right – no class. How about: "President Arrives as Mafia Gathers." Still not right, but Smythe was smiling.

* * *

Back at his desk the next morning, Smythe's euphoria was fading as he contemplated steps to bring in the story, assuming there was one. He rubbed his face and squinted at nothing in particular.

It would be a church wedding, but he wouldn't waste his time there. Any notables – notables of the sort he was interested in – would shun the church in favor of the privacy of the reception at Scalia's home. They'd probably stagger their arrivals to town and might not even use the Portland airport. He could end up chasing in circles. No, the reception had to be his target. But how to cover it? Security would be tight. He could never fake his way in. And even if he could, what good would it do? He needed pictures – and good ones. He wasn't skittish, but neither would he take pointless risks. If caught with a hidden camera, he'd end up with nothing but lumps for his efforts.

He spent the rest of the morning putting the finishing touches on his regular Sunday feature and then ducked out for lunch. When he returned, his mind had settled. It might be a wasted trip, but so what? The worst that could happen was he'd see Kennebunkport for the first time and maybe get in some sailing or deep-sea fishing. But if his hunch panned out, it could be the biggest story of his career. He had to go. What he needed was a good photographer who knew the area. He buzzed his secretary.

"Yes, Mr. Smythe?"

"Grace, bring me that directory of newspaper companies." Then he called the bookkeeping department. "Betty, this is Samson Smythe. I need a check pronto for five thousand. No, make it for eleven. Charge my source account. That's right. Make it payable to me. I'll pick it up."

In a few minutes, his secretary brought the directory, and he turned to "K". He vaguely recalled that the *New York Times* had purchased a local paper in the Kennebunkport area some years ago. Yes, there it was: The *York County Coast Star* in Kennebunk. He wrote the name on a scrap of paper and stuck it in the side pocket of his sport jacket with his flight guide.

In Chicago, particularly in the newspaper business, the more confidential a matter was the quicker it made the rounds. Smythe's penchant for secrecy verged on paranoia. Until his story was ready for press, he would hold

38

information of his trip on a need-to-know basis. No one at the paper fit this category.

"Grace, I'll be out for a few days. You have a nice holiday."

"Thank you, Mr. Smythe."

He picked up his check and stopped first at the bank. "How would you like that, Mr. Smythe."

"Ten one-thousand-dollar bills. The rest in fifties, twenties, and one roll of quarters."

He walked up Michigan Avenue toward the Gold Coast until he found a vacant phone. He checked his flight guide and called the airline. The only evening flight to Portland, Maine was sold out and no standbys were being accepted. He settled on a flight to Boston. He'd stay at the airport hotel and make the 85-mile trip to Kennebunkport in the morning. Satisfied, he called the *York County Coast Star.* The sun was beating down and he felt the sweat collecting under his shirt.

"I'd like to talk to your top photographer."

"That would be Loring Mills. Who may I say is calling?" asked the crisp, efficient voice.

"It's a personal matter."

"One moment please, I'll see if he's available."

Smythe drummed his fingers on the side of the phone box.

"Hello, this is Loring Mills."

"Mr. Mills, I'll come straight to the point. I have a matter that's highly confidential. I understand you are very discreet."

"I am when the occasion requires. You tell me who I'm talking to and I'll tell you how discreet I am."

"This is Samson Smythe of the *Chicago Tribune.*"

Mills dropped his guarded tone. "What can I do for you, Mr. Smythe? I read all your columns."

"Work with me, I hope. Are you free tomorrow and Saturday? And do you moonlight?"

"I can be available, and I do private work."

"One more question. How well do you know Kennebunkport?"

"Like the palm of my hand."

The perspiration was now pouring down Smythe's face but he ignored it. "Good! I'm staying in Boston tonight. Driving up tomorrow. Do me a favor and find me a place to stay tomorrow night."

"I'll do it. Look forward to meeting and working with you."

"Loring, keep this to yourself. Tell no one. And book the reservation in your name."

"I understand." Mills didn't, but he was now too excited to ask questions.

It was now after 4:00 p.m., and Smythe's flight would leave O'Hare Field at 6:45. Smythe took a taxi home.

At his house, he told the cabby to wait and hurried inside. He decided against packing a suit. Some extra slacks and the summer sport jacket he was wearing would fit the informality of a summer resort. As he headed for the front door, he sensed he was forgetting something. Of course, his binoculars.

The taxi was heading west on Dempster Street and had crossed the sanitary canal into Skokie when Smythe remembered something else he'd forgotten. He hadn't left a note telling his wife and daughter where he would be. *Oh well,* he told himself, *I'll be back home before they will.*

CHAPTER 8

The one-hour time difference and a delayed departure from Chicago put Smythe into Boston's Logan International Airport at 11:00 p.m. He went directly to the car rental counter. "I'm very sorry, Mr. Smythe, we simply have no car of any kind."

He checked with three other companies and received the same response. The proximity of Boston to the summer resorts of Cape Cod and southern Maine, combined with the start of the long holiday weekend, meant reservations were required well in advance. At the last rental counter, the representative suggested a limousine service. One left the airport hotel hourly and stopped in Portsmouth, New Hampshire. From there, he could catch a taxi for the 35-minute, $65 ride to Kennebunkport. After that, he would rely on Loring Mills for transportation.

When he saw the long line at the registration desk, he was glad he had called personally for a reservation. He waited a half-hour for his turn, only to be told that the hotel was over booked and his reservation could not be honored. "We do have one two-bedroom suite left."

"I'll take it," Smythe growled, wincing at the $375 price tag.

Dropping his things in his suite, he went to the cocktail lounge. *This has all the makings of a first-class boondoggle,* he reflected, as the waitress delivered his third vodka. He was ready for a fourth when he saw two men sidle to the crowded bar just in front of him. They were decked out in suits which would easily exhaust his entire clothes allowance for two years. The shirts and ties alone would be a strain.

He studied the men's profiles. They were undeniably good-looking, but vaguely sinister. Stretching, as one does after a long plane flight, each seemed completely relaxed. They laughed about something and turned to face the bar. Smythe continued to look at their backs. Was there something familiar about the older one, or was his imagination trying to convince him that this wasn't a wasted trip after all? He could have sworn one of the men mentioned Kennebunkport.

The men finished their drinks and turned again. As they did, Smythe quickly swiveled in his chair so he was no longer facing them. *Sonofabitch!*

That's Frank Scozzari from New Orleans.

When he awoke next morning, Smythe felt like he had a ball of cotton in his mouth. He checked out of the airport hotel early and caught the first limo for Portsmouth at 7:00 a.m. He could have used about three hours more sleep, but he had to avoid the risk of running into Scozzari at the check-out desk. Besides, last night's encounter had his adrenaline flowing. His instincts were shouting he was on the verge of an explosive exposé. *First Magaddino and now Scozzari!* Who else would come out of the woodwork before this weekend was over? Adrenaline notwithstanding, exhaustion took over, and Smythe nodded off in the rear seat as the limo sped along the coast toward Maine.

"Well, here we are," said the cabby, twisting in his seat. "This is Dock Square. Anyplace in particular you wanna get out?"

"I need to make a phone call," Smythe replied, while he made mental notes of the square's layout.

"We'll go 'round the corner to The Landing. They have a public phone."

Smythe collected his suitcase from the trunk, paid the cabby, and located the phone. He fished through the pockets of his green sport jacket until he found the paper on which he had written the name of the newspaper, Mills's name, and the telephone number.

"Loring, this is Samson Smythe. I'm at a place called The Landing in Kennebunkport."

"You must have left Boston early."

"I did. Thing is I don't have wheels. There were no rental cars available."

"No problem. I got you a place at Austin's Inn. You can see it from where you are. Look across that little tidal inlet at the edge of the parking lot."

Smythe turned. Across the inlet was an alleyway of small shops with a three-story blue-gray wood building. "I see it. Looks nice."

"Check in and I'll meet you in, say, forty-five minutes at The Landing. It has an outdoor deck overlooking the river. Good place for breakfast."

"I'll be there."

Smythe claimed the reservation Mills had made and registered as "Paul Simes," paying cash. He went to his room, changed to shorts and sneakers, took his binoculars, and left the inn. Dock Square was already crowded with tourists.

He walked the short distance to the bridge and stood watching the activity on the river. Some boats were heading upriver with water skis past the tall steeple of the South Congregational Church. As he watched, more boats appeared pulling the skiers. They crisscrossed back and forth over the boats' wakes, dropping their tow lines just short of the bridge. The bright morning sun reflected off the water. *Very pretty! Tricia and Jan would love this.*

After a few minutes, Smythe walked to The Landing and up its outer stairs to the deck. He had left the hotel in Boston before breakfast was served, and he was hungry. He placed an order for ham, eggs, and home fries, and, while waiting, watched a sightseeing boat pulling from the dock for a four-hour "Whale Watch."

He was starting his last piece of toast when he saw a small, fine-boned figure of a man with light hair and a pleasant, boyish face talking to the hostess. Man? He looked more like a high school student. Smythe returned to his toast.

"Samson Smythe?"

Smythe looked up in surprise, then stood and extended his hand. "Loring, good to meet you. Sit down. Do you want something to eat? Some coffee?"

"Some iced coffee and a blueberry muffin would be good." Mills seemed chipper, but a bit anxious.

Smythe studied the fragile young man for a moment. He was fair-skinned, and his delicate features seemed almost effeminate. But this was balanced by a surprisingly deep voice and firm grip. "This is a beautiful place," said the visitor, "Do you have a house in Kennebunkport?"

Mills pulled up a chair. "We just bought. Nerve-wracking business, but we love it." His eyes rolled.

"Expensive?"

"When your wife's expecting and you're used to renting, it is. We bought a small place that needs a lot of work. It's on School Street about two miles from here."

"How long have you been with the paper?" Smythe asked.

"Eight years. Seems like it's been forever."

After the waitress had brought his iced coffee and muffin, Mills started his questions. "What's this all about? And why all the hush-hush?"

The people at the adjoining tables paid their bills and left. It was after 10:00 a.m. and the two men had the deck almost to themselves. Smythe popped a stray homefry into his mouth without answering Mills's questions. "I'll get around to that. What's your situation? Are you still free today and tomorrow?"

"No sweat. I took the rest of today off. Don't have anything going until Tuesday."

"Have you told anyone I'm here?"

"No. You said not to."

"How about your wife?"

"Samson, I said I haven't told anyone. You may be a famous crime reporter, but your paranoia is showing."

"O.K., O.K." Smythe was pleased with Mills's irritation. He didn't need a sycophant just now. "Do you know the Scalia family?"

Mills weighed his answer. "Not personally, but I know who they are and I've seen them around. If we're talking about the same people, they own the house next to the president. They bought it last December, as I recall. Let's see, his name is Vito. He owns or runs the biggest investment business in the state."

"He's the one. Has a daughter, Camilla?"

"I'm not sure of the name. But I know he has a daughter. They keep pretty much to themselves. The story is they moved here from New York City."

"Did you know his daughter is getting married tomorrow?"

"No, I didn't. There hasn't been anything in the paper about it. Are you sure?"

"That's the word I have. The reception is supposed to be at the house."

"Jeez, that's funny," Mills said, rubbing his chin. "You'd think there'd have been a story. It's a small town, and he's big in the business community."

"Maybe there will be one after it's over," Smythe replied, with a faint smile.

Things were falling into place. "So that's why you're here. You're covering the wedding."

"Not the wedding, the reception."

"And you want me to take pictures."

"Exactly."

"Does Scalia know this?" Mills asked, pushing his chair from the table to cross his legs.

Smythe eyed the remains of Mills's muffin. "No. Are you gonna eat the rest of that?"

"Yes, I am. Do you have an invitation?"

"Nope."

"Then how're we gonna get pictures?" Mills uncrossed his legs, leaned forward in his chair, and stared steadily at Smythe. "Samson, what's going on? Why is the *Chicago Tribune* – wait a minute, does your paper know anything about this?"

"Not yet."

"Why not?"

Smythe forced a smile. "Loring, let's leave things at that. There may be a story in this and I need pictures of the reception. Do you want in?"

"Let me think," Mills said, finishing the muffin. "This is something I should probably tell my paper about. I moonlight, as you put it, but not on news stories."

Smythe's voice sharpened. "Absolutely not. No one – and I mean *no one* – is to get wind of this."

Mills forced a smile. "I'll be honest with you, Samson. Working with someone of your reputation is tempting. But I'm getting an uneasy feeling about this."

That's it, thought Smythe. *He bit. Time to land him.* "Loring, let's move out. We can talk more about this in your car."

Smythe signaled the waitress and paid the bill. He chatted with her for a moment before following Mills to the parking lot. At the car Mills asked, "What now?"

"Let's talk about moonlighting and a young man expecting his first baby who has just bought a house," Smythe replied. He took off one of his sneakers, fingered the ten $1,000 bills, and slowly peeled off five. Mills eyes widened as Smythe handed him the bills. "There will be five more – that's right, five – when we get the pictures. How's that uneasy feeling?"

"What feeling? Where to?"

"For starters, let's cruise by Scalia's place."

Mills pulled onto Ocean Avenue and drove along the river past the village green, the Godens' house, and a string of quaint New England inns. Each inn displayed a No Vacancy sign. Passing the Colony Hotel, the road curved left and wound along the ocean's rocky shore. On the right was St. Ann's Episcopal Church, a century-old stone structure with green lawn to the ocean's edge. Looking over his shoulder to the southwest, Smythe could see, across the water, Mount Agamenticus dominating the horizon. "This is breathtaking, Loring. Is that Walker Point up ahead?"

"Yep. You'll get a good view of the president's spread as we get closer. Now, see up ahead. If the president was here, there'd be roadblocks on both sides so you couldn't drive by. You'd have to stop and explain yourself, you know, like you lived in one of those houses on the left."

"How are people gonna get to the reception?" Smythe asked, moving his head from side-to-side.

"No problem. We're taking the scenic approach. If you come from the other direction, the roadblock isn't until after Scalia's place. From town, that's the quickest way to go."

They passed the Secret Service guardhouse protecting the entrance to Walker Point. They had gone another 200 yards when Mills slowed down. On their right was a narrow driveway through the woods. There was no sign of a house, only a large metal gate. Inside the gate stood a smaller version of the guardhouse at Walker Point. Two men were standing next to it. Mills came to a stop. There was no shoulder on the narrow two-lane road, and the sightseeing traffic was heavy in both directions. Soon, they could hear the blare of horns behind them. "Jesus," Smythe exclaimed, "is that the entrance to Scalia's place? It looks like a fortress."

"That's it. The gate and guard station were put in after he bought it."

"O.K., let's move on before we attract attention."

Mills drove a quarter mile, turned right onto Creek Road, and stopped in a small clearing. "Loring, you're gonna earn your money. Have you ever been on the grounds?"

"Once. On a lark, the real estate agent we were using took us in for a look when it was on the market. The house is a mansion and it's surrounded on three sides by woods. It has a big yard – three acres at least. Runs down to the ocean. Most of the yard is on the left side of the house, so that's where the reception will be – assuming it doesn't rain, which it's not supposed to. Of course, it could be inside."

"Not a chance! With a layout like that it'll be on the lawn. Anyway, no one's gonna get past that gate without an invitation. We'll have to go through the woods. Who lives next door?"

"The Mintmires, and they're out of town."

"How do you know?"

"He's the biggest General Motors car dealer in the state and the paper's biggest advertiser. One of his daughters, Nancy, works for the paper during the summer. They left yesterday to visit friends on Cape Cod."

"Let's drive into their place and have a look."

Mills turned the car around and headed back to Ocean Avenue. They turned left into the Mintmire driveway and a few moments later they were parked in front of an old three-story yellow Victorian in mint condition.

With Mills hurrying to keep up, Smythe covered the grounds in long strides. They stopped when the lawn ended and was replaced by a small pebbly beach which centuries of erosion had carved in the craggy shoreline.

Smythe turned to the right and walked to the end of the beach where his path was blocked by enormous boulders. He bent his tall frame low for balance and picked his way to the top. He turned and waved for Mills to follow.

They stood surveying the scene until Smythe asked, "How far are we from Scalia's place? I can't see anything but rocks."

"I'd say a good hundred yards."

"Does he have a beach like this?"

"Not that I recall. Besides, the tide's coming in. Tomorrow afternoon this whole stretch will be surf."

"O.K., we try the woods."

Smythe led the way. They were into the woods when he knelt to tie a sneaker. "Loring, what's so funny?"

"See all this nice lush ground cover?"

"Yeah. What about it?"

"It's poison ivy."

Smythe cursed and rose quickly to wipe his hands and knee with a handkerchief. They went another twenty-five yards. "Sonofa–" Both men stopped abruptly. They had almost walked headlong into a fourteen-foot-high chain-link fence. "What the hell?" Smythe nearly shouted.

"I'd say we've gone about as far as we're going," Mills observed.

Five minutes later they were back where they started. "This thing runs all around the property," said Mills. "Looks new. Scalia must've put it up."

Smythe studied the fence and then reached up for a handhold.

"You're crazy if you think I'm going over that!" Mills said emphatically. "We'll either get our asses blown off or we'll end up in jail for trespassing."

"You're right."

"Samson, forget the whole thing. This is impossible. You can have your money back." The words were no sooner out than Mills regretted them. The money was burning a hole in his pocket and the thought of another $5000 made his head spin. The $10,000 would cover nearly a year's mortgage payments and ease an already badly strained budget that had caused him more than a few sleepless nights. But Smythe seemed to have ignored his precipitous offer.

"Loring, let's get back to town."

They returned to the car and headed for Dock Square. "What now?" Mills asked.

"I wanna see Scalia's place from the water. Saw a sightseeing boat pulling out while I was having breakfast. Where does it go?"

"Out the Kennebunk River. Then it turns left and goes past Walker Point. You can get a good view of Scalia's house."

"Perfect! How often does it leave?"

"I'm not sure. Maybe every four or five hours. But there are three or four of them. They're in and out all day."

Smythe's spirits rose a little. "Let's take one. We can get some sandwiches and beer and make an afternoon of it. Do you have your camera equipment handy?"

"It's in the trunk."

* * *

The sightseeing boat was crowded. Most of the passengers had moved to the port side as it approached Walker Point. Many had cameras; some, including Smythe, were using binoculars. Mills's camera began to click at the first sight of the Scalia property.

"You have plenty of film?" Smythe asked.

"Four rolls."

"How effective is that zoom lens you're using?"

"Very! When you see the pictures you'll think you're standing on shore."

"Good! We want everything – shoreline, houses, the grounds."

"I've got you covered," Mills answered, smiling.

"Make sure you get some panoramic shots, too."

"I understand."

"And get –"

"Hey, Samson, lighten up. I know the routine. Believe me, I won't miss anything."

CHAPTER 9

Except for Smythe and Mills, the offices of the *York County Coast Star* were deserted. It was after 6:30 p.m. and Mills was developing the film. From time to time, he emerged from the darkroom with pictures. Smythe arranged them on a long table.

"Loring, you have a touch. These pictures are sensational! You didn't miss a thing. Problem is you were right. We're not gonna get anything from the ocean side. Maybe a plane or helicopter is the only alternative."

Mills put a quick end to the idea. "You can forget that. When the president's in town, you can't get clearance to come anywhere near that area."

Smythe studied the pictures for several minutes and then began rearranging them as Mills watched over his shoulder.

"Loring, look here," he said, pointing to a group of photos of the shoreline from Walker Point to the Mintmire house. "Those trees aren't as tall as I thought they were. Notice the tree line. Here the trees are tall. But follow along. They get shorter the closer you come to Scalia's place. It looks like there was a fire at one time near his property. The trees are short – almost stunted."

"So?"

"Now look where I'm pointing. Isn't that the corner of Mintmire's house. It's barely showing."

Mills leaned over the table. "Uh huh. It's the only three-story house in that stretch. There's one part that seems to be above the tree line."

"Get me a ruler."

Mills rummaged around his desk. "Here, use this T square."

Smythe aligned one edge of the T square, and drew a line from the small exposed section of house on a downward angle corresponding to the top of the tallest tree. The line touched down at the shoreline before the Scalia grounds. Then he studied the pictures again. "Which one of these close-ups of Mintmire's house would you say shows that corner?"

"This one."

Smythe studied the picture Mills handed him. "Shit! There aren't any. Wait a minute! Yeah, that looks like a small window. It's almost on the roof.

Must be an attic up there."

"No way," declared Mills, as if reading Smythe's mind.

"Loring, we have to get into that house."

When he replied, Mills's deep voice seemed to crack, and he almost stuttered. "Jesus Christ! We can't just break in. For God's sake, he's the paper's biggest advertiser. We're caught, I lose my job – not to speak of going to jail."

"Loring, where's your newspaperman's balls?"

"Where they're supposed to be, and that's where they stay."

Smythe bent over and again shed the sneaker. He peeled off two bills and laid them on the table. "There's two more. Not bad, huh? Now let's stop arguing and go for dinner. When it's dark, we'll have a look."

Mills rolled his eyes. He was going to object, but the words didn't come.

* * *

After leaving the newspaper, Smythe and Mills drove along Summer Street and then across the bridge into Kennebunkport. In Dock Square, they hung right and followed Ocean Avenue to Mabel's Lobster Claw. There, Smythe devoured two lobster rolls and an order of onion rings, washing them down with three Molsons. Mills, sitting opposite, poked his fork aimlessly at a mound of fried clams. His stomach felt like it was in his mouth. Finally, giving up, he looked out the window and said in a barely audible voice, "It's as dark as it's gonna get."

The two men returned to Mills's car and continued their drive out Ocean Avenue toward Walker Point. When they were abreast of Mintmire's driveway, Smythe told Mills to stop and let him out.

"Loring, you go park on that side street we were on this morning. While you're gone, I'm gonna look around. Don't forget your camera."

When Mills left, Smythe began a slow walk around the large house. He tried the front and back doors. Dead bolts! All the ground-floor windows were locked. He carefully examined the doors and windows with a pencil-size flashlight. There were no signs of an alarm system. Then he noticed the garage addition. The door was secure but the latch on the decorative window was barely in place. He tested the top frame. It fit loosely in the sash. The vibrations from a series of rapid up-and-down pulls caused the latch to slip open. He raised the window and climbed into the garage. The door from the garage to the house was locked but not with a dead bolt.

By the time Mills had parked and returned to the house, Smythe was inside. When Smythe saw Mills walking up the driveway, he went back out through the garage to the yard, closing the unlocked door and window behind him.

"Loring, over here."

"What's the situation, Samson?"

Smythe noted a more upbeat tone in Mills's voice and decided he had better not spook him. "I tried the doors, but everything seems to be locked."

"Did you try the garage?"

"No, I was about to do that. Where is it?" Smythe blandly asked.

"Must be on the other side."

He let Mills lead the way. "Ah, shit, that's it. The garage door is locked too," Smythe said, with resignation.

"Hey, Samson, this window is open." A moment passed. "So is this door."

"Well, how about that!"

They went through the laundry room and kitchen into the front hall and then up two flights of stairs to the third floor. "O.K. Loring, you got us in here, now let's find that window. None of these is high enough."

"Look there on the ceiling. There's a pull-down ladder."

A minute later they were in a hot, stuffy, unfinished attic, so close to the roof that it was little more than a crawlway. Suddenly, there was a loud flapping sound. Then another. "Jesus!" cried Smythe. He sprung from his crouch, striking his head sharply on a beam.

"Calm down, it's only bats. There's the window."

Smythe rubbed gently. "I'm getting a lump on my head the size of a baseball."

"That's nothing! Wait 'til tomorrow. With the sun beating down on this roof, it'll be like a furnace up here."

"Doesn't seem to be bleeding. I'll survive. Move over a little so I can see." Smythe focused his binoculars. "This will do it! We're golden! I can see most of the yard. Here, have a look."

Mills took the binoculars. "You're right. Hey, two people just came out of the house. It's almost like day with this moon."

"Let me see. Yeah, one of them has a cane. The other one is younger. Loring, is there enough light to get a picture?"

"Sure, I have a roll of infrared."

Fifteen minutes later they were drenched with perspiration. "That's enough. Let's get to your office and develop these. They'll give us an idea of how good the ones tomorrow will be."

"Samson, you'll think you're standing in the yard." Mills was suddenly surprised at how easily he had forgotten he was a housebreaker and inwardly cursed the easy morality that hard cash had brought.

* * *

"Well, neither of these guys is Scalia," said Mills, as he emerged from the darkroom with the fresh prints. "Must be visitors."

Smythe took the prints from Mills. Glancing at the top one, he felt a sudden tightening of his stomach as he recognized Gabriel Buffalino.

Noting Smythe's interest, Mills demurred. "Samson, I'm bushed. Call it a day. It's almost eleven."

"All right, phone your wife and tell her you're on the way."

Twenty minutes later, Mills dropped Smythe off at Austin's. "What's for tomorrow?" he asked.

"Pick me up here about ten-thirty. I've got no idea what time the reception will begin, but it probably won't be before noon. We can cruise by Scalia's place every so often until we see people begin to arrive. I don't wanna be in that attic any longer than we have to be."

When Mills left the inn, Smythe turned toward the entrance, changed his mind, and walked instead to The Landing cocktail lounge. If seven $1,000 bills and the anticipation of three more had dispelled Mills's uneasy feeling, Smythe's had just begun. Apart from taking on something he might not himself be able to handle, he was drawing in Mills and now, in a sense, even the unwitting Mintmire. *Maybe a few strong belts will help me sleep,* he thought.

CHAPTER 10

After having spent the previous evening drinking bourbons by himself in the bar, Samson Smythe had spent a very restless night but by 6:00 a.m. was wide awake. He lay staring at the ceiling, debating whether to return to Chicago after the reception or stay another day. Nervous and on edge, he wondered if an extra day might help him unwind.

After a half-hour staring at the ceiling, he dropped a leg over the side of the bed, pushed himself up, showered, dressed, and went outside to face the crisp morning air. Except for an occasional jogger, Dock Square was deserted. Deciding he had a hangover and needed a walk, he followed Ocean Avenue to the breakwater and parked himself on a huge hunk of granite – the better to watch the river and oceanfront coming alive. It was the sort of day in Maine when the deep-blue ocean glistens, white puffy clouds float lazily across the sky, and pounding waves send plumes of spray high above the rocks. With the breeze coming from the ocean side of the breakwater, the occasional boat bound from the river to the sea seemed to slide by noiselessly, and only the occasional screech of a gull provided counterpoint to the rhythmic pounding of the surf. Samson sat and soaked it in.

Glancing at his watch, Samson was startled to see that the hour had slipped to nearly 9:00. Both refreshed and hungry, he hastily slid from his granite perch and set out for breakfast at The Landing. He wasted no time ordering and, after swallowing the last of a hearty breakfast, returned directly to his room. There, he put his binoculars, a small tape recorder, a pad of legal-size paper, pencils, aspirin, and a towel into a small carrying case and by 10:30 was outside waiting for Loring Mills. Mills arrived on schedule and they set out once again on the now familiar route to the Mintmire home.

By 1:30 the two men were in their crow's nest by the open attic window. Smythe was scanning the Scalia grounds through his binoculars, while Mills fitted and adjusted his camera equipment.

The grounds had been transformed since last evening. A dance floor was in place, and the orchestra was tuning up. The lawn, its expanse largely unbroken last evening, was now dotted with tables and chairs, blue and yellow umbrellas, clusters of potted flowers, and several food and beverage kiosks, each with two servers putting the last touches on the exact placement of bottles, bottle openers, ice chests, glassware, condiments, utensils, napkins, and what else Smythe could only guess. Servers hovered over two long buffet tables, already spread with cold buffet fare. Near one end of each long table a row of already ignited burners awaited chafing dishes of hot food that were just now being carried from the kitchen. Off to the right, but now hidden from the field of Smythe's binoculars, was a large area reserved for parking, where attendants were already arranging in compact rows the cars and limousines dropped at the front entrance by early arriving guests.

As he scanned the scene, Smythe was pleased with the sharp image he was getting of the faces below, and he assumed that Mills would, if anything, get even greater detail on film. His view panned again the busy party scene, coming at last to rest on the porch. As it did so, a figure in satin and white lace appeared through the door with two other figures. Camilla turned, kissed her father and mother, and drifted down the stairs to the lawn.

"O.K., the yard's getting active. Here's the drill," said Smythe, as he and Mills wiped their dripping faces with towels. "I'll be talking into this tape recorder. Don't let that distract you. Focus on the reception line. After that breaks up, divide the yard into sections. Get close-ups of people section by section. When you complete a full sweep, I'll tell you when to begin the next one based on the number of new arrivals. Oh, and keep the camera inside the window. We don't want any reflections from the sun giving away our position." Mills didn't respond. "Something bothering you, Loring? Mintmire will never know we've been here."

"Something is bothering me, and that's not it. You're not leveling with me. When you clammed up yesterday, I thought I had it figured out."

"Oh yeah, like what?"

Mills ignored Smythe's sudden change of tone and plowed ahead. "That the president was going to be there. But that doesn't make any sense the more I think about it. The White House wouldn't keep something like that a secret. So I ask myself, why does a hot-shot crime reporter want pictures of everyone at a reception – the 'notables', as you put it? Now I'm sighting on that lawn and it's beginning to look like goddamn Little Italy. And all that sweat pouring off your face isn't just from the heat. This is a fucking mobster shindig; and if we're caught, we're in deep shit! Tell me I'm wrong," he challenged.

Smythe sat up from his prone position at the window and looked at Mills while he undid one of his sneakers.

"Jesus, here we go with the sneaker bit again. So I'm not wrong."

"Loring, I won't know until I see who all shows. Here's the balance. Now stop whining and earn it."

Mills was torn. His street sense told him he was playing too dangerous a game. Trespassing in the home of his employer's best customer was one thing, but spying and photographing people he was now convinced might be – in the words so often used by Smythe in his columns – "outfit thugs" was quite another. On the other hand, he had come this far and he didn't relish being pegged a quitter. After all, working with a nationally known reporter couldn't help but enhance his position at the paper. But when all was said and done Smythe had found his Achilles heel. He simply couldn't resist the $10,000. Smythe was right. It was time to stop acting like a wimp. Mills's camera came to life; Smythe began speaking into his tape recorder.

"Kennebunkport, Maine, Saturday afternoon, July 4, 1992. I woke at 6:00 a.m. to a perfect summer day. The kind we pray for when we're on vacation. The President of the United States arrived here this morning. He might be in the midst of a round of golf, or plowing the waves in his gas-guzzling Cigarette Boat, or meeting with some foreign dignitary. If I had to guess, I'd say he's just plain relaxing at his summer home at Walker Point. But others are covering that story. What I'm about to tell you is what's happening at this very moment on the lush oceanfront lawn of the president's next-door neighbor, Vito Scalia, a local investment tycoon, pillar of the community, and the father of the bride. He's hosting a wedding reception for his daughter, Camilla. What's so newsworthy about that, you ask? Maybe nothing. But this reporter's instincts tell him that before this afternoon is over, we will have observed a gathering of organized-crime chieftains as unprecedented as it is brazen. As I speak, my associate is making a pictorial record. He's the –"

Mills interrupted with a soulful plea. "Samson, for God's sake, don't use my name!"

"O.K., O.K.! Calm down and keep on that reception line." Smythe reactivated his tape recorder. "Bingo! There's Joe Zicari and Bartolo LaDuca. I think that's – yes, Dominic and Paul Falcone. Further down the line I can see Sam Mancuso and Natale Migliore, and behind them Thomas Riccobono. My God! This is unbelievable. There's Joseph Ormento and John Profaci. Yep, there he is, Frank Scozzari. He's talking to Gabriel Buffalino and Tony Rosato."

For the next hour, the silence was broken only by clicks and the whir of film being fed through Mills's camera and the cryptic recitation of names by

Smythe, as he thumbed his tape recorder off and on:

Ignatius Bonanno	Michael Alaimo
Patsy Monachino	Joe Catena
Roy Cannone	James Larasso
Thomas Castellano	James Chiri
Salvatore Sciortino	Mark Colletti
Louis Turrigiano	Thomas Sciandra
Ben Lagattuta	James Civello
Peter Bonventre	Francis DeSimone
Charles Tornable	Al Siciliano
Damian Monachino	Carmine Cucchiara
Anthony Guccia	Vitale Genovese
Nick D'Agostino	Luke Mannarino
Contenze Guarnieri	Luke Majuri
Joe Carlisi	Dominic Filardo
Angelo Magliocco	Matthew Oliveto
Frank Evola	Lorenzo DeMarco
Don and Vito Valenti	James Ida
Augustus Miranda	Louis Osticco
Lou Montana	Santo Lombardozzi
Vincent Ravino	Sam Riela

By 3:30 p.m., Smythe and Mills had made three trips from their perch to cool themselves and drink water. Smythe's breathing had become heavier in the sweltering heat of the sun-baked attic.

"Loring, keep shooting at that table in the back of the yard where the man with the cane is sitting. Our friends have been stopping there one by one since the reception line broke up. It's almost like they're paying homage to the pope. Shit! I wish I knew who he is."

After another half-hour, Mills took the zoom lens off his camera and began packing his case. "Samson, that's it! I've seen enough, and Lord knows I've heard enough. I'm out of here, with or without you. If I never see that place again, it'll be too soon."

"Fair enough. You've done good. Let's police the area and get moving. I've got all I need for now."

The two men left the house the way they had entered. Smythe locked the door from the garage to the house behind him and closed the window. They walked in silence toward Creek Road, where Mills had parked his car. Their silent ruminations were miles apart.

The young newspaper photographer felt twitching in the center of his back. Were unseen eyes boring into him? Were the scenes he had photographed as sinister as he imagined? *I haven't heard the last of this,* he thought. *I wish I could forget those faces.*

The crime reporter, for his part, was savoring what would surely be the biggest scoop of his career and praying that nothing unforeseen would spoil it. *Sweet Jesus, what a story! The possibilities seemed damn-near endless.* He wondered which of the guests was Patsy Magaddino.

"Where to now?" Mills asked, when they reached the car. The two were still toweling off as though they had spent the afternoon in a sauna.

Smythe ran a hand through his hair and squinted. "Let me think. I was planning maybe to stay over 'til tomorrow. But now I'm thinking I'd rather get home. I'll have the house to myself. By Monday I can have a first draft done. There's a six o'clock flight to Chicago from Portland. Can you stop at Austin's while I get my things and then drive me to the airport?"

Mills started the car and headed toward Dock Square, looking constantly in the rear-view mirror. "When do you think your story will hit the papers?"

"It depends when this friend of mine returns from Atlanta." Smythe craned his neck to look through the back window for a moment. "I need to run the pictures by him. There were people there I'm sure I didn't recognize. Like the geezer with the cane everyone seemed to be brown-nosing. He must be really big to command that kind of attention. I mean, those guys I made are heavies in their own right."

Mills pulled up at a stop sign and turned to face Smythe. "Shit, Samson, you have enough for a barn-burner with what you've got. Those names you were rattling off sounded like they came from a Palermo phone book. Maybe you could do it in installments. You know, an initial story and a sequel or two."

Smythe slapped his knee. "Goddamn! That's a good idea, Loring. In fact, it's a great idea. I'll do it! You seem to be loosening up, by the way."

"Distance does that." Mills underlined his comment by pressing the accelerator. They screeched from the stop sign.

"Loring, please see we get out of this alive. And where did you come by that 'Palermo' bit?"

"I wasn't born yesterday. Sonofabitch. The president's next door neighbor. What a story! Too bad the president wasn't there."

"By time I've finished my story, the reader may wonder if he was. Hey, slow down! You've made your point."

Mills let up on the accelerator but kept his eyes moving to the rear-view mirror. "Samson, you're a prick with ears. Just remember, don't use my name or anything that might identify me."

"But it would help you at your paper." Smythe turned again toward the rear window.

"I don't need that kind of help. Remember, I live here with my wife. Give me your word or you don't get the pictures."

"You have it, Loring. Don't look at me out of the corner of your eye like that. I keep my word. From here on, you're a confidential source. And until the story breaks, not a word to anyone about my being here."

They pulled up to Austin's Inn. Both men felt sudden relief, as if they had just emerged safely from a combat zone. While Mills waited in the car, Smythe took a quick shower and changed into slacks and his sport jacket. In twenty minutes, they were headed north on the Maine Turnpike. They rode in silence until they were approaching Saco. Then Smythe gave Mills his final instructions, with Mills interjecting questions.

"So when I've made the prints I'll send a set, with the negatives, to your home address by Federal Express tomorrow," Mills recapped. "After I let you off, I'll go to my office and start developing right away."

"Are you sure you don't mind working tonight?"

Mills felt his mouth go dry, but he managed to shoot back, "Hell no! That's what you paid me for, and I'll feel better when they're out of here. Where do I send the second set?"

"I'll write it on my business card. Be sure to put the card in with the pictures." Smythe paused and ripped a small piece of paper from his legal pad. "I'm trying to visualize that number," he muttered to himself. He wrote one on the paper and crossed it out. He wrote again. "That's it!" Then he wrote the name and mailing address on the back of his business card. He crumpled the small piece of paper in his left hand. When he couldn't find the ashtray, he laid it on the seat.

"Here's my card with Hundley's address. Send his set by regular mail. He probably won't be back home until the end of next week sometime."

"What about the boat pictures?" Mills asked. He took the card and put it in his shirt pocket. His hand trembled enough that Smythe noticed.

"Send them to me. No need to make a set for Hundley. You'll have all you can say grace over with today's and last night's."

Mills pulled up in front of the airline terminal, and the two shook hands. "Well, Samson, this has scared the piss out of me. But it's been worth it."

"There were some tense moments. That's for sure. I'll send you a copy of the story. The first one should make the Wednesday paper."

"Thanks. Do me a favor and autograph it. Someday I can tell our kid what a crazy bastard you are."

"I'll do it." Smythe bent low and pushed himself from the car. As he did, his hand encountered the crumpled scrap of paper and inadvertently forced it down behind the seat cushion. He reached into the back seat for his suitcase, gave a parting nod, and walked away.

Mills jumped from the car and called after him. "And one other thing. You jimmied the window and door in the Mintmires' garage, didn't you?"

Smythe stopped and grinned back. "Loring, a guy has to get up damn early to put something past you. Let's just say they were careless."

CHAPTER 11

Shortly after Smythe and Mills had left their post at Mintmire's attic window on July 4, 1992, but long before the reception had wound down, Patsy Magaddino paid his respects to his host and apologized for his early departure.

"Vito, what can I say? It's been beautiful. I'm sorry I've had to change my plans, but I better take that six o'clock from Portland that connects in Chicago. I can be back here by Monday."

"Patsy, I understand. I'll arrange a ride to the airport. Are you sure Monica and Gina wouldn't rather stay here with us? Gina was a beautiful bridesmaid, by the way."

"And Camilla and Maria were glowing. But no, you're too generous, and we already have the rooms at the Colony. Gina wants to lounge around the salt-water pool. The men, you know!"

"I know. Perhaps we will be attending a similar event in San Francisco one of these days."

The men embraced again, patting each other on the back.

* * *

Samson Smythe, in the Portland Airport, finally reached the head of the line at the ticket counter and asked for a coach seat. "I'm sorry, that flight is completely sold out in coach. I have one seat left in first class," the United ticket agent advised.

"I'll take it."

"The name?"

Smythe's paranoia took over. "Simes. Paul Simes."

"How will you be paying for your ticket, Mr. Simes."

"Cash."

"Your seat assignment is 3A. We should be boarding in fifteen minutes. Do you have any luggage?"

"No, just carry-on." Smythe took his ticket and headed toward the cocktail lounge.

Twenty minutes later, another man approached the same counter. "Yes, we have your reservation, Mr. Madigan. How will you be paying for your ticket?"

"Cash."

"Your seat assignment is 3B. That flight is now boarding. You will connect with United flight 175 in Chicago for San Francisco. Do you have luggage to check?"

"No. This will fit under the seat."

* * *

When Smythe was settled, he took out his tape recorder and legal pad, breathed a sigh, and in a moment was completely engrossed. When the plane reached cruising altitude, the man in seat 3B spoke. "When are you coming up for air? You're working mighty hard."

Smythe regarded his neighbor for a moment. "Sorry to be so quiet. I'm working on a sale's presentation I have to give on Tuesday." Then his bladder told him that the two beers he had downed before boarding would not wait for Chicago. "Excuse me, I have to use the john."

Smythe put his tape recorder in his pocket, turned his legal pad face down, and began to slide past his seatmate. For a fraction of a second he hesitated, thinking he should take the pad, but dismissed the thought for fear of conveying a wrong impression. As he reached for the handle of the lavatory door, he changed his mind and started to return for the pad, but saw the man had reclined his seat and appeared to be dozing. *Relax*, Smythe told himself. He opened the door and entered the lavatory.

When he returned to his seat, he saw that the man had left his seat for a stretch at the rear of the cabin. Smythe picked up his pad and continued writing, alternately pressing the small recorder to his ear.

* * *

"Vito, this is Patsy."

"Patsy, where are you? I thought you'd be on your way by now."

"I am. I'm calling from the plane. We have a problem. It's pure luck I found out. The guy sitting next to me is Samson Smythe. He doesn't know me but I know him."

"The crime reporter for the *Chicago Tribune?*"

"He's the one," Magaddino replied.

"Are you sure?"

"Positive. The stewardess called him Simes but it's Smythe. I've seen his mug in the papers often enough, and he testified before the San Francisco Crime Commission a coupla years ago and his face was all over TV."

"So what's the problem?"

"He knows about the wedding reception and he's doing a story. From the time he got on the plane, he's been writing on a legal pad and listening to a tape recorder. What got me curious was he has a sketch. It looked familiar. Then I figured out what it was. It's the layout of your lawn. You know, tables, reception line, dance floor, bars. He has names next to some of the tables and he circled the one where Don Salvatore was sitting. Then he had to go to the head. He took the tape recorder but he left the legal pad. I only got a quick look, but it was enough. Vito, take my word, Smythe has the whole nine yards. He had to have been there."

"That motherfucker!" Scalia roared. "But that's impossible. Everyone, and I mean everyone, was screened at the gate. Gabriel and I watched the people during the whole reception. There were no outsiders."

"Vito, I'm telling you –"

"O.K., O.K. I don't doubt what you're telling me. He's a resourceful whore. Let me think. Patsy, how long before you land in Chicago?"

"We're due in a little over an hour. But the captain just came on and said there are thunder storms in the area, and everything's being delayed. Knowing O'Hare, that means at least an extra half-hour, probably more."

"Good! Good! By the time he gets off the plane and reaches the terminal, we're talking two hours. What flight are you on?"

Magaddino took his boarding pass from his suitcoat pocket. "United 350. Do you want me to get off with him?"

"Yeah, do that. We'll have people at the gate and a car."

"All right, I'll be on him like glue. But on the outside chance we get separated, he's wearing a green blazer, yellow sport shirt, and light-tan slacks. He's about six-four or five with sandy hair. They can't miss him. If somebody's gonna be meeting him, I'll switch my watch to the right wrist."

"Patsy, we need that story and his tape recorder." Scalia's voice was calm, but precise.

"Don't sweat it, Vito. They're not going anywhere."

"And, Patsy, one other thing. The whoremonger violated my – our – privacy. Make sure he never does it again."

Magaddino felt perspiration forming on his brow and upper lip. This had suddenly gotten very heavy. But he drew an inward sigh of resignation. "I understand. Make sure the people meeting us do."

* * *

They were thirty minutes from Chicago. Smythe put his tape recorder and writing materials away and signaled the flight attendant. "I think I'll have a vodka and tonic." He then began to think about the fast-moving events of the past three days, while he looked out the window at lightning flashing in the distance.

"Very good, Mr. Simes. How about you, Mr. Madigan, can I get you anything else?"

"A ginger ale please. I'm Pat Madigan," said Magaddino, extending his hand toward Smythe.

Smythe turned from the window and took it. "Paul Simes."

"Paul, do you live in Chicago?"

"The suburbs. Evanston. How about you?"

Magaddino's mind's eye visualized the Chicago-area map in the flight magazine he had quickly studied. "We're almost neighbors. I live in Kenilworth."

Smythe made no pretense of attending to the small talk. His mind was obviously elsewhere, so the two men flew on in silence. Finally, they were taxiing to the gate when Magaddino asked, "Is anyone meeting you, Paul."

"No." Normally an outgoing gregarious person, Smythe began to feel self-conscious about the way he had been rebuffing the pleasant man's efforts to be friendly. It was time to make amends. "Do you wanna share a cab?" he asked.

Magaddino smiled warmly. "That won't be necessary. My son is picking me up. We can give you a ride. Evanston's right on the way. The cab line will be a zoo with this rain."

Smythe cocked his eyebrows. "That's damn thoughtful, Pat. I'll take you up on it."

He and Smythe left the plane together, and Magaddino's eyes immediately picked out the two men in business clothes nonchalantly standing fifty feet apart in the crowded corridor outside the gate area. They didn't stir, but their eyes told him they knew the wait was over. Magaddino raised his left wrist slightly and one of the men began walking toward the passenger terminal.

The other walked to a nearby newsstand. Scalia hadn't skimped. These men were the very best at what they did.

They were passing a men's room when Smythe stopped. "I need to take a quick one."

"I'll wait here for you."

Once Smythe was inside, the man with the paper stepped in front of Magaddino, his back turned. "Good to see you again, Angelo. He doesn't suspect anything. Thinks my son is picking me up. We're supposed to be dropping him off in Evanston. Told him I live in Kenilworth. I'm Pat Madigan, by the way. Under no circumstances can he leave here alone."

Angelo then turned toward the wall as he spoke. "It's a slate-green Taurus wagon. Directly across from the taxi stand. Just follow the baggage claim signs. And don't worry, Mr. Magaddino, he ain't goin nowhere. You'll be covered until he's in the car."

Angelo lost himself in the crowd. When he was past the security check points, he joined the second man for a moment and received a package. He walked quickly to another men's room. He went to a stall, opened the package, and removed a snub-nosed revolver equipped with a silencer. He left the men's room and waited. When he saw Magaddino and Smythe approaching, he nodded to the second man.

* * *

An airport policeman walked up to the Taurus wagon. "Hey, buddy, can't you see the signs? Get moving."

"My passengers will be right out." He reached into his coat pocket for his Chicago Police Department shield.

"Oh, sorry, Lieutenant. Anything I can do?"

"No thanks. Everything's under control."

* * *

Smythe and Magaddino walked toward the sliding doors to the street. Smythe hesitated for a moment, but kept walking. He felt a growing uncertainty. Why, with this story in his briefcase, was he accepting a ride from a perfect stranger? Despite the rain, the cab line was moving smoothly. There would be, at most, a five-minute wait. He had already thrown money around like a drunken sailor. What was an extra $40 or $45 – $55, maybe, with tip? Now they were crossing the street toward the waiting wagon. Smythe suddenly made his decision.

He turned to Magaddino with a tight smile. "Pat, I've changed my mind. I'll take a cab. I'd feel more comfortable not putting you to the trouble."

Magaddino raised his voice to be heard over the roar of a departing plane. "It's no trouble," he shouted. But he recognized Smythe's irrevocable change of heart. He responded by seizing his forearm as Smythe turned to leave. Smythe tried to break free but Magaddino now had him by the shirt collar.

Angelo and his companion, close behind, instantly read the scene. They closed the gap in long, fluid strides and pushed Magaddino aside. Now, each of Smythe's arms was held in a vise-like grip. He could feel something hard near the base of his spine. He opened his mouth, and his brain transmitted the message to scream. Before it could be received, the silenced revolver coughed twice from beneath the newspaper. The hollow-tipped wad cutters shattered the spinal column and disintegrated into a mass of lead splinters, grinding Smythe's insides to pulp. The two men held the body upright and carried it the few remaining feet to the open back door of the wagon.

The policeman turned. "Everything all right, Lieutenant?"

"Yeah. The guy had too much booze. Happens on those long flights."

* * *

Vito Scalia, Don Salvatore, and Gabriel Buffalino were waiting anxiously in the den. A blue haze of cigar smoke hung over the silent figures. They were watching the phones, willing one of them to ring, when a yellow light flashed on the console. Scalia's hand shot out, and he had the receiver in hand before the ring. He listened without interruption.

"Smythe was one of the best. I'll give the bastard that. He made damn near everyone except me, Don Salvatore, and a few others." Magaddino paused for a moment, and Scalia beamed.

"Patsy, what can I say, old friend. You did good. We're all in your debt." Scalia turned to the others. "Everything's under control."

"Hold on Vito! I still need to tell you. I listened to the tape. There's a loose end. Someone was with Smythe and took pictures."

Scalia sprang to his feet. "Gesu! That fucker invades my privacy and then takes pictures of my guests! Didn't he have the film with him?"

"No, he didn't. Probably left it behind for his partner to develop and send to him. Now, –"

"Sonofabitch! It could be anybody. Patsy, we need those pictures and negatives," Scalia hissed.

"Vito, let me finish. I think I know where to look. We went through his clothes and found a piece of paper in his sport jacket. It . . . ."

CHAPTER 12

Loring Mills was in his office at the *York County Coast Star*. He had been working without a break since back from dropping Smythe at the airport. His camera equipment was on the floor and two sets of photographic prints were in two neat piles on his desk. He put one set and the business card in the plain manila envelope addressed to Hundley with Smythe's home address in the left corner. Then he took it to the mail room and weighed it. The postage machine was locked, so he used stamps. As he returned to his office, he saw a man standing in the doorway. He thought the building was deserted, and the sight of the man startled him so badly he began to tremble. The man turned when he heard him. He was of average height, about fifty, a little dumpy in the middle, wore horn-rimmed glasses, and had a meticulously trimmed beard.

"Whew!" Mills exhaled in relief.

"I thought I saw your light on," said Cameron Herd, the paper's chief editorial writer. "Why are you so jumpy?"

"It's nothing. Figured I had the place to myself. You gave me a start, that's all. What're you doing here?"

"Picking up some stuff for my next two columns. Laura and I are headed for Nantucket tomorrow. Some friends invited us for the rest of the month. I was just on my way out."

"Jeez, Cameron, that sounds like a great trip. Do me a favor. You go by the post office. Would you put this in the mail box?"

Herd took the Hundley envelope and left. He made a stop at a convenience store for some items his wife had asked him to pick up. By the time he reached home, he remembered he had forgotten to mail the envelope. He began to back from his driveway, but stopped. I'll mail it when we get to Nantucket, he decided. Tomorrow's Sunday, so it won't make any difference.

* * *

When Herd's car rounded the corner as he left the *Star*, another car with two men pulled into the *Star*'s parking lot. They turned off the headlights and sat for a time watching the building. They wore gray silk suits and dark turtlenecks. Their Burberry trench coats were folded neatly on the back seat.

"I don't see any sign of a security guard, do you?"

"No. That could be Mills's car over there. It's the only one in the lot."

One of the men went to the car and returned. "It's locked." He opened the trunk and removed a long narrow strip of metal looped at one end. "I'll take care of this. You go have a look around."

In less than a minute, the man was inside Mills's car. He opened the glove compartment and removed the registration certificate. He rejoined his companion. "It's his car. He must be inside."

The other man pointed. "Probably in that office. It's the only light. How you wanna handle this? Everything's locked."

"We wait until he comes out. Then he takes us inside."

* * *

Mills looked at his watch. It was almost 11:30 p.m. The heavy flow of adrenaline had given way to near paralyzing fatigue. He put the second set of pictures and the negatives in the envelope addressed to Smythe. All that remained for tomorrow was to find a Federal Express drop. Then he would stop at the bank's teller machine and deposit the $10,000 which he was carrying, as had Smythe, in his sneaker.

He put the envelope under his arm, turned off the lights, and left the building. Suddenly, two men materialized from nowhere. Mills froze as they blocked his path. Beads of perspiration formed on his forehead, and he began to shiver.

"You're working late, Mr. Mills."

"Later than I like. What's it to you?"

"No games, Mr. Mills. The tougher you make it for us, the tougher for you."

Mills looked from the corner of his eye to the street twenty yards away. Two cars passed. A smile crossed the face of one of the men. When Mills spun on his heel and bolted, the man's leg snaked out. Mills's feet were swept from under him and the envelope flew in the air. The man fielded it with one hand and helped him to his feet with the other.

"Now, Mr. Mills, let's go to your office where we can talk."

Mills inserted his name-coded card into the receptacle at the door and the men followed him inside. When they had climbed the stairs to Mills's office, one of the men pulled Mills by the nape of the neck and drove a knee into his groin. As Mills lay writhing on the floor, the other man opened the envelope and removed the pictures and negatives. He began to compare each picture with the corresponding negative, marking them with matching numbers.

"What was that for?" Mills gasped.

"So you won't decide to be a rabbit again. I don't want to use this." The man slipped a black ebony stiletto from a sheath taped to the side of his leg, snapped his wrist, and watched the stiletto imbed itself in the carpet a fraction of an inch from Mills's outstretched hand.

When the other man was satisfied that each picture and negative matched, he asked, "Did you develop these here?"

"In the darkroom across the hall."

"Show me."

For the next forty-five minutes, the men methodically searched every inch of Mills's office and darkroom, while questioning him about his activities for the past two days.

Mills's voice quavered. "I've told you everything I know. Here, take the damn ten thousand." He removed his sneaker and held out the money. "What harm's been done? You have the pictures and the negatives. I'll never say a word to anyone. God Almighty, I don't even know the people in those pictures."

The men ignored the money and said nothing. Finally, Mills lifted his head and looked directly at his two tormentors. His voice no longer quavered. "You have to believe me. Like I told you, Mr. Mintmire doesn't know a thing about this. He was out of town and we broke into his house. You can check for yourselves."

"We will. One last question, Mr. Mills. If you don't spin us, you're home free. You sent a set of these pictures to someone else, didn't you?"

Mills's mind raced. *How did they know about the second set for Hundley? Did they see Herd leave with the envelope? They obviously don't have it. If they don't, they have to be guessing about what was in it. If I tell them, what will they do to him? They can't do anything. It's already in the mail. Hell, they didn't see him. But what will they do to Hundley? If I don't tell them, will they use Priscilla to make me talk? I don't even know this Hundley. I owe him nothing. Will they really let me go if I tell them?*

"Mr. Mills, I asked you a question."

Mills looked directly at his questioner. "I was just thinking. You're going to kill me anyway." As he heard his own words, the terror became a metallic taste in his mouth, but his voice stayed even. "So it doesn't really matter what I tell you. But I swear you're wrong. You have the only set of pictures. Smythe told me to make only one set. That was part of the deal. He didn't want anyone stealing his story. That's why he made me send the negatives."

One of the men walked slowly to where Mills was sitting, yanked him to his feet by the front of his shirt, and again kneed him in the groin. He held him upright while the second man pummeled his kidney area. Then they bound his hands and feet to a heavy chair, and covered his mouth with tape. "Pull down his pants," said one of the men. He lit a cigarette. Mills shook his head rapidly and his eyes swelled. The tape was ripped off.

The men regarded him for a moment. "Let's have it!"

"Please, I'm telling the truth. There are no other pictures."

An hour later, the men carried the inert Mills to their car and deposited him in the trunk.

"Well?"

"I'd say we've squeezed him dry. Either that, or the little rabbit is a very hard case. What do you think?"

"Doesn't matter. What matters is we're absolutely certain. I'd feel better if we grabbed his wife."

"Can't do it. You heard what the don said."

"Then drugs."

"No. I don't trust them. Better, let's get him on the boat."

* * *

It was 3:00 a.m., Sunday, July 5th, when the two men took Loring Mills aboard the fishing boat at a commercial dock in Kennebunkport. The man carrying Mills laid him, not ungently, face up on the deck. The two men quickly tied lengths of line to his hands and feet, lashing him spread-eagle between two stanchions and a pair of rings.

As the boat cast off and headed for the open sea, Mills's eyes opened and his mind began recording the details of his new surroundings. The boat was pitching gently, pale smoke puffing from the blackened stack with each throb of the engine. Mills could see the well-worn grain of the deck extending beyond his cheek, a boathook carefully stashed inside the gunnel, several coils of yellow nylon line, a gaff resting just beyond Mills's extended right arm, a neatly stacked trawling net, a hand net held loosely by hooks protruding from below the back window of the cabin, a steel drum in which holes had been randomly punched, a large green ice chest.

After twenty minutes with the throttle open, the boat slowed. The smaller man opened the green chest, removed a pick, and began honing its point with a small whetstone. He tested the point with his thumb. The larger man then knelt on the deck, straddling Mills's right leg. Suddenly jamming his right knee into Mills's groin, he deftly inserted a small block of wood between Mills's jaws as the jaws parted in scream. The smaller man, now kneeling on Mills's right, inserted the pick, bringing its point to rest on the bearing surface of one of Mills's molars. Then, with the heel of his hand, he drove the pick through the tooth into the nerve below.

"Now what do you say, little rabbit?"

Mills shrieked. But, though tears ran down his cheeks, he made no further sound. He found his mind focused, not on the pain, which he had expected, but on the image of the steel drum, holes punched in its sides, resting on the deck. The drum strangely composed his mind, and some inner kernel of stubbornness, which he would never have divined, kept him from giving the two men what they wanted.

The men repeated the process on three more teeth, pausing between each to see if Mills would speak. Finally, the frail man's heart simply gave out. The men stuffed his body in the drum, secured its top, and rolled it over the side. Bubbles rose from the punched holes, and, within thirty seconds, the drum rested on the ocean floor.

* * *

Vito Scalia and Gabriel Buffalino walked the grounds that early Sunday morning in pajamas and robes. The manicured lawn was strewn with small remnants of yesterday's reception. Vito had the envelope of pictures and negatives under his arm. He gave it a pat.

"So, Gabriel, grandfather's men assure us that we have the only set of pictures and negatives. They were quite thorough."

Buffalino frowned in distaste. "Like animals, is more like it. That kind of brutality was unnecessary. The poor little bastard was obviously too frightened to lie. He told them everything else. If there'd been another set of pictures, he would've told them straight out."

"I told them to be sure. Could they have been more sure?"

"Vito, sometimes you go too far. Anyway, we have the pictures, and the only two people with any knowledge are removed. I suggest we put the matter

71

to rest."

Scalia kicked at an Havana cigar butt. "There's one piece of unfinished business."

"Oh?"

"Mintmire."

Buffalino felt his stomach tighten. "Mintmire! Vito, you can't be serious. He doesn't know a thing. They broke into his house, for Christ's sake!"

The two men stopped and Scalia turned to his brother-in-law. "But suppose he was here? What then? Besides, I'm not so sure he didn't give them a key before he left. Grandfather's men say there's no sign of forced entry. I agree with you that he probably wasn't in on it, but what if he was? He needs a message he won't forget. Gabriel, stop clenching your fist. You make me nervous."

"I make you nervous!" Gabriel exploded. "Mother of God, Vito, have you lost your fucking mind! You can't be thinking of doing him too?"

"No, nothing that crude. He is my neighbor."

They began walking again, and Buffalino quickly arranged his thoughts. "Before you go any further, let me remind you of Goden. Don't be fooled by the fact that he's now a small-town cop. You read his dossier. The New York book on him is that he's tough, resourceful, and imaginative. Goden has a nose for trouble. When he gets fixed on something he doesn't let go. You're in his town, and these are his people. We have a good thing going here. The last thing we need is to have him asking questions. Mills was one thing, but Mintmire is too much. I told you I thought it was a mistake having the family here, and that –"

Scalia put his hand up. "Gabriel, I value your counsel. What's happened proves you right to be concerned. But forget Goden. Mintmire needs a message."

"Maria is right. Someday that temper of yours is going to –"

Scalia put his hand up again, as if dealing with an unruly student. "Let Grandfather decide. You're staying 'til Wednesday, so let's think it over."

Buffalino spoke with defeat in his voice. "What will you tell him? Not that it matters. You have him wrapped around your finger."

Scalia was restored to good humor. "A message for Mintmire is a no-lose proposition. If he wasn't involved, we lose nothing; if he was, our future privacy will be respected."

CHAPTER 13

It was Sunday, July 5th, the day after the Scalia wedding, and Tom and Sarah Goden were on their screen porch drinking coffee and reading the Sunday newspapers. It was another gorgeous day. There was a steady hum from the auxiliary engines of sailboats fighting the incoming tide on their way out the river to the ocean. Tom watched the boats and returned to his reading. "Hey, Doll, there's a piece in the *Portland Press* about the Scalia kid's wedding yesterday. It says the reception was at the house. Do you know anybody who went?"

"Amos got an invitation but couldn't go," Sarah replied, looking up from her own paper.

"Why weren't you invited?"

She turned a little wistful. "Because I don't know him that well and I don't do any legal work for him. Wish I did, though, he's making it a very good year for Amos. Scalia's legal bills are close to one hundred thousand a month."

Tom stood and stretched. He wore only a faded red swimsuit low on his lean hips. He was still in good shape, his stomach flat, and he could pinch less than an inch. "I'd like to get a look at that spread of his. Hear he's spent a small fortune on it."

"Honey, I keep telling you to go make a courtesy call. You're the police chief. He's a pleasant person. Amos likes him. Says he's real easy to deal with."

Tom looked at his wife while he mulled over the suggestion. She was wearing a simple one-piece mauve swimsuit and sandals. Her creamy white complexion had turned nicely bronze under the protection of sunscreen.

"Maybe I'll do that. How about inviting them to dinner some night? I'll toss on some steaks. We could include the Mintmires." He moved to her chair and nuzzled the smooth curve of her breasts.

She pulled gently at a few hairs on his chest, then ran her hand over the nape of his neck. "Let me think about that. He's the firm's biggest client. I don't wanna look like I'm kissing up to him."

At 10:00 a.m., as they were leaving the house for the beach, the phone rang.

"Tom, it's Priscilla Mills for you. I think something's wrong."

He put down the beach chair and blanket and took the receiver from Sarah. "Priscilla, how are you?"

"Chief, I'm sorry to bother you at home but it's about Loring. I've tried everywhere. Oh, God," she sobbed, "I just know something's happened to him. I –"

"Priscilla, you calm down, you hear! Why do you think something's happened to Loring?"

Tom heard a muffled choking sound, then a pause before her answer. "Because he was working at the paper last night. It must've been important. He said he might not be home until after eleven. I haven't heard from him. I've been calling the paper since three-thirty this morning. Someone finally answered. His car is in the parking lot but there's no sign of him. I've called the hospitals but they don't know anything. I'm so worried I could scream. That's why I called you. I'm sorry."

Tom began to pace as far as the phone cord would allow. "Nothing to be sorry about. You should've called sooner. Let me think for a second. Are you calling from home?"

"Yes."

"All right, you stay there while I call the station. Then I'll be over to see you." He forced a reassuring smile as if she could see it.

"Thank you, Chief. Please hurry."

Sarah moved close and put a hand on Tom's arm. "Has something happened to Loring?"

"I don't know. He worked late at the paper last night and never came home. His car's there but no Loring."

Her hand tightened. "Oh, my God! Priscilla must be frantic."

"She is, and with good reason. That little guy worships her. With her expecting and all, he'd never worry her like this." He dialed the police station, impatiently moving from one foot to the other.

"Kennebunkport police."

"Roy, this is Goden."

"Good morning, Chief. See you Mike. What can I –"

"Is that Magruder?"

"Yeah. He's just leaving."

"Put him on."

"Hello, Chief."

"Mike, what time did you come on?"

"Two a.m. I switched with –"

"Never mind that. Did anything come in on bad accidents or fatalities."

"No. It's been quiet for the Fourth of July weekend. What's the problem?"

"Priscilla Mills just called. Loring's dropped out of sight. He worked late at the paper last night and never came home. His car's there but he's gone."

"Jesus! That's not like him," Magruder observed.

"I know it isn't. I'm heading over there now."

"O.K., I'll get right on it."

Tom paced beyond the reach of the phone cord and the phone fell off the table with a crash. Sarah quickly replaced it. "Also, call the paper and tell them to stay out of his office. I don't want anything touched. Same with his car. If the state police and the hospitals don't have anything, put out an all points."

"Isn't that jumping the gun a little? I mean –"

"No it isn't. I don't like the feel of this, and the sooner we get cranking the better. Tell the state police we need a lab team. Find out how soon they can send one."

"Will do. I'll stay in touch."

Tom hurried upstairs to change. He opened the closet and looked at a row of navy-blue, hunter-green, tan, and maroon blazers, and slacks in various shades of gray – his business clothes. The police-chief uniform was in the back, reserved for parades and ceremonial occasions. He selected navy-blue and charcoal gray, quickly changed, and hurried to his car. Priscilla's call had touched off not only professional alarm, but personal concern. The photographer for the *York County Coast Star* and his pleasant wife were a young couple he and Sarah were very fond of.

* * *

The small three-bedroom house of Loring and Priscilla Mills was in various stages of repair. There was a smell of fresh paint and some of the walls had swatches of wallpaper taped to them. Priscilla sat on the living room sofa in a brightly flowered smock nervously fingering her wedding band. Her blond hair was nicely combed and she looked very pretty, but the rims of her soft blue eyes were red and swollen and her face was waxen.

"Priscilla, honey, tell me everything you know about Loring's activities the past few days. You could begin by telling me what he was working on at the paper that was so important he'd be there late at night on a holiday weekend." Tom flipped open a note pad and pulled a chair to face her.

She shrugged in frustration. "That's just it – I don't know. When he came home from the office Thursday, he seemed excited about something. I asked about it and he sort of pooh-poohed. He did say he might have something that could mean a little extra money. Friday morning he tore out of here full of it. He called later in the morning to say he would probably be gone from the office for the rest of the day. Then he called again and said he wouldn't be home for dinner and might be working late. When he got home it was after eleven and he was very preoccupied. His shirt was damp, like he'd been perspiring. Something was really bothering him, but he wouldn't talk about it. That night he –"

"Are you sure he'd been at the paper?"

There was a quick look of challenge. "Oh, yes. He smelled sweaty, but he also had the smell on his hands and clothes he gets working in that darkroom. And he didn't smell of perfume or anything like that."

"Hell, Priscilla, I wasn't suggesting –"

She bit her bottom lip until teeth marks showed. "I know you weren't, but I want to cover everything. Loring's a good man. He'd never cheat on me," she sobbed. The tears rolled from her eyes, ruining the light touch of makeup.

"I know that," Tom said softly.

"I'm sorry. Give me a moment. Where was I? Oh, yes. He tossed and turned all night. This morning – Oh, God, I mean yesterday morning – he sat around the house until about ten. I knew he'd been keeping something from me. I got a little testy with him, you know, told him he shouldn't be keeping things from his wife. He gave me a big hug and patted my stomach. Said the job he was working on would be finished by the end of the day." She wiped her eyes and looked at Tom.

"Then he nearly floored me. Said he was being paid ten thousand dollars. He kissed me good-bye and that's the last I saw of him. He called a little after six to say he'd be working late again to finish the job and not to wait up for him. When it got to be ten-thirty or so, I began to worry. Then he called again and told me he'd be home in an hour. He sounded – I don't know – relieved. He said everything was fine and to go to bed. It was about three-thirty when I woke up. I thought I heard Loring calling me. I put a robe on and went downstairs. But –"

She began to cry softly. Then she wiped her eyes again and bit on her tissue. "That's everything. The rest I told you on the phone. There's no need to fool me. I know something terrible has happened to Loring. I've resigned myself to that. Now the hard part is not knowing what."

"Priscilla, I know how those things work. We've pulled out all the stops. Don't you go giving up hope. Do you feel up to answering some questions?" Tom turned a page and put the note pad back on his knee.

Her lips quivered and for a moment she looked helpless. Then, folding her hands in her lap, she steadied her gaze. "Yes, of course."

"Did Loring do work on the side?"

"Sometimes. He did family pictures, some weddings and such."

"This ten-thousand-dollar job – I assume it had nothing to do with the paper?"

"That was my understanding. The paper pays him a decent salary but not that kind of extra money."

"Now, someone was going to be paying him. Was that person working with him on the job or was Loring working on it alone?"

There was another frustrated shrug. "I don't know. He just wouldn't tell me anything."

"When he left the house Friday and Saturday, did he say he was going to be meeting somebody?"

"No."

"What was he wearing on Saturday?"

"A navy-blue summer shirt, tan shorts, and white sneakers."

"How about Friday?"

"He wore a new sport coat and tie. He even started to put on a suit then changed his mind. I told him how nice he looked."

"I assume he had his camera equipment with him both days?"

"Oh, yes. He always carried it in his trunk."

"When he left Saturday, did he take anything unusual with him?"

"No. Wait a minute. Yes. Well not really unusual. He got to his car and then came back into the house for a towel."

"Why a towel?"

"I don't know. He just breezed back in and out."

"Is there still a guard on duty at night?"

"No. The paper changed that last month. Now you use a security card to get in."

"You said something was bothering him Friday night that he wouldn't talk about. But when he left Friday morning, he was, how would you say it – upbeat?"

"Exactly."

"If you had to take a wild guess, what sort of thing would you say was bothering him?"

Priscilla began twisting her wedding band again. Then she rose from the sofa, walked to the window, and stood for a moment, her hands clutched, watching the busy traffic on School Street. Wiping her eyes, she returned to the sofa.

"Something was eating at him real bad. I don't have to guess. He'd done something he wasn't proud of."

Tom rose from the chair and sat down on the sofa to face her. "Knowing Loring as well as I do, I wouldn't think that," he said firmly. "But this has been very helpful. I'm going over to the paper now. If we haven't learned anything by later today, you stay with us tonight."

They stood up, both knowing nothing more could be accomplished just now. Trying to smile her gratitude, she managed to say, "Chief, that's not necessary."

"I wish you would," Tom persisted.

"No need. My sister is going to be here any minute to stay with me."

Tom took her hand and squeezed it for a moment. "One last thing, do you have a set of keys to Loring's car?"

"Yes, I'll get them." He watched her hurry from the room as he put his note pad away. Nothing she had told him was anything but discouraging. Helpful, but discouraging.

CHAPTER 14

Later that Sunday afternoon, Tom was in Loring Mills's office when the lab man entered.

"That's about it, Chief, we'll be done with the car in a few minutes. What specifically are you looking for? We vacuumed everything here and in the car. Prints are a hodgepodge. You know, give us some direction."

"That's easy. Just tell me where Mills is," Tom snapped. The state cop was short and fat, with buggy eyes. Tom had worked with him before. He was first-rate at what he did, but he had the irritating habit of asking you questions to which he had the answers, or thought he did.

"Just like that?"

"Yeah, just like that. I'm particularly interested in this damp spot on the carpet."

"I thought you would be. Do you think someone grabbed him?"

"Yes I do."

"How do you figure that – apart from the stain itself?"

"He called his wife from here to tell her he'd be home in an hour. His car started right up today. This means he didn't have car trouble last night. So we have two possibilities. He could have decided to disappear on his own. But if he did, why would he call his wife? She's pregnant with their first child and he loves her. He wouldn't do that to her. I know this guy. So what's left?"

"I follow you. We'll do our best."

* * *

"This everything?" Tom asked, viewing the flotsam from Mills's car lying on a plastic sheet in the parking lot.

"That's it," replied one of the technicians. "Nothing but that sweaty towel, sunglasses, tissues, and the stuff from the glove compartment – owner's manual, registration, and a repair bill. Nothing in the trunk but the usual spare-tire equipment."

"How about the ash tray?"

"Empty."

"Work the towel over good – real good." Tom crouched and examined the items carefully, moving things with the tip of a pencil. He was about to rise, but stopped.

"Where did you find this piece of paper?"

"It was crumpled up inside a small rip in the back of the front-seat cushion. We found it when we removed the seats. Almost missed it."

"Did it look like it had been there awhile?"

"Hard to say. The writing looks fresh."

Tom took out his note pad. "The first entry has been crossed out. It looks like '460'."

"Yeah," the technician agreed.

"The second one is good and clear: 'R L 160H'," Tom observed.

"That's what it looks like to me."

He thanked the lab team and went back to Mills's office. Twenty minutes later he left the building and started the short drive to Kennebunkport. As he neared the bridge, there were lines of bumper-to-bumper traffic in both directions. Tourist season had come with a vengeance. As he inched his way toward Dock Square, he studied his notes once more. It was time for some brainstorming.

Entering the police station, he found Lieutenant Carl Tito and Sergeant Mike Magruder in the kitchen drinking coffee. Magruder had been on duty for nearly sixteen hours but looked surprisingly fresh. They had both been on the phones nearly non-stop. Tom gave them a wave, and they followed him to his office. While they finished their coffees, he gave them a play-by-play account of what he had learned from Priscilla Mills and of events at the paper.

"It has to be connected to that ten grand," observed Magruder. "Friday morning he's on top of the world minus ten big ones. Friday night he's looking at ten grand but he's in the dumps. The only thing that makes sense is he didn't like what he had to do to earn it."

"Then what?" Tom pushed.

Magruder tapped his fingers on the arm of the chair for a moment. "He either wouldn't perform, in which case he pissed off the buyer, or he did perform, but not to the buyer's satisfaction. Or, he did a top-notch job and the buyer didn't want him around to talk about it. I'd say its the third possibility."

"Carl?"

80

Tito nodded his craggy head in Magruder's direction. "Mike's right. Loring makes contact on Thursday. Gets his marching orders on Friday, and they bother him. But he does the deal anyway on Saturday. And Saturday night he delivers whatever he was working on – most likely pictures – and gets smoked for his efforts."

"That rings," Tom agreed. He rose and seized the back of his desk chair with both hands. "But there could be another twist which lets the buyer off the hook. Suppose the buyer hired Loring to get pictures of something or someone. Then the target of the job finds out and grabs Loring before he can deliver." Tom paused, then continued.

"You know, one of the things that's starting to bother me is Priscilla. What if the target thinks she might know something?"

Tito leaned forward. "Do you want to put a car on her?"

"Yeah. Do that." Tom's lowered tone meant *now!* Tito and Magruder hurried from the office.

When Tom opened his note pad to continue brainstorming, his eye hit the entry he had made of the letters and numbers from the crumpled scrap of paper. When Tito and Magruder returned, he pointed to the entry. "What do you make of that?"

Tito and Magruder studied the page. "I'd say it's the license number of a rental car," Tito replied. "Every state uses 'R' as the first letter."

"So would I," Magruder agreed. "Where did you get it?"

"From a crumpled piece of paper the lab boys found in the back of the front-seat cushion in Loring's car."

"Is it his writing?" Tito asked.

"It seems to be – what little there is. Before I left, I compared it to some writing in his office. Looks similar. Right now we don't have shit, so let's make some wild assumptions."

"That's easy," said Magruder. He stretched his long legs from the chair and studied the tips of his Timberlands. "Loring is doing the deal and comes across a license number. Maybe it's the customer's. Maybe it's the target's. Whatever. It's important so he writes it down and puts it in his pocket. Then he's in his car when the deal begins to unravel. He needs a hiding place in a big hurry. So he stuffs it down behind the seat."

"Sure. The ashtray's empty, so that's no good. And the glove compartment is too obvious," added Tito. "But why didn't he write down the state?"

"Who knows?" replied Tom. "Maybe he didn't have time. What's more likely is the car was too far away. He wrote three numbers and crossed them out. So he must've had trouble getting it right. I'll ask Vince Inserra to get the Bureau on it."

Magruder put a hand over his mouth for a moment to stifle a yawn that had been building. "What I can't figure is, let's assume we have the right slant on this. What the Christ could Loring have known that was so important it might have cost him his life?"

"When we know that, we'll have our collar," Tom surmised. He ran his fingers lightly over the long scar on his cheek, then turned to stare out the window.

* * *

The telephone rang in Evanston, Illinois. "Hi, Mom, I'm glad you called. Have you talked to Dad?" asked Jan Smythe.

"Not since Wednesday. I've been at the Lake of the Ozark's with grandmother and her friends. We just got back to Kansas City. Stayed an extra day. Why do you ask? Isn't he home?"

"No. I just got back myself this afternoon."

"He's probably working late on something."

"The house doesn't seem like there's been anyone here. And there's no note."

"You know how your father is when he's on a project. Go upstairs and see if his suitcase is in our closet. He could be out of town."

Jan returned to the phone two minutes later. "You're right. It's not there. I've been out for dinner. Maybe he called then."

"You'd think in his business we'd have one of those message machines. Everyone has one. Don't worry about him. I'll see you tomorrow."

CHAPTER 15

Amy Mintmire was bright and lively like her mother. She was also a business major with visions of someday running the family automobile dealership. This was the third summer she had worked for her father, Neil.

The Mintmire dealership was open until 9:00 p.m. six nights a week during the summer months. At 9:45 p.m. on July 7th, Amy and the last of the sales people completed the closing routine, locked up, and went their separate ways. Ten minutes later, two men moved quickly through the darkened lot, molding small globs of plastic to gasoline tanks of strategically selected cars. When done, they turned their attention to the gasoline pump and the two buildings containing the sales offices and the service and repair facilities. Finally, they placed a battery-operated timer set to detonate the latticework of dormant charges at 11:30 p.m.

As they were leaving, one of the men frowned. "There's no guarantee this will blow. We're working with surplus shit. Better to juice it from here."

"He knows that. But he told us to be at the house when it goes."

* * *

Abbey Mintmire was in the living room with a book. She was a striking woman in her early forties, with dark hair that fell to her shoulders, alert eyes over a slightly prominent nose, full lips, and a firm jaw. When she heard her daughter's car enter the garage, she took off her reading glasses and walked to the kitchen. It was 10:25 p.m.

"Hello, Mom. Where's Dad?" Amy asked, shedding the jacket to her business suit and walking over to kiss her mother.

"He's in bed. I think the trip and the drive home last night caught up with him. Anything happen?"

Amy opened the refrigerator and foraged for a snack. "Yeah. It was a pretty good night, actually. We – Damn!"

"What's wrong, dear?"

Amy slammed the refrigerator door. "I forgot to set up the cash drawer for the service shop. Millie won't be on until noon and I promised I'd take care of it tonight. I have to go back. Dad's playing golf in the morning and I'm going on that sailing trip."

Her mother managed to combine a smile with a frown. "Can't you get up early and do it?"

Amy grimaced. "We're leaving early as it is. I'd much rather do it tonight."

"If you wait a couple of minutes, I'll go with you."

Amy's grimace turned to a smile. "Thanks, Mom, I'd like the company."

They arrived at the dealership at 11:15 p.m. Abbey looked at model cars in the showroom while waiting for her daughter. At 11:29 p.m., Amy called from the front door: "O.K., Mom, I'm done. Let's blaze!"

Abbey smiled at her daughter, then chuckled to herself. *Such a descriptive idiom!*

They walked across the lot and were about to enter Amy's car, when a tiny light glowed bright red. The doubtful detonator functioned perfectly. Ten miles away the blasts sounded like the staccato booms of a fireworks display. Twenty miles away they sounded like rumbles of distant thunder. The shrapnel from the cars exploding all around them killed Amy instantly. Abbey's last sight was of the mutilated body of her daughter.

Twenty-five miles away, on a beach in Kennebunkport, three men listened for the explosions. As the sound rumbled over them, one muttered through clenched teeth, "Messagio recapitato!"

CHAPTER 16

By 5:00 p.m. Tom had cleared his desk of routine paper and was again fretting the possibility of a link between the Mintmire bombing and the disappearance of Loring Mills. When Tito and Magruder appeared at his door, he waved them in. Seated, they glanced at each other before either spoke. Tom steeled himself.   "What do you have?"

"The preliminary lab results just came," said Tito. "We've been over them. Here."

Tom scanned the three-page report. His stomach roiling, he looked up sadly.

"I guess the urine on the carpet is Loring's. If it is, we pretty well know why he fouled himself. But that's, that's —"

"Water over the dam," completed Magruder.

"For now," said Tom, rising and then sitting back down. "What do you make of the insulation fibers in his towel?"

"We talked about that. Insulation and a sweaty towel mean someplace hot. Do you have a partially finished attic at home?" Tito asked.

"Yeah, we do. And it's unbearable in the summer."

Tito pointed a finger toward the ceiling. "Take a look when you get home. You'll probably find that the floor area is packed with insulation. If it isn't, you're losing a lot of heat in the winter. We figure Loring was in an attic or a loft. Someplace like that."

Tom moved some papers absently, then chewed on his pencil eraser. Not looking at the two men, he struggled for something to say. "We still haven't found anyone other than the waitress at The Landing who recalls seeing him?"

"That's right," Tito replied. "Loring had breakfast there with someone on Friday. All she remembers without a picture is that the guy was tall, fairly good-looking, and had light hair. She waited on him again Saturday morning, but he was alone. We picked up something else this afternoon. Joan Austin just got back in town. She says that last Thursday Loring made a reservation in his own name. Then on Friday morning a man calling himself Paul Simes checked in and claimed the reservation. He checked out late Saturday afternoon. He didn't give his address, and she didn't press for one because he paid cash. She remembers that he was over six feet, pleasant, had a squint and a thick wad of bills. We figure this Simes is the one Loring had breakfast with at The Landing. Inserra can check the airlines. Simes might've taken a flight after he checked out of Austin's."

"That fits too," said Magruder. "Austin said he didn't have a car, which could mean Loring drove him around. Probably picked him up and dropped him off. I'd say Portland is the best bet."

"One other thing," said Tito, "the paper still hasn't reached Cameron Herd. They can't get an answer at the number he left."

* * *

The northeaster was still punishing the Maine coast when the Godens finished dinner. Tom was making coffee while Sarah stacked the dishwasher.

"Tom, I just can't understand why you think the disappearance of Loring is connected to the Mintmire bombing." She added the last of the silverware and reached for detergent.

"I'm not sure I understand. It's just that my gut tells me the two are related. How, I don't know; maybe it's the timing."

Sarah closed the dishwasher door and punched the button. "But there is no timing. Loring disappeared Sunday afternoon – two days before the bombing. And the Mintmires weren't even in town that weekend."

Tom poured the coffee and they moved to the living room. "What I meant was you have two Kennebunkport families who get harshed back to back. How often does that happen?"

"But so what! You talked to Neil, and he hardly knows Loring and hadn't seen him for months."

Tom's eyes narrowed. "You may have put your finger on it."

"On what?"

"Neil was involved in whatever Loring was doing but doesn't realize it."

"And where do you get that?"

"It's the timing again. If Loring was tortured, he could have implicated Neil. But in what?"

Sarah frowned. "If Loring implicated Neil, he sure as hell did the same to Simes. Right now I wouldn't be thinking about what Neil did. I'd be worrying about Simes."

"You're right."

86

CHAPTER 17

It was 6:30 Saturday night, July 11th. Tom was on the flagstone patio arranging a fresh bag of charcoal, lighter fluid, and his cooking utensils next to the Weber grill. He looked up when he heard the Scalias' four-door silver Mercedes turn into the driveway. Vito turned off the engine and moved smartly around the car to open the door on the passenger side. Out slid a pair of long tan legs, then a white summer skirt cut well above the knees, and a purple breast-hugging blouse. Maria Scalia stretched for a moment, saw Tom, and waved. *A piece of work,* he thought, walking toward them. Vito flashed a smile. He was in yellow bermuda shorts and a black Polo. Tom's usual summer shirt had an alligator. Vito extended his hand and the muscles of his tan arm rippled. Tom stuck out his own muscled arm and the two locked hands in a hard grip.

* * *

Tom strode through the back door into the kitchen, flourishing a tray weighted by four pieces of blackened meat. His face flushed from the heat of the grill and his second gin and tonic, he put the tray down and pushed the hair from his eyes. He wore a red apron with blue lettering: "Function In Disaster. Finish In Style!"

"Tom," chided Sarah, "there's enough steak to feed an army; and they look like you cooked them with an acetylene torch. I've told you: Don't use so damn much charcoal."

"Now, Doll, a good steak requires a crust," Tom replied, tweeking each piece of blackened meat with his barbecue fork.

Sarah threw up her hands and rolled her eyes. Vito half-smiled; Maria grinned.

Poking fun at Tom was a good ice-breaker, and he was loving it. So she poked again.

"When we first moved here, the first thing Tom did was buy an outdoor grill. He's the ultimate meat-and-potatoes man. Thinks Bearnaise sauce is a French conspiracy to ruin beef. He usually beats me home, and the first thing he does is light the damn Weber. I swear, I'm going to hide it so we can have a decent meal. What do you think, Vito, you were out there with him – doesn't he get the fire too hot?"

Vito smiled and feigned a slap at his neck. "It did keep the mosquitoes away."

"He does the same thing in the winter. The neighbors think he's crazy. Oh, well, let's go eat. At least they smell good."

When Tom had put a steak on each of four heated plates, Sarah added fried onion rings, au gratin potatoes, and green beans. With Sarah leading, the four carried their plates to the dining room, where separate servings of caesar salad, hot french bread dressed with garlic butter, and an opened bottle of red wine waited on the dining table.

Salt air and alcohol had sharpened their appetites and they attacked their food with zest. "Every time I serve a meal like this, I swear it's the last," said Sarah. "It's downright unhealthy."

"You and Tom couldn't look healthier, and the food was delicious," Maria responded, sipping the last of her wine.

Their bantering continued until Sarah directed everyone to the living room for coffee. There, the mood became more serious.

Vito was sitting on the sofa with an arm and faultlessly manicured hand draped casually along the back. "Sarah, we saw you and Tom at the Mintmire funeral yesterday. Wasn't that the saddest event you've ever attended?"

"Just about."

Maria put her coffee down. "What a tragedy!"

The tone and pace of Tom's voice were tightly controlled. "Makes you wonder. First, a good kid like Loring Mills disappears. His wife's given up hope of ever seeing him again. Then a classy guy like Neil Mintmire gets his family blasted. It's senseless."

"Do you have any leads on either?" Vito asked.

Sarah, listening intently, now sensed some sullenness in her husband's voice. "Naw. All we know is that Mills just dropped from sight; and the Portland P.D. hasn't made any progress on the Mintmire bombing. About all we can hope for is a lucky break."

Vito took his arm from the back of the sofa and, looking squarely at Tom, leaned forward. "I don't know that I can do anything to help, but if there is, just holler."

"Thanks, Vito, I'll keep you in mind."

The two couples spent the balance of the evening talking of life in

Kennebunkport, the effect of the recession on Vito's business, the presidential campaign, and the like. When Sarah pressed for details of the wedding and the reception, Maria complained that too many of Vito's customers and not enough friends were there.

As the hour edged to 11:00, Vito was studying the long ash building on his bootleg Havana. "Sarah, I had a meeting yesterday with your partner, Amos St. John. I'm sorry to hear he's retiring."

"So are we. He's been planning to retire for a year now. I think the only reason he stayed on was because of your account. That's taken up all his time."

"Well, I've met with two other law firms, and they've been giving me a pretty hard sell. I had to be impressed."

Sarah knitted her brow. "Vito, what can I say? It's your investment business. Do what makes you most comfortable. I know our firm can deliver as well as any firm in Maine, but it's your decision."

Before Vito could resume, Maria interposed. "Will you lay off the business bit! Sarah, I apologize for Vito. It's been a lovely evening, and I don't know why he's putting a damper on it."

But Vito would not be put down.

"Who's putting a damper on it? You haven't heard me out. Sarah, if I decided to stay with your firm, who would get credit for the business?"

She thought a moment. "Actually, no one. We have what's called an 'origination fee' system for new business. It's paid to the partner who brings the business in. But since you're already Amos's client, you'd become a firm account and the fee would be spread among all the partners. Actually, 'fee' is a misleading term. What it means is that for every dollar a client is billed, the partner who brought in the client receives a certain percentage regardless of whether he or she does any work on the account. It's the way rainmakers are rewarded."

Vito allowed himself a Santa Claus smile. "What would happen if I told your firm I was going to remain a client only so long as you were a partner and that if you left my business would follow you?"

Sarah, now seeing where Vito was leading, saw a string of dollar signs. "Then I'd become the originating attorney on all your legal business."

"So, even if you didn't work on my account you'd get the origination fee?"

"That's right."

"How much is the origination fee?"

Sarah hesitated. "Thirty percent. Vito, what are you driving at?"

He moved his cigar over an ashtray and tapped it with his little finger, studying the ash as a philatelist might study a rare stamp. "In a second. So, if my business and personal legal expenses totaled a million a year, you'd get three hundred thousand?"

Tom steadied one hand with the other as he returned his cup and saucer to the coffee table.

"That would be the gross amount. I have to bear my share of the law firm's overhead, but I'm already doing that. So yes, you're right, I'd get an extra three hundred thousand if the firm's net profit were large enough to cover it."

"Sarah, I've heard a lot about your legal work – not just from Amos, but from business people and other lawyers – and I like what I've heard. I'm meeting with your firm's executive committee on Monday."

"I know. I'm a member."

Vito brought the cigar to his lips, revived its glow, and, forming an O with his lips, sent a string of smoke rings marching over the coffee table. "Then act surprised when I tell the committee I'm staying with the firm on the understanding that you get the credit as originating partner."

Sarah tied the last loose end. "Vito, you understand that I won't be working on your affairs. I do mostly criminal law matters."

"I understand. Just make sure I get the best."

"Depend on it," she assured.

* * *

A half-hour later, the Scalias made their goodbyes, and the Godens saw them off as the Mercedes backed from the driveway onto Ocean Avenue for the short drive home. Returning inside, Sarah was in a state of shock as she numbly walked to the living room, sat again in the chair across from the sofa, and looked at Tom.

"Tom, honey, make us a nightcap. I need one."

"I'll bet you do." He went to the kitchen and returned with gin and tonics. "Is that one-million figure realistic? Hell, even half that means you bag an extra one hundred fifty thou."

She took the drink and rattled the ice cubes before taking a long swallow. "Yes, it is realistic. I told you we've been billing him close to one hundred thousand per month. An investment firm that big generates an enormous amount of legal work. From the way he was talking, I get the feeling he's also going to steer some friends and customers our way. Three hundred thousand could be the minimum."

Sarah moved to the sofa, next to Tom. "Jesus, Doll, you could retire. I mean semi-retire. You know, just go to the office and clip your Scalia coupons."

She put down the drink and frowned. "What I'm wondering is why's he doing this?"

Tom had a quick answer. "That's easy. It doesn't cost him anything. You're a partner and a manager in one of Portland's top firms. If he's not paying your firm, he's paying another one. This way he gets someone he has confidence in to take a personal interest in his account. Don't underestimate your reputation. He wasn't bullshitting. He obviously likes you, and being married to the police chief doesn't hurt. Christ, with Vito as a client you'll probably end up being the chairman of the executive committee."

"Chairwoman," she corrected. "I might even get used to his filthy cigar smoke."

* * *

Maria looked at her husband as he maneuvered the Mercedes from the Godens' driveway. "Vito, you seem to have enjoyed yourself tonight – especially when you told Sarah Goden you were about to make her one of the richest lawyers in the state."

He momentarily took his eyes from the road and turned his head. "Maria, I always enjoy doing nice things for people."

Her tone stiffened. "I know why you're doing it. But don't underestimate her; and don't underestimate him. Those two can be hard cases."

"I know that. But the attorney-client privilege can be a very valuable tool; and I don't lose anything by having them as friends. I like their style."

"So do I. It would be nice to make some real friends in the town."

"Sounds good," he replied perfunctorily. "Did you believe Goden when he said he had no leads."

Maria felt her cheeks flush. "Vito, you son of a bitch, I told you I never wanted to hear about that again! I've heard enough to make me sick."

His tone remained conversational. "Not so sick that you're ready to give up the life I provide you."

"Vito, fuck off. Don't tempt me."

"I asked you a question," he reminded her.

"Yeah, I believed him. But you'd better pray he doesn't get one. If he does, he'll never get off your back. Gabriel warned you and you wouldn't listen. At times, you can be a goddamn animal." She was watching her husband and saw the blood drain from his face. The ugly insult suddenly seemed hollow.

Vito drove into the garage and turned off the lights and engine. Maria was opening her car door when he roughly seized her left arm. "This is why you'll never leave me, you bitch."

In a single movement, he slid across the seat and turned Maria, lifting her onto his lap until she straddled him. Then he tore off her blouse and brassiere. He hiked her skirt to her waist and ripped off her panties. He pushed her away and shifted his tongue to her nipples while he squeezed her breasts until she cried out in pain. Despite the pain, her nipples gradually became erect. Holding her by the hair with his left hand, he removed his right hand from her breast and ran it up her thigh, insinuating his middle finger. Maria began to moan. She ground her hips against his hand. Then she pulled his head from her nipple and plunged her tongue into his mouth. Their moans became guttural.

As he erupted within her, and her jolting orgasm joined his, she shivered with the sense of his domination. The question began to form. "How can he own me so completely?"

CHAPTER 18

On Friday, July 24, 1992, Tom arrived home at 6:00 p.m. Tilting with windmills was all he could think of to describe the four unproductive days that had passed. R L 160H – or was it 460 – had become a cunning opponent whose identity, it seemed, would remain a secret.

Sarah wasn't home yet. He changed into worn jeans, a faded denim shirt, and battered Nikes. Then he opened a can of beer and carried it to a lawn chair in the yard.

Tom sat watching the Kennebunk River and the boats returning to their moorings. Holding the beer in one hand and massaging his temples with the other, he replayed for the hundredth time the events which had transpired since the frantic call from Priscilla Mills. What was he missing? He had built an investigation entirely around unproven assumptions: Paul Simes had hired Loring Mills to take incriminating pictures; Mills had been discovered, tortured, and murdered; before his death, he had written down and hidden a license-plate number; and Mintmire was involved somehow and had been punished. So what did Tom have? A series of meaningless letters and numbers on a discarded scrap of paper.

Tom ended his fruitless ruminations when he heard Sarah's car enter the driveway. She came through the house and joined him. She was in a fitted dark-brown suit and off-white shirt, with a single strand of pearls and matching earrings, her hair pulled back, and wire-rimmed glasses.

"Hi, how was your day?" he asked in a flat voice.

"Good! Very good! This Scalia account is a gold mine. You sound down in the mouth. Still no progress?"

He tried a smile, but it came out a grimace. "Nope. We're spinning our wheels trying to figure out what the hell those numbers and letters are. Inserra's gotten nowhere with them. Neither has Jerry Borghesani. I'm beginning to think we'll never know."

Sarah put her briefcase on the flagstones and pulled up a lawn chair, bending down to kiss him first. "You going to stay with it?"

"Of course. We don't have anything else."

"I think your assumption that Loring hid that paper is right. I mean, think about it. How often do you stuff things down behind the seat? I know I never do. It's too sloppy."

He groaned, then drained his beer. "Jesus Christ! I should run an investigation based on your housekeeping habits?"

"It's human nature," Sarah persisted. "You might do that in someone else's car but not in your own."

"If you say so. Maybe it was some passenger, maybe Simes, who did it. Then where are we? Aw, shit, let's talk about something else. You want a gin and tonic?" he asked, without enthusiasm.

"Sounds good. Get me one while I change." She rose and rested her hand on his arm for a moment before going in.

Sarah returned in khaki walking shorts and a white summer-weight sweater. Her hair was down and brushed to a high gloss. Some extra makeup and softer glasses completed the transformation. "It's a beautiful night. Why don't we drive over to Cape Porpoise for dinner."

He looked at his pretty wife and smiled. "I'd like that."

* * *

Maybe it was the effect of a leisurely dinner at a table overlooking the harbor, but on the drive toward home Tom briefly shed the pressures and frustrations of the past weeks. He was about to turn left on Ocean Avenue but changed his mind and turned right. "Dock Square looks active. How does an ice-cream cone sound?"

"Wonderful!"

Cones in hand, they walked around the square licking at dribbles of chocolate and strawberry. "It looks like The Copper Candle is crowded, and it's after ten," noted Sarah.

"David must've had a good day. I see him in the window. Let's go over and say hello," Tom suggested.

They entered the store and chatted with David Armstrong for a few minutes. "I think I'll browse a bit," Sarah said. "Do you have anything new and exciting?"

"Some new Portuguese candlesticks," the shop owner replied. "I'll show you. Be right back, Tom."

The two walked toward the rear of the store, while Tom lounged by the check-out counter. "Has it been busy tonight, Megan?" he asked one of the summer employees.

"Yes, Chief, the way we like it."

"Did you have a good year at college?"

Before she could answer, they were interrupted by two customers with merchandise. Tom watched their purchases being bagged. Then one of the customers asked, "Do you have a business card?"

"Certainly," Megan replied. She reached under the counter and handed one to the woman.

After the customers left, Tom asked, "Why do you keep those under the counter? Wouldn't it be better to have them where people can see them?"

"They're too expensive. If you keep them on the counter, everyone ends up taking one. Lots of people collect business cards."

"Well, in that case I'll take one," Tom said, with a grin. "Hey, Megan, I'm only joking," he protested.

"I know you are, but take one anyway."

Tom took the card, gave it a perfunctory glance, and absently put it in his pocket.

* * *

Monday, July 27, 1992. First there was a persistent line of thunderstorms. Then the plane had mechanical difficulty. It was six hours late departing Atlanta, and so it was 2:00 a.m. before Dick Hundley finally arrived home. But he was a morning person and by 7:00 a.m. he was up and about. He took bread and bacon from the freezer and prepared breakfast. Then he made a grocery list and puttered around. At 8:30 a.m., he looked at his watch and reached for the phone.

"Good morning, Lieutenant Cain's office."

"Joyce, this is Dick Hundley. Is he in?"

"Just arrived. I'll put you through."

After a short pause, Cain came on. "Dick, you back home?"

"Yeah, Ronnie, but didn't get in until late. Got hung up in Atlanta half the day. Any word on Samson?"

"Zilch! This fucking thing has us buffaloed. Feel sorry for his wife and kid. Don't have to tell you, it's looking bad. We simply don't have shit at this point. We still figure he was heading for Cape Cod. What more can I say?"

"I understand. Keep in touch, you hear."

"Don't worry. I get anything, you'll be the first to know."

Hundley hung up and shook his head. He sat for a time, suddenly feeling lethargic. Then he pulled himself together and drove into town for his groceries and mail. Two hours later he was back at his bungalow, putting groceries away and then getting out his fishing tackle. On the way out the door, he glanced at the large bundle of mail which had accumulated since his trip to Atlanta on July 1 – most of it obvious junk. He left it unopened.

Hundley returned from fishing at 2:30 p.m., showered, and began sorting his mail. He was nearly to the bottom of the large pile when he saw it – a bulky manila envelope with Samson Smythe's home address in the left corner.

* * *

On Monday morning, Tom pulled into the Kennebunkport Police Department at 8:45. He sat in his car for a moment, not eager to begin a workweek like the last. Inserra was right; they had come up dry. But acceptance of this unarguable conclusion would be immobilizing. He sat for a moment with the engine running, then put his car back in gear and drove toward Dock Square.

"Good morning, Jean," Tom greeted the Allison's waitress.

She fluffed her hair a bit and flashed Tom a smile. "Good morning, Chief, what'll it be?"

He forced a smile in return. "Coffee and a coupla well-done english muffins."

After thirty minutes watching tourists through the window, he signaled for his check and reached into his money pocket. As he pulled out a small roll of bills, the Copper Candle business card fell to the floor. Picking it up to return it to his pocket, his eyes focused on the address:

10 Dock Square
P.O. Box 460C
Kennebunkport, Maine 04046

The number 460 seemed to leap from the card. "Jesus! It's the same number," he muttered. "No, it's the one crossed out."

"You talking to someone I can't see?" asked the waitress, handing him the check.

"Oh, Jean, thanks," he replied, ignoring her remark. He paid the check and hurried from the restaurant. He jogged up the street to the post office, card in hand.

"That's right, Tom," said the postmaster, "the letter after the number would correspond to the first letter in the name of the individual or business holding the box. Some offices use a letter, some don't. But we don't have letters preceding the number, so I have no idea what the letters 'R L' would signify. Sorry. And we don't have a box 160H or 460H. You could put a request into Washington for a national search. Would take some time, though."

"Thanks, Vern, I might do that."

Tom returned to his car and drove to the police station. Without responding to the receptionist's greeting, he strode to his office and shut the door, only to find himself pacing back and forth with the Copper Candle business card and his notebook entry "~~460~~ R L 160H" both in hand. Finally, he sat down and shook his head in frustration.

A few minutes later, Edna brought him his mail. He thumbed through it aimlessly until he came to a piece from a police association soliciting contributions. He was about to discard it when a portion of the address caught his eye: Rockville Center, New York 11570. An idea began to develop. He buzzed his secretary again.

"Edna, you have a Rand McNally Road Atlas out there someplace. Bring it in, please."

In a moment, Edna came into Tom's office with the battered atlas. "Here you are, Chief. It's two-years old."

"Thanks, Edna, it'll do. Tell Tito and Magruder to see me when they get back from court."

He turned quickly to the back section, titled "Index to United States Counties, Cities and Towns." After some forty minutes of study and note-taking, he put the atlas down.

He was reviewing his handiwork when Tito and Magruder entered. "Gentlemen, keep your fingers crossed. I think we're onto something."

"You going on a trip?" Magruder asked, nodding toward the open atlas.

Tom stood up, a single sheet of paper in his hand, and began pacing again. "Too early to tell. Get out your note pads. There are seven towns in the United States with two-word names beginning with the letters 'R L'. Take these down. Red Level, Alabama; Round Lake, Illinois; Red Lake, Minnesota; Red Lodge, Montana; Red Lion, Pennsylvania; Rib Lake –"

"What's the last one?" asked Tito.

"Rib Lake –"

"No, the one before that."

"Red Lion, Pennsylvania."

"O.K. Keep going."

"Rib Lake, Wisconsin; and Rice Lake, Wisconsin. Got them?"

"Yes."

Tom pointed to the black notebook lying open on his desk. "Now, look at this notebook entry, this business card, and this police association letterhead. Then tell me what comes to mind. Take your time."

Tito and Magruder rose from their chairs and studied the items, switching their eyes from one to another and then back again. Finally, Tito exclaimed: "Sonofabitch! It's a –"

Tom stopped him with a quick wave of his hand. He waited a few moments more. "What's taking you so long, Mike? I had it in an hour."

Magruder scratched his head. "I was just trying to figure out why Loring would have written down a post office box. A license plate I can understand. But a box number?"

"That's all I wanted to hear," said Tom. "We agree on what it is. Now let's find out what it means. I'll call the first three. You split the last four. Tell the postmasters it's a missing person investigation and that it's critical we find out who holds that box. If they give you any shit, don't argue. We can always turn it over to Inserra."

* * *

At 5:00 p.m. they reassembled in Tom's office. He was frowning. "I hope you had better luck than I did. Red Level and Round Lake don't use letters. And Red Lake has no 160H."

"We struck out too on Red Lodge, Red Lion, and Rib Lake," reported Tito. But –"

"Shit!"

"Chief, let me finish. That's only six. Mike just heard back from Rice Lake, Wisconsin. Tell him."

Magruder grinned. "They have a P.O. Box 160H. It's in the name of one Richard Hundley. Here's the really interesting thing. He's a retired cop."

Tom exploded to his feet. "That has to be Dick Hundley!"

"You know him?" Tito asked.

Tom grabbed his head with both hands. "Know him! For Christ's sake, I flew to Chicago for his retirement party. I can still feel the hangover. Let me tell you something about him. In the late fifties, or maybe it was the early sixties – whatever – the Chicago P.D. was rocked by a scandal like you wouldn't believe. Anyway, –"

"I remember that," interrupted Tito. "Those bastards were acting as lookouts for burglary gangs."

"Yeah, that sounds right. The point is, Mayor Daly figured he had to do something drastic. So he brings in this professor type as the new commissioner. Orlando Wilson was his name. He was smart enough to know he couldn't fire all the deadwood, so he isolated the hacks and went on a national recruitment program for new blood. Wilson set up an intelligence division as part of his reorganization, and recruited Hundley from the San Diego P.D. to head it. Hundley built files that would make the Bureau drool. Jesus, when I was at the New York P.D., the word was that if you needed something and didn't have it in your file, you called Hundley. The guy was a walking criminal encyclopedia. Hell, if I'd thought of it, I would've sent him the pictures of Gambini and Lumbardino. But what was Loring doing with his address?"

"Give him a call," Magruder suggested. "Here's his number. It might be another coincidence."

"Don't even think it," Tom snapped.

The two men watched while he dialed.

"Hello."

"Am I speaking to Dick Hundley, formerly of the Chicago P.D.?"

"Yes."

"Dick, this is Tom Goden."

"Tom, this is a surprise. How's life treating you in Kennebunkport?"

"Can't complain. How about yourself?"

"Pretty well. What can I do for you?"

"I'm not sure. Do you have a coupla minutes?"

"Of course."

Tom drew a deep breath. "Let me fill you in on a situation we have here." For the next ten minutes, Tom summarized the events since the Sunday-morning phone call from Priscilla Mills. "So, Dick, I was wondering why Mills had your box number. Do you know him?"

Hundley's tone turned guarded. "No, I don't know this Mills."

"How about Simes?"

"Never heard of him."

"What do you think –"

"Tom, there's nothing to talk about. I told you, I don't know either one of them."

"But," Tom began and then stopped. His tone turned frigid and his face burned. "I understand, Dick. Sorry I bothered you."

Hundley's tone softened. "No bother. Look, if you can spare the time, why don't you pack a bag and come out here for a day or two. The fish practically jump into your boat."

There was a long pause. *What is Hundley trying to tell him? Is he being a smart ass? It is completely out of character,* Tom decided. *But why? Only one way to find out.* "You're on. I can leave first thing in the morning."

Hundley sounded relieved. "Good! Your best bet is to fly direct to Minneapolis-St. Paul. From there, it's about a ninety-minute drive to Rice Lake. Call me when you know your flight, and I'll meet you at the airport."

"Wouldn't it be easier for you if I just rented a car?"

"Not a chance. I'm retired, Tom, remember? I have time on my hands."

"Thanks, Dick. Looking forward to this. I could use a break. Get back to you with my flight number."

When Tom hung up, Tito and Magruder looked quizzical. "Your guess is as good as mine," he replied to their unspoken questions. "He said there was nothing to talk about. But I don't believe him."

"There's some mean fishing in northern Wisconsin," Tito observed. "Why don't you send someone with more experience?"

CHAPTER 19

Tom's 7:00 a.m. flight from Portland reached its cruising altitude and the captain came on. "Good morning, folks. Sorry for that bumpy ascent. But we're fortunate. The tower reports this will be the last flight to leave Portland. There's quite a northeaster blowing and the airport is now officially closed. From here, we expect a smooth trip and an on-time arrival in Minneapolis-St. Paul. So sit back, relax, and enjoy the flight."

On leaving the gate area in Minneapolis, Tom immediately spotted Dick Hundley. He was hard to miss. His cherubic sunburned face and full head of whitish-blond hair belied his age. He had almost no neck, and his head seemed to rest between his shoulders atop a squat fireplug of a body. His arms were too long, as if nature had decided at the last second to produce a short man, but forgot the necessary adjustments.

The men pumped hands. After small talk about the flight and the weather, they walked through the terminal to the short-term parking lot and Hundley's car. The ninety-minute drive north and then east to Rice Lake went quickly as they moved through a network of small rivers and lakes, lush pastures, and an endless series of dairy farms. Their conversation ranged widely, but never touched the purpose of Tom's trip.

After turning onto a narrow dirt road, they drove nearly a mile before coming to a winterized bungalow at the edge of a sparkling lake. It was a long, one-story structure with a porch facing the lake and a pier. A twenty-two foot Boston Whaler tugged impatiently at its line. Entering the house, Tom found a large living room, with a work table and desk at one end and shelves crammed with police memorabilia, books, and files. The kitchen and dining area were off the living room, and beyond were three fair-sized bedrooms.

"Tom, you can stow your things in the first bedroom on your left and change into something comfortable."

When Tom returned, Hundley had finished making sandwiches and was taking beer from the refrigerator. "This is a great spot you have, Dick. But are you ever off by yourself!"

That evening, Tom called Sarah. "Catch anything?" she asked.

"Yeah. Some bass. Had them for dinner. Cooking wasn't like yours, but they were good."

"Anything else?"

"A lot of sun. It seems you were right."

"He's feeling you out?"

"Looks that way. Dick says to say hello."

"Well, make the most of it, honey. Enjoy the fishing."

When Tom returned to the living room, Hundley was in a large over-stuffed chair. Tom sat down across from him and stretched his legs. The two men looked at each other for a moment.

"Tom, you're pissed and I don't blame you."

"I am a little. But I have a smart wife. She warned me you might play it close to the vest, not knowing whether you could trust me. You must be sitting on something awfully fucking important to jerk me around for a whole day."

"I am, and I've decided to trust you. I guess I have to."

Tom leaned forward. "What do you mean?"

"I think you'll see. You'll also see I'm playing a long shot. Have you heard of Samson Smythe?"

"Smythe? Smythe? Oh yeah, isn't he the missing crime reporter for the *Chicago Tribune*?"

"He's the one. Samson and I are old friends. He called me the morning I left to visit my daughter in Atlanta. Wanted information on Patsy Magaddino. I was in a hurry and we only talked for a minute."

"Who's Magaddino?"

"A Mafioso from San Francisco. We didn't have time to talk, but Samson seemed excited about something. Figured he might be doing some story involving Magaddino. When I got home from Atlanta yesterday and went to the post office for my mail, there was a large envelope from Samson containing pictures – pictures some people would do anything to get their hands on."

Tom put his coffee mug on the floor and leaned forward again. "Of what?"

Hundley put a hand up. "In a minute. You'd think that in his business Samson would be pretty good with a camera. But he was so bad it was a standing joke. Whenever he worked a story he always had a photographer with him. Then when you called yesterday and told me about this Mills and Simes, I played a hunch."

Now Tom was on his feet. "You think Simes is Smythe and he got Mills to take those pictures – whatever they are?"

"That's right. It could be a coincidence they disappeared about the same time, but why else would Mills have my box number? I figure Samson gave it to him. But there's one thing that doesn't fit."

"What's that?" Tom asked, impatient to see the pictures. It was almost as if Hundley, despite what he had said, didn't fully trust him.

Hundley continued, "The envelope has a Nantucket postmark dated July sixth. So if Mills took the pictures on July fourth, it isn't likely he took them around Kennebunkport."

"You're assuming the pictures were taken in Nantucket?"

"Yeah. You have the postmark plus some of the pictures have what looks like the ocean in the background. That's what doesn't fit. Seems Mills was one place and Samson another. But I still can't shake this feeling that Mills and Samson knew each other and were collaborating on this. I don't know where Mintmire fits in, if at all."

"Dick, why don't you show me those pictures. Otherwise, we're talking in a vacuum."

"I'll show them to you on one condition."

"What's that?"

"Promise there'll be no public disclosure, and that only people we agree on will be told about them."

Tom challenged, "If I promise, how do you know I'll keep it?"

"That's my worry, not yours. I told you I trust you. Give me your word and you see the pictures. Refuse, and you won't."

Tom rubbed his chin and narrowed his eyes. How could he agree to let Hundley restrict his use of evidence that might be vital to a prosecution? Yet what choice did he have? Fifteen minutes earlier he had nothing. Now he had a jumble of clues and pieces falling into place faster than he could have imagined.   "O.K., you have it."

Hundley smiled, rose from his chair, and left the room. "Be back." He returned carrying a large envelope, and Tom watched as he took out a handful of pictures and started arranging them in rows on his work table.

Tom hovered over the pictures, scanning them.

"Good sharp detail. Professional, no question." Hundley stood silent.

Tom began to study the pictures more carefully. "It looks like a party of some kind. It could even be – " Suddenly, Tom froze. He stared at one picture. His eyes raced over others. He picked up two, then three. His face flushed, he cleared a space on the table and laid three pictures next to each other. "Jesus Christ!" His eyes continued to race. Selecting four others, he cleared more space, until he had seven pictures lying side by side. "Sonofabitch!"

"What is it?"

"Let me see that postmark," he replied, ignoring the question. "Yeah, it was mailed from Nantucket. But these pictures were taken in Kennebunkport."

"Are you sure?"

"Positive. You're looking at pictures of the Fourth of July wedding reception for the daughter of Vito and Maria Scalia. That's Vito, that's Maria, and that's their daughter, Camilla," he said, pointing. "That's their house in the background. And unless I miss my guess, here's Scalia talking to Tony Rosato. He's –"

"No need to explain. I know who Rosato is. Do you know the others?"

"No, but something tells me you do."

"I'll get to them. But first, who is Vito Scalia?"

"I think I'm going to wish I didn't know. Shit! Look here. Isn't that Gabriel Buffalino?" He jabbed a finger at one of the pictures.

"Yeah, but get back to Scalia."

"O.K. Scalia moved to Kennebunkport from New York in December or January. He bought the house next to the president's summer place."

Hundley's eyes widened. "You mean he and the president are next-door neighbors! No wonder – sorry. Keep going."

"Scalia bought the biggest investment firm in Maine. Sarah's law partner handled the deal. That's about all I can tell you. He and his wife are friendly enough, and we've gotten to know them a little. Had dinner with them twice recently and enjoyed it. Of course, he made that easy."

"How's that?"

Tom hadn't taken his eyes from the pictures, but now he looked up at Hundley.

"Sarah's partner just retired. Scalia was his client. Instead of taking his business somewhere else, Scalia said he wanted Sarah as his lawyer. This means that even if she doesn't do any work for him, she gets a percentage of all the billings. He's the firm's biggest client. Sarah's sittin' pretty."

"Nice!"

"Something else. In January, I ran into two of Rosato's men in Kennebunkport – Carlo Lumbardino and Carmine Gambini. Now I'm thinking Rosato must've been in town to see Scalia. Dick, it's time you tell me what I'm looking at. Is this an outfit party?"

Hundley drew a breath. "It's that and more. It was before your time, but did you ever hear of the 1957 meeting in rural Apalachin, New York? The media called it the biggest gangland gathering in history."

Tom's eyes were drawn back to the pictures, and he decided he needed to sit down. "I've heard of it. Some New York state troopers decided something was up and set up roadblocks. They bagged thirty or forty outfit types. The media had a field day with it for years. As I recall, everyone said they were only visiting a sick friend."

Hundley returned to his own chair. He seemed to relax, and his voice dropped into a more conversational tone.

"Good memory. The papers were full of stories about a crisis in law enforcement evidenced by a brazen criminal convention to divide territories. It never proved out, but the stories had their effect. The Attorney General created a special group on organized crime, with an unwritten directive to get convictions – any convictions – against the people at the Apalachin meeting."

"So what happened?"

"Well, special grand juries were impaneled and a national investigation began. The Apalachin crew were hauled before the grand juries. Instead of taking the Fifth, they all gave cock-and-bull stories – like just stopped by to visit a sick friend, or got stopped by car trouble when passing through for a vacation in Canada. And that's what almost got them. Most were indicted and convicted for conspiracy to obstruct justice and to commit perjury – both of which they'd done. But their convictions were all reversed on appeal, and the court rapped the government's knuckles good for deliberately creating a climate in which everyone assumed what the government couldn't prove – that the Apalachin tea party was a convention of crime bosses working out deals."

Tom picked up his coffee mug but decided against a refill. "Was it?"

"A few were heavies; most, only lieutenants. But their meeting and its fallout hurt their business. The publicity made terms like the 'outfit' and 'Mafia' household words. It spawned movies and TV series. Caused the FBI and police departments to create special anti-racketeering units. It's ironic in a way – all this because of a meeting of second-stringers."

Tom was once more drawn to his feet and back to the array of photos. Pointing, he asked, "Are you saying Apalachin was small-time next to this."

Hundley's tone hardened. "That's exactly what I'm saying. There's never been anything close to this. What you're seeing is – how can I put it – the Mafia's board of directors for American operations and, unless I miss my guess, both the chairman and the chief executive officer."

Hundley rose and joined Tom at the table. Pointing to one picture after another, Hundley for the next forty-five minutes poured forth information gathered from years of investigation and research. The pictures came alive. Facts, figures, rumor, anecdotes, relationships, reputations all merged to form the picture of a monopoly that had insinuated itself, like a virus, and was now controlling the management and profits of organized crime in the United States.

"Who's this guy?" Tom asked, pointing. "He's in a lot of the pictures. Everyone seems to be stopping at his table. It's almost like a second reception line."

"I was saving him 'til last. He's from Palermo, Sicily. Salvatore Natale Scalia."

"Chairman of the board?"

"That's right. If I had to bet, I'd say he's Vito Scalia's grandfather."

Tom winced. "That makes Vito the CEO?"

Hundley's tone turned professorial. "Not necessarily. But something else does. For years, there's been scuttlebutt about someone like Vito Scalia. Someone in this country bigger than Magaddino. Even bigger than Buffalino. A financial genius. These people know the kind of heat Apalachin caused. So you have to ask yourself why they'd expose themselves by showing up together at the same place – and why at this particular place? A few wouldn't attract attention. But believe me, this is the whole goddamn clan."

"So, why did they?"

"Two reasons. First, arrogance. These people aren't street hoodlums or outfit enforcers. They're not even mob bosses in the usual sense. They're powerful, wealthy, well-connected members of their communities. Most have never spent a night in jail and have no arrest record. If any do, it's ancient history. They clawed their way to the top through the so-called victimless crimes – prostitution, gambling, labor racketeering – crimes with willing victims. They're two levels removed from the violence and extortion, and they know that the law can't touch them. They infiltrated legitimate businesses through threats and violence that can't be traced to them, and now they're reaping the rewards."

"What's the second reason?" Tom asked.

"Respect for the host, Vito Scalia. Despite their arrogance, these people would never risk another Apalachin fiasco without good reason. Only one person could command the respect necessary to bring them. I'd say the president has himself quite a neighbor!"

Tom's stomach tightened. The room suddenly felt too warm, then too cool. "Jesus! Things're falling into place. I think Sarah's got a murderer for a client."

Hundley arched an eyebrow. "Smythe and Mills?"

"Yeah. Are you certain it was Smythe who sent you these pictures?"

"Seems so. His business card was with them and the return address is his."

"Did Smythe ever use an alias?"

"I don't know, but he was paranoid about people knowing what he was working on before his stories were ready, and he loved the cloak-and-dagger games. This Paul Simes has to be Samson Smythe."

"I'll need a picture. We've got at least one witness and probably two who saw Simes. One may have seen him with Mills."

Hundley thought for a time. "I have some decent ones. But you told me Simes flew to Chicago from Portland that Saturday night. If that's true, then why were the pictures mailed from Nantucket? I mean, it's damned unlikely he would have flown back there from Chicago. Unless –"

"– he didn't mail them," Tom completed. "Let's back up for a minute. We assume Smythe hired Mills to take the pictures. It's an afternoon reception. Shit! It's staring me in the face."

"What is?"

Tom opened his black notebook, ignoring the question for the moment. "We know Simes – or Smythe – was in Kennebunkport on that Friday morning and checked into an inn using a reservation Mills made. He checked out late Saturday afternoon and took that six p.m. flight to Chicago. Based on what we learned from his wife, Mills was using the darkroom at his paper to develop pictures he took that weekend. We know Simes didn't have a car, so we assume Mills drove him to the airport. Now look here. We also know from these security-system records that Mills didn't enter the newspaper building on Saturday until six-fifteen."

"So, assuming Simes is Smythe," Hundley interjected, "he flew to Chicago without the pictures because Mills didn't start developing them until after six-fifteen."

"Exactly!"

"That still doesn't explain why they weren't mailed from – where's the newspaper office?"

"Kennebunk."

"From Kennebunk. Why Nantucket?"

Tom, again rubbing his chin, let the question pass.

Hundley picked up Tom's notebook and began scanning the entries. "I see Mills didn't leave the building until eleven-thirty p.m., then reentered three minutes later, then didn't leave until one-fifteen Sunday morning. Do I read it right?"

"Yeah," Tom replied, not looking up.

"And it's during that period you think Mills was grabbed and tortured?"

Tom, now suddenly attentive, thought he saw light at the end of the tunnel. "That's how we see it."

"Tom, if you're right, then Mills couldn't have mailed me the pictures. Wait a second, what's this entry? 'Herd in 10:00 p.m. out 10:30 p.m.'"

The light went out. "He's one of the newspaper's editorial writers, Cameron Herd. He's on vacation and the newspaper hasn't been able to reach him. I haven't pushed it. That was a fuck-up. Mills gave the envelope to Herd to mail. I'd bet my life on it. But I just had something else and lost it."

"Was he the only other employee on the premises that night?"

"According to the records."

"Where'd he go?"

"Cape Cod. We have a phone number but there's been no answer. Dick, go get a phone book."

Hundley went to a closet and returned with a book.

Tom leafed through his notebook. "It's area code 508."

Hundley turned pages for a moment. "Let's see, 508. Yeah. That area code does include Nantucket Island." Now it was Hundley doing the pacing. "We have some major pieces of the puzzle in place. The obvious question is how did they learn about Samson? We could assume Mills told them."

Tom shook his head. "Mills wouldn't need to tell them. There must've been a second set of pictures, probably with the negatives because none were found at the paper. Smythe had Mills send you a set. He'd want a second set for himself. Where would he have Mills send them?"

"To his home. I'm certain something would've leaked by now if those pictures were floating around. I'd say Scalia has the only other set plus the negatives."

"This means that when Mills was grabbed he probably had an envelope like this one, only addressed to Smythe. To me, the question is how did someone get onto Mills?"

"That's a better question," Hundley agreed. "Look at these pictures. They look like they were taken by someone at the reception, but I can tell you they weren't. The angle's wrong. They were taken a fair distance from the Scalia property from a position above the yard. And another thing, the photographer wasn't spotted."

"How do you know that?" Tom asked.

"If he had been, we wouldn't have these pictures. Let me see those entries again. O.K., Mills entered the building at six-fifteen p.m. and left at eleven-thirty, when he was grabbed. Herd left with my envelope at ten-thirty. The only thing that makes any sense is somewhere in the period after Samson boarded his flight he was discovered. My guess is he had a welcoming committee waiting for him in Chicago and that's how they got to Mills. Tom, are you with me?"

"Yeah. I see where you're going. Smythe could've gotten careless during the flight. Maybe he was celebrating his exposé, drank too much, talked to the wrong person. Maybe before he boarded." Tom made a note to have Inserra check the other passengers.

Hundley nodded. "It's possible. Samson likes his tea."

Tom frowned. "I think you'd better get used to referring to him in the past tense."

"You're probably right."

"Would Scalia be capable of mounting that kind of operation so quickly?"

The sudden gleam in Hundley's eyes suggested a black respect or even perverse admiration. "Those people play hardball and are capable of damn near anything. They can mount a small professional army with a few well-placed phone calls. You're talking about a government within a government. There aren't many major police departments or government agencies where they don't have listening posts. They spend money to corrupt government officials like IBM spends for research and development."

That hit home. "Is Scalia trying to corrupt Sarah with his legal business?"

Hundley mulled that one over carefully. "Not exactly. 'Compromise' might be a better word."

"She'll have to be told about these pictures and what they mean."

"Certainly. Now let's talk about –"

Tom suddenly exploded to his feet. The light had come back on. "Of course!"

"What now?"

"Mintmire. I think I see the connection. You say the pictures were taken from above the yard. How far away would you say?"

Hundley walked to the table and studied the pictures. "A hundred yards, maybe a hundred fifty. Why?"

Tom tore a blank sheet of paper from his notebook and began sketching squares signifying houses and arrows showing lines of sight. "Neil Mintmire is Scalia's neighbor on the other side. He has a three-story house with an attic and window facing Scalia's yard. Neil's a good friend and I know his house well. It's the tallest one in the area. Mills's wife told us he was sweaty and smelled of the darkroom when he got home Friday night. Saturday he took a towel. The lab boys found insulation fibers in the towel like you find in attics."

Hundley studied the paper for a moment, then nodded to himself and looked up. "When Scalia and his people got their hands on the envelope they figured out the pictures must've been taken from Mintmire's place. Maybe Mills or Samson let it out. Scalia decided to send Mintmire a message he wouldn't forget."

"But they were all away for that weekend," Tom said, with a catch in his voice. "They left on Thursday before Smythe even arrived. Neil didn't know what was going down. Your friend probably broke into his place. The bastard hooked a kid with a pregnant wife, then he gets himself killed, along with Mills and Mintmire's wife and daughter – all for a goddamn newspaper story about people who don't mean shit to anyone but you and a few others."

Hundley put a hand up. "I won't argue with you. And you're right about one thing. Mintmire didn't know about the pictures because if he had, he'd be dead. As I say, it was a message."

"Why send a message if he wasn't involved?"

"To tell him that if he did let his house be used to spy on Scalia's place, he'd better not do it again."

Tom clenched his teeth. "Sonofabitch! You even think like them."

Hundley stared at him. "I've been at this a long time. Put your anger where it'll do some good."

Tom smiled apologetically. "Can you come back to Kennebunkport tomorrow for a few days? We've done all we can from here. I want you to tell Sarah what you've told me. Then we need to get in high gear."

"Yeah. I'll come." Hundley yawned and returned the smile. "I'm bushed. Let's get some sleep. We can pick this up tomorrow."

Tom had put off asking the obvious. "Do you think they know you have these pictures? Smythe or Mills could've told them."

"Not a chance." Hundley yawned again and began turning off lights. "If they did, we wouldn't be talking. Damn, I can't keep my eyes open."

Tom was not through with questions, but Hundley was already heading for bed. He sat for a moment, one dark thought pursuing another, until his mind somehow pictured Sarah's law partner, Amos St. John. The thought bubbled: *Wouldn't he shit his venerable pants if he knew his biggest client was parking Mafia money?*

CHAPTER 20

It was late in the evening after a desultory effort to do justice to the dinner Sarah had cooked for Tom and Dick after their arrival from Wisconsin. Leaving the dining room, they looked again at the photographs neatly arrayed on the living room floor. Tight lipped, Sarah poured their coffee. Seething with anger, her self-control served only to build the pressure of her fury. When she finally spoke, it was a shout compressed to a hiss.

"That cocksucker! That ruthless bastard! Just two weeks ago he sat here and asked what he could do to help. Then he offers to make me his lawyer. And I snap it up like a bull frog going for a fly! That arrogant son of a bitch thinks he can corrupt me with his filthy business, and he very nearly did!"

At first, the two men sat stunned by the ferocity of her explosion. Then Tom, followed by Hundley, erupted in the first honest laugh he had in nearly a month.

"Doll, I told Dick you were a sweet homebody. I'll have to wash your mouth with soap." This served only to turn Sarah's rage, for the moment, from Vito and herself to her two immediate tormentors.

"Kiss my ass! You're worse than Vito Scalia!" Suddenly sobbing, Sarah let the tears flood that she had held since Priscilla Mill's call that Fourth of July weekend.

* * *

Despite Tom's misgivings about the ethics of the relationship, Sarah kept Vito Scalia as a client. She decided, with both foreboding and vague exhilaration, that she could outplay Vito at his own game. And so Tom kept his date to go with Vito on the fishing boat, and both Godens kept their date for dinner with the Scalias.

The morning after their late evening conversation, the Godens and Hundley were up and dressed early. It was Thursday, July 30th, and in two days native Mainers would begin wondering where the summer had gone. The three were sipping coffee in the kitchen. "Are you sure you don't want some breakfast?" Sarah asked.

112

"Positive," Tom replied. "We'll have something at The Landing. I'd like to catch the waitress who waited on Simes. Joan Austin too. They may recognize these pictures of Smythe. Then we take a look at Neil's attic."

Sarah frowned. "How do you plan to do that without him asking a lot of questions? If he finds out you suspect Scalia, you'll have another murder on your hands."

"We're meeting him this morning. I'll introduce Dick as a criminologist I've asked to review the case to be certain no one is missing anything. He'll give Neil some mumbo jumbo about maybe someone tossed the house while they were away. One thing'll lead to another, Dick will want a look around, he'll notice the entry to the attic, and, being thorough, he'll say he wants to check it out."

"That's not exactly mumbo jumbo," Hundley observed. "More like it is in politics – a little creative deceit."

"But there's enough truth to it," Tom observed. "Well, we have to run. I'll call you later." They kissed and held each other in a tight embrace, ignoring Hundley.

* * *

"Betty, are you absolutely certain this is the man who had breakfast with Mr. Mills?" Tom asked The Landing waitress.

"Chief, I'm positive. He came in the next morning alone, and I waited on him again. You don't forget the big tippers, and he was a big tipper, I'll tell you! This is the guy. He had sandy hair and one corner of his mouth turned up when he smiled – just like in this picture."

Joan Austin was equally emphatic. Besides the sandy hair and peculiar smile, Smythe had a habit of squinting even in the absence of sunlight. It was an additional feature Austin recognized immediately. "That's Simes, no question about it."

He covered the distance to his car in long, buoyant strides. Hundley hurried to keep pace with short, rapid steps. "That salts it away," said Tom. He maneuvered from the small parking lot into Dock Square. "Simes is Smythe, and he was here with Mills. There's no doubt about it."

"And that means you figured it right. It was Smythe on that six p.m. flight to Chicago. Mills drove him to the airport and then went back to the paper to develop the pictures. The goons were waiting for Mills when he left at eleven-thirty. That also means Samson probably let the cat out of the bag either just before he boarded or during the flight."

"It looks that way. Dick, we're gonna be coming up on Neil Mintmire's place. Do you have your script down?"

"In a general way. I'll play part of it by ear."

But pretense was unnecessary. As Tom drove into Mintmire's driveway, he saw Mintmire approaching in his car. They stopped next to each other. "Tom, you're early. I've got to run in to Dock Square. Nancy's left for work, but the back door is open. Go in and make yourself at home. I'll be right back."

"Take your time, Neil, we're in no hurry."

They parked in front of the house, waited a minute to make sure Mintmire had no second thoughts, and then hurried to the attic. "Goddamn!" exclaimed Hundley. "It's like a sauna up here. No wonder Mills was sweating. Watch your head."

The men crouched low and moved to the window. "That's Scalia's house," said Tom. "You can see most of the grounds. What do you think? This is the only place with this view."

"Fits. This has to be it," Hundley replied. He reached his hand into a space between two floor boards and pulled out a swatch of light-gray material. "And here's your insulation."

"Shit!" Tom cried.

"What's wrong?"

"I got a splinter in the heel of my hand. There's something between these boards I can't quite reach. Look where I'm pointing. See it?"

"Yeah. Let me give it a try. My hand's smaller." A few moments later Hundley was holding a small piece of yellow cardboard with some imprinted black lettering. "It's the lid to a box of film. If anyone needs confirmation, here it is."

They had left the attic and were in the living room when Mintmire opened the front door. The physical presence of this first-generation Scot was intimidating – six feet tall, broad shoulders, thick neck and chest, ham-like hands designed to crush rocks, and a craggy face topped with an unruly shock of gray hair. But his eyes, bloodshot from lack of sleep, carried no threat. Tossing his rumpled sport coat on the sofa, he waived to his two visitors back to their chairs.

"Thanks for coming. Hope I can help."

Tom led off.

"Neil, we appreciate your talking to us. As I've told you, we're stumped.

You've got no personal enemies, and there's no apparent reason why your business would be bombed. But there must be some reason, and if we can find it we may have a lead to who did it. We're convinced it was done by a professional in this sort of thing – probably two. This way of sending a message is the kind of thing we've seen done before by some of the goons in organized crime. Anyway, I thought it might help to bring in somebody who knew more about this sort of thing than I do. That's why I've asked you to talk to my friend Dick Hundley. He probably knows more than anyone else in the country about these kinds of crimes. He'll have to ask you a lot of details about your business, your personal life, and your family. I hope you understand."

"I understand." The burly Scotsman's head dropped into his hands. The three sat silent as tears seeped through his fingers.

"O.K. I'm ready."

Commencing softly, Hundley questioned the Scot carefully, pausing, as needed, to allow Mintmire to respond. Tom, who was assiduously taking notes, interjected only an occasional, clarifying question. Finally, Hundley ran out.

"I guess that does it. Thanks, Mr. Mintmire. I truly appreciate your patience. Is their anything else you think you should add?"

"No, nothing else."

Mintmire stood by the door as the two men left. Tom turned. "Neil, we'll do all we can."

"I know you will."

* * *

As the two men drove from the driveway onto Ocean Avenue, Hundley let out a deep breath. "That was tough. Your friend Mintmire is a class act."

"Like Sarah told you. That's one reason she erupted like she did last night."

"Do you think she'd actually –"

Hundley's question was cut short by the crackle of Tom's police radio. "Chief, this is Tito."

"Carl. We're through at Mintmire's and heading in. What's happening?"

"We just got a call from the Wells P.D. They have a badly mutilated body that could match the description we put out on Loring Mills. It was dredged up late yesterday at the entrance to the harbor."

"Jesus!" Tom gripped the steering wheel, his knuckles white. It had to be Loring's body. He knew that by now it would be on some examining table, its wounds gawked over by cops like himself in voyeuristic fascination with the visible results of sadistic torture.

"Chief, are you still there?"

"Yeah, Carl, I'm here."

"Do you want us to handle this?"

"No, I'll take care of it." He switched on the car's roof lights, activated the siren, and began to increase speed. Then he cut the lights and siren and let up on the accelerator. "I suppose there's no need for that now," he mumbled.

Hundley gave Tom's forearm a supportive grasp. "Take it slow, Tom."

* * *

Vince Inserra walked into the sparsely decorated conference room adjoining his FBI office. Jerry Borghesani of the Maine State Police and the Justice Department's Page Moore were waiting. The three men were speculating about the reason for the hastily called meeting until Goden and Hundley arrived thirty minutes later. The necessary introductions made, Tom gave a brief but graphic account of the discovery of Mills's body.

"Now that we have that out of the way, let's hear what this is all about," said Inserra. "Tom, it's your show. You have the floor."

Tom slung his tan blazer over the back of a chair and addressed the room. "Dick and I called you together because we think we know who's responsible for the Mills murder, the Mintmire bombing, and the disappearance of Samson Smythe."

"Smythe?" Inserra interrupted. "You mean the missing crime reporter?"

"That's right."

"You think Smythe was hit, too?"

"Yep. And not only do we think we know who's responsible, but we're confident we know why."

"Where does Simes fit in?"

"Smythe is Simes, or was."

"Hey slow down," Moore interrupted, with a hand wave. "Maybe you'd better start at the beginning. This is going right by me."

"Keep your pants on." Tom opened his black notebook to the chronology-of-events section. "I'll give you the entire background, and then I'm gonna turn things over to Dick Hundley. Let's begin with the telephone call I received from Priscilla Mills on Sunday morning, July 5th."

Step by step, Tom traced the investigation, concluding with his trip to Rice Lake. Moore wrote quickly, circling dates, underscoring certain matters, and drawing arrows connecting related items. Only twice did he interrupt for clarification. Inserra and Borghesani were equally attentive. While those three bent over their note pads, Hundley sat rigidly with his eyes fixed on some imaginary spot across the room, his fingers peeked like a steeple.

"That's an impressive piece of work, Chief," complemented Moore. "Now, suppose we find out what's in that envelope Dick's hanging onto for dear life. Must be the one Herd mailed from Nantucket."

Hundley rose from his chair and shed his sport jacket. Now everyone but Moore was in shirt sleeves. "It is." He began spreading the pictures face down in prearranged order on the conference-room table. The others crowded around. "Gentlemen, three people – four, if you include Smythe – have died to date because of these pictures. When you see them you'll understand why and know who's responsible." He turned over the first four. "Now, these are pictures Mills took of Vito Scalia and his wife and daughter," he began.

With each picture Hundley turned up, the atmosphere in the room became more charged. Finally, turning the last, he sat down next to Tom, and the two men looked at their small audience and waited. Moore broke the silence.

"Amazing! It's fucking incredible! This Scalia is a piece of work. He marries off his daughter on a day the president's in town and holds the biggest mob convention in history right under his nose. He gets pissed when someone finds out, murders two newspaper people, and bombs his neighbor's business, killing the neighbor's wife and daughter in the process. This guy has balls bigger than an elephant's."

Moore turned a page of his legal pad, pulled a green felt-tip pen from his jacket pocket, and began to write in bold block lettering. With one finger, he pushed his reading glasses back to the bridge of his nose; then pausing, he looked up. "The first thing we have to decide is obvious. What do we do with these pictures? They're a goddamn powder keg. If we go public with them, we dirty Scalia and the media has a feeding frenzy. But they don't show a crime. Only motive. So Scalia and his guests ride out the storm. That's not worth giving up the element of surprise, at least not at this point. The less Scalia knows the better. But sitting on these pictures creates a problem for Vince and me. If we disclose them to our superiors, then somewhere down the line I'm afraid we'll get a leak."

Inserra tugged at his chin. "So, how do we handle that?"

"Easy! They belong to Dick Hundley. We forget we saw them. You have a problem with that, Vince?"

The FBI man stared at Moore without answering. He didn't like being told to forget what he'd seen. Finally, he nodded. "Not really. I'll only be following my lawyer's orders. Dick, you lock those up somewhere, you hear?"

Hundley nodded and began collecting the pictures. This sudden recognition of his property rights seemed too cavalier, too convenient – and too dangerous. But he said nothing.

"O.K. Let's talk about how we orchestrate this thing," Moore continued. "We have to assume that barring some stroke of luck, we're not gonna make a homicide case against Scalia. Finding who did the actual hits is one thing. That's tough enough. Getting the hitter to implicate Scalia will be next to impossible. This means –"

"Wait a minute," Tom interrupted. "What's this impossible bullshit?"

"I said 'next to impossible.' Of course, we could get lucky while they get careless. In the meantime, we'll begin a full-field investigation of Scalia and his business interests. But before we do, I'll check with other federal agencies to see if one of them already has something going. If so, we can piggyback on that. Scalia might figure that the increased activity is all part of the earlier investigation. I'll start with IRS and work from there. Maybe we can catch that bastard on something else and squeeze his nuts."

"Start with the SEC," Tom suggested.

"O.K., I will. You know something I don't?"

"He's in the securities business, isn't he?" Tom replied. "Let's get back to these pictures. I think we need some agreement as to how long we sit on 'em. If you'd seen what was done to Mills, you'd understand why. That Mafia butcher isn't gonna live in my town indefinitely without people being told who he is."

Borghesani nodded. "I'd have to agree with Tom. The pictures will lose impact the older they get."

Moore looked up from his legal pad, trying to conceal his impatience. "That's just the point. We need maximum impact. This presents three scenarios. First, assume we get extraordinarily lucky and build a homicide case. Then the matter resolves itself. We hold them until the trial. Scalia's lawyers will make an opening statement to the jury claiming their clients had no motive for the killings. Then we blind-side them with the pictures. The second scenario assumes we're only able to make a white-collar case on a technical violation of some federal or state criminal statute. The pictures become irrelevant and inadmissible at trial. Without the sex appeal the pictures provide, we can figure that Scalia, as a first-time offender, could walk with no conviction or, at most, get a suspended sentence."

"So what happens to the pictures then?" Hundley asked.

"We poison the atmosphere by releasing them to the media just prior to the indictment. You could argue that the timing wouldn't be exactly kosher, but it would be damned effective! The media would go after those pictures like a vampire after blood. Judges and prospective jurors would gobble up that kind of story. Then the third scenario assumes Scalia has covered all his bases so that we don't develop any case against him. If that happens, then again the matter resolves itself. We release the pictures, hold a press conference, convene special grand juries. Mark him for what he is. Make him a pariah."

"Page, what you say makes sense," said Hundley. "But you still haven't addressed Tom's problem – and mine."

"You mean what're we talking about in terms of how much time we allow for each scenario to run?"

"Exactly."

"Well, the pictures are your property so you have the last say. My suggestion is that we give ourselves six months and then see where we are. A decent full-field investigation covering all the possibilities can't realistically be done any quicker. Vince, am I right?"

"That's pushing it, but it's possible." Inserra began to elaborate but was interrupted by a buzz from the intercom. "Good, show him to my office. I'll be right there." Then he turned to the others. "Why don't we take a break. We've been at this for over three hours. This shouldn't take too long."

Inserra returned to the conference room thirty minutes later. "One of our special agents just gave me the passenger information Tom wanted on that Portland United flight to Chicago. We may be close to some pay dirt. Paul Simes – or Smythe – had a seat mate name of Patrick Madigan. They both paid cash for their tickets. Madigan was one of four passengers booked through to San Francisco. But he left the flight in Chicago and took another United flight three hours later. Twenty-four hours after that, he took a return flight from San Francisco back to Portland. That would have been Sunday evening, July 5th. Dick, in the rundown you gave us, didn't you say that Patsy Magaddino is from San Francisco?"

"Yeah. He's the one Smythe called me about."

"O.K. I'll have one of the Bureau's pictures of him enlarged, and we'll show it to the flight attendants. With three different crews involved, someone might recognize him. We'll circulate it with the Smythe pictures."

"I think we'd better get moving on long-distance phone records," Moore suggested. "If Magaddino called from that flight to Chicago, he could've called collect. Then according to the script, Scalia would've called the Chicago welcoming committee. Those records could be a gold mine. Vince, do you see any problem getting a look at them without a subpoena?"

"Nope. I have a reliable source in the phone company's security department." Inserra thought a moment. "It seems to me we're talking about two different teams here. The one that did Smythe and the one that did Mills and Mintmire's business."

"That's what the timing would indicate," Hundley agreed. "You should check the airline passenger manifests for that period for flights from and to Italy and Sicily. Salvatore Scalia wouldn't have traveled alone. Maybe we can piece together who his bodyguards were. They could be the second team."

"No problem for the U.S. carriers," Inserra said. "It could take some time for the Italian carriers. Tom, you look skeptical."

Tom was absently rubbing the scar on his cheekbone. "Just thinking. I'm supposed to go fishing with Scalia on Saturday, the day before the funeral service for Loring Mills."

Moore put his pen down and grinned. "I like that. Keep the date. If you and your wife can stay cool, it may help keep Scalia from figuring we're onto him. But remember, he's a suspect and you're a law enforcement official after his ass. Don't try to trick him into any statements or we'll never hear the end of it if we ever bring him to trial."

"Don't worry, I know the drill. If he accidentally falls overboard, I'll even throw him a life preserver." Tom worked up a black scowl for Moore's benefit. But it was the FBI man who reacted.

"Jesus Christ!" exclaimed Inserra, "don't even joke about that."

Borghesani flashed a rare smile. "You got a better idea?"

"I think it's time we call it a day," said Moore. "I could use a drink."

CHAPTER 21

It was late Saturday afternoon, August 1st. Vito Scalia sat in the den with the phone pressed to his ear. He hadn't showered, and his tanned face and dark, wind-tossed hair were flecked white with dried ocean spray. His mood had been pleasant when the conversation with his brother-in-law began, but he now reacted irritably. "Gabriel, I'm telling you, finding Mills's body doesn't mean shit. I can't figure why that bothers you so much."

"It's the fact that there was a slip-up. Where else did Don Salvatore's people get careless? That's what bothers me – that and you screwing around with Goden and his wife. Jesus, a fishing trip!"

"Nobody could predict three storms in a row that big. They dumped him five miles out, for Christ's sake. And being tight with the police chief and having his wife as my lawyer are the best wiring we can have. Whenever they think they're onto something, it'll show."

"Or they just might teach you a lesson in poker."

"Goddamn it, Gabriel, I read these people. Goden had a few beers on the boat today and got talking. Believe me, he doesn't have squat."

"You don't know that. Goden's a good cop. He wouldn't tell you if he did, no matter how good a friend he thought you were."

"Listen! I spent over an hour with his wife yesterday. We had lunch. They can't both be that good. And you're forgetting one other thing."

Buffalino sighed. "What's that?"

"Without those pictures, there's nothing to arouse their suspicion."

"O.K., you've made your point. But I still think we should consider precautions."

"Gabriel, because of our personal involvement, I can understand your concern. But the soldiers followed our orders and are to be rewarded. They're our people. Grandfather personally vouches for their silence. He'd never approve."

"You're pretty loose with the 'our personal involvement' bullshit. You gave the orders, not 'us.' In fact –"

Scalia snarled and sprang to his feet, dragging the phone cord behind him. "Don't be a yellow whore! You knew what was going down. I have a

WILLIAM A. CAREY AND ST. JOHN BARRETT

good mind to – " He took a deep breath and exhaled, bringing himself under control. His voice softened. "Gabriel, no recriminations. We've been through too much together. This matter will pass quietly, I promise."

Buffalino relented and signaled a truce by softening his own voice. "I wish I could be as certain. In the meantime, I think we should reconsider precautions – as I suggested."

Scalia, reflecting, decided his brother-in-law was right. "I will. And, by the way, have we made any progress at the Justice Department?"

"Yeah. We should have a replacement functioning by the end of the month."

"What's taking so long? I thought this was only a lateral transfer."

"It is. But the Organized Crime and Racketeering Section requires a higher security clearance. That means another FBI check. Mario picked a bad time to have a heart attack. A ten-year asset down the drain!"

* * *

The *Portland Press* on Sunday beat its editorial breast. "We are outraged and dismayed at the gangland-style violence that has now claimed its third Kennebunkport victim. The inability of local law-enforcement officials to solve the tragic Mintmire bombing augurs ill for the apprehension of the jackals responsible for the Mills atrocity. We urge these officials to recognize their limitations and seek the assistance of the Federal Bureau of Investigation, with its superior skills and resources."

Sarah Goden handed the newspaper back to her husband. "Doesn't that bother you, Tom?"

"Not at all. I couldn't have written it better."

"You mean it gives Inserra and Moore some cover?"

"That's right. If Scalia's intelligence is as good as Hundley says, then he's bound to find out they're thrashing around up here. Now he'll know why."

Tom looked at his watch and downed the last of his coffee. When Sarah had finished hers, they left the house for Loring Mills's funeral, which was scheduled to begin in just thirty minutes at Saint Ann's Episcopal Church. It was a warm and humid day. The sky was darkening and thunder rumbled in the distance. Tom didn't think he would ever feel hatred to match what he now felt for Vito Scalia. He was wrong.

* * *

For the next two weeks, the investigation moved quickly. On Monday, August 17th, Inserra reported to Tom that two flight attendants on the Portland to Chicago run had positively identified Smythe's picture – the hair, the crooked smile, and the squint. They remembered he spent nearly the whole flight writing and listening to a small tape recorder. They also made Magaddino. One of the attendants, an old-timer, thought he looked like Caesar Romero. Inserra agreed.

"Jesus, Vince, are you that old?"

"Late-night movies. Anyway, Magaddino did make a call from the plane. She remembers that clearly. The other one remembers that she served them drinks less than an hour from Chicago. She saw the two of them shake hands like they were introducing themselves. When they landed, Smythe and Magaddino left the plane together. Seems you and Hundley had this figured. There was a collect call to Scalia's number from that flight at seven-fifteen. Then there were two calls from Scalia's phone to a Chicago number – one at seven-twenty-five for two minutes and the second at seven-thirty. The second one lasted fifteen minutes."

"Whose number is it?"

"No one's. It's a public phone in a very busy north-side Italian restaurant."

Tom nodded to himself. "One of those deals! It probably has an out-of-order sign on the phone booth, or the coin slot is taped over. A private phone with a public number."

"Exactly. Our Chicago office checked it out. The restaurant is owned by a corporation which is a subsidiary of another corporation which in turn – well, you get the picture."

"Any luck with the flights from Italy?"

"We're part of the way. Salvatore Scalia flew to New York from Palermo via Rome on Thursday, July 2nd. He returned on Wednesday, July 8th – the day after the Mintmire bombing. We tried to narrow the search for his traveling companions by identifying people who were on both the July 2nd and July 8th flights. But that hasn't gone anywhere because there isn't anyone else who was on both flights."

"How about other flights?" Tom asked. "They might've read our minds and decided to split up on the return."

"We're working on that. Getting back to Magaddino. We canvassed the expensive lodgings in the area. He took two rooms at the Colony Hotel on Friday, July 3rd and checked out on Tuesday, July 7th. The registration was for Mr. and Mrs. and daughter. I'd say Smythe was the victim of pure chance.

For some reason, Magaddino had to be in San Francisco that Sunday. So he takes the Saturday-night flight and ends up sitting next to Smythe. They're waiting for him in Chicago, find out about Mills and the pictures, and the rest we know, or think we do."

"Vince, we know! Proving it is another thing."

* * *

Puffs of white smoke swirled behind the large plane's tires as the Alitalia 747 touched down at New York's JFK airport. The plane taxied toward its gate. Impatient passengers in the crowded coach section began rummaging for their belongings preparatory to the initial dash down the aisles and then the interminable wait as over three hundred people worked their way in single files through the two exits. One man, however, sat quietly, as he had during the entire flight, staring out the window at nothing in particular. He looked at his watch again. It would be over two hours before his connecting flight to Minneapolis-St. Paul. Then he would have another wait of nearly two hours for his final connection to Rochester, Minnesota.

The man waited until the last passengers were deplaning. Then he rose, took a single suitcase from the overhead bin, and walked slowly to the exit. Once inside the teeming international terminal, he cleared customs without incident and took the shuttle bus to the domestic terminal. He hesitated at the first bar. He had had no stomach for the inflight meal, but knew he should eat something. He hesitated a moment longer and then moved on reluctantly to a restaurant. He would force down some food and hope it stayed down.

An hour later, two men watched him board his flight. They waited until the plane had backed from the gate and joined the line of aircraft heading toward the runway. Then one of them walked quickly to a phone.

* * *

A week went by. It was August 24th. Page Moore pored over his steadily growing file on Vito Scalia. The information-gathering was being spearheaded by the FBI's Portland office and was proceeding with the utmost discretion. But it was thorough – SEC filings, tax returns, real estate transactions, personal relationships, social security and self-employment filings, passport applications, airline manifests, and a myriad of other documents and information. The raw data stored in the government's computer banks and electronic archives was awesome, and Inserra knew which buttons to push.

The most intriguing data was on the gigantic incomes disclosed by the tax returns. Scalia had undergone periodic IRS audits, but each time with the same result – no fraud and little, if any, additional tax liability. The possibility that Scalia was a tax-cheat appeared nil. That was one risk he avoided. But the seed of an idea began to sprout in Moore's mind.

Moore's secretary buzzed. John Devitt, Assistant Attorney General in charge of the Criminal Division, was on the line. Devitt and Moore were old friends and Devitt was Moore's superior in name only. "Yeah, John, what's happening?"

"That lateral from the Tax Division will be on board tomorrow."

Moore crunched down in his chair and ran his free hand over a cache of candy bars at the bottom of his desk drawer. He selected a Milky Way. "Simone?"

"He's the one. Find something for him to do. He's supposed to be very bright."

Moore wasn't impressed. "Why does he want this section?"

"I don't know. Maybe he's been watching Godfather movies. One of his senators pushed, so as of tomorrow he's yours. You got the referrals on that Maine bombing and newspaper photographer?"

"Yeah. I've looked at them. Very nasty!"

"Can we do any good?"

"Too early to tell. The Bureau's Portland office is working it."

"Well, keep me posted. The thing has generated a lot of press, and the A.G. will be asking for a report."

Moore hung up the phone and chewed thoughtfully on the candy bar. His failure to inform Devitt about Scalia and the pictures was making him uneasy. It wasn't that he didn't trust his friend, but Devitt would feel pressure to pass such volatile information up the line, and the chance of a premature leak would increase exponentially. Still, he would have to be told at some point. When he was, he would be royally pissed at having been kept in the dark.

It was after 7:00 p.m., and Moore had lost his momentum. He sighed deeply, leaned back in his desk chair, and closed his eyes.

* * *

Page Moore was a native of West Virginia. He'd been raised in poverty in the state's strip-mining country, but poverty didn't dull his brilliant mind.

Attending the state university on a competitive scholarship, he graduated valedictorian of his class. Moore was nothing if not totally unpredictable. For no apparent reason, he enlisted in the Army on graduation day and enrolled in paratroop school. He was in decent shape then. At the end of his enlistment, he went to law school at the University of Pennsylvania. His law degree in hand, he married and opened a practice in Beckley, West Virginia. As court-appointed counsel, he argued and won two landmark criminal cases in the United States Supreme Court. With several lucrative offers from major law firms, he accepted one in Washington, D.C., and for the first time in his life had money in his pocket.

Five years later he told his wife he was tired of being just another establishment lawyer. He was going to resign and join the Justice Department.

"And I suppose that's not the establishment," his wife retorted.

"Maybe, but with a big difference. With the department you actually enforce the law. You don't make a fortune overcharging fat cats intent on breaking it. They figure there's no law that can't be evaded, including murder and mayhem."

So, Moore made the move and became one of the country's premier criminal prosecutors. Gone was the possibility of big tax write-offs, money, power, status, and tuxedos. Not once did his wife rail at him for consigning them to middle-class mediocrity, but she never let go her resentment for his career decision.

Two years ago, their only daughter married. That was his wife's signal to divorce and marry a senior partner in his old law firm. He was not surprised, but neither was he ready. He could not accustom himself to an empty house, and he sometimes worked until 1:00 or 2:00 a.m. at the Justice Department, then slept on his office couch. Tonight he was feeling particularly melancholy. Perhaps his wife had been right; perhaps he was just an eccentric, overweight underachiever.

* * *

Moore snapped from his reverie and turned his mind to the work at hand. A breakthrough in the Scalia case would dissipate his malaise, and he intended just that. After all, they had landed John Gotti, and he was only a foot soldier compared to Scalia. They did have those Hundley photographs – and what a trial they would make! Torture, bombing, murder – all designed to conceal the fact that Scalia was the Mafia's fair-haired boy and it's financial guru.

There had never been and probably never would be a criminal trial to match it. But where was the hard evidence?

He opened the folder containing the names Inserra had given him of passengers on Salvatore Scalia's incoming flight who had returned to Sicily on July 8th or within a day before or after. There were nineteen names, a manageable number. Tomorrow he would call Interpol to begin the winnowing.

Moore heard growling and patted his stomach. It was time for some Chinese food. He collected the folders from his desk, locked them in a file cabinet, and left his office. He walked out the Justice Department's main entrance onto Pennsylvania Avenue, turned right, and hailed a cab for the eight blocks to Chinatown. When his cab pulled from the curb, a car waiting near the entrance pulled in behind it.

After Moore entered the restaurant, the car that had followed waited twenty minutes. Then one of two men in the car entered the restaurant, returning five minutes later. "He's eating alone," he told his companion. "I think we can call it a day."

* * *

On Tuesday, August 25th, at 3:00 a.m., Tom and Sarah were wakened by the screech of their bedside telephone. Tom, raising on one elbow, looked at the luminous hands of the clock, ran a hand through his hair, and lifted the receiver. Even in his business, calls at this hour were rare, and they invariably brought news he would rather not hear.

"Yes, operator, I'll take it. This is Chief Goden." He listened intently for the next half minute to the whispering voice at the other end of the line. Then a click.

Tom slowly replaced the phone. Sarah, rubbing her eyes, turned to Tom. "What was that all about?"

"I'm not sure. It could be a sick joke by someone who wants to see me make an ass of myself. This guy calls collect and says he's Dominic Silento, whoever that is. Then says he's calling from his room at the Mayo Clinic. Claims he's a patient and he's being watched, but wants to talk to me about – and these are his words – 'the little rabbit with the camera'."

Sarah bolted upright. "My God! Did he use Loring's name?"

"No, he didn't. Then he said he'd leave it to me to figure a way to talk without getting him killed. That's all there was. He hung up before I could

127

say anything. His English was nearly perfect, but he had an accent. Talked real quiet and in a hurry, like he was afraid someone might walk in on him any second. He didn't waste a word."

"Why don't you call back and see if he's really a patient."

Tom thought a moment. "Think I'll hold off on that. If he's for real and he's being watched, someone might have long ears. The name Silento doesn't ring a bell, but there are so many Italian names floating around I can't remember them." He reached for the phone again.

"Who are you calling at this hour?" Sarah asked.

"Vince Inserra. I've a feeling this won't keep."

* * *

An orderly walking along a corridor at the Mayo Clinic passed Dominic Silento's room and suddenly stopped. He heard what sounded like someone talking. He waited a moment and then quietly opened the door a crack. The figure on the bed was lying with his back to the door. The bed clothes rose and fell slightly with his rhythmic breathing. The radio on the nightstand was playing softly. Without speaking, the orderly closed the door and moved on. It was just past 2:00 a.m., Central time, six hours before his relief came on.

CHAPTER 22

The cool of dawn lay over the city as Tom Goden and Vince Inserra shook hands in front of the Federal Building in Portland before riding the elevator to the FBI floor. Once in Inserra's office, Tom strode to the window for the calming effect of its familiar view. He could see Casco Bay and its cluster of islands, the sun rising behind them through a thin bank of fog. "It looks like another beautiful day. The tourists will be happy."

Inserra stifled a yawn with the back of his hand. "Forget the tourists. What is it that couldn't wait until a decent hour?"

Tom turned from the window and related the abrupt one-way conversation with the mystery caller. When he was done, Inserra let out a low whistle. "Well, what do you think?" Tom asked.

"Impossible as it may seem, I'd say the chances are good that you heard from one of Salvatore Scalia's people." Inserra unlocked a file cabinet, removed a folder, and spread the contents on his desk. "These are the passenger manifests for those Italian flights I told you we were working on. By comparing names, we've narrowed it down to nineteen or twenty probables – people who were on Scalia's incoming flight on July second and who returned to Sicily within twenty-four hours of Scalia's return flight. This is the list," he said, pointing to a single sheet.

Tom studied it a moment before his eyes riveted. "There he is! D. Silento. If Hundley is right, he could be one of the hitters or know who they are."

"There's only one way to find out. We have to confirm that he's there and then get you in and out unnoticed."

"Can you manage that?" Tom asked.

"With a good show from you, it's possible. But first we call Moore and Hundley."

Ten minutes later they were on a conference call.

"Silento?" Moore shouted. "With a D?"

"That's right," Tom replied. "Dominic Silento. Vince showed me a passenger list that –"

"I have the list," Moore interrupted. "What did Silento tell you?"

Tom repeated the words that were burned in his memory. The ensuing silence was finally broken by Moore. "Maybe this is our break. Dick, what's your read? Is someone playing with us?"

"Your guess is as good as mine," answered Hundley. "We won't know until we talk to him. But we have the problem that he says he's being watched."

Tom's mind was churning. "He probably is. Assume Silento traveled to Kennebunkport with Salvatore Scalia. So he's on the scene when he's unexpectedly needed. They get back to Sicily, and Silento finds out he's in bad shape, maybe even dying. Salvatore is from the old school. He takes care of his people. So he arranges for Silento to go to the Mayo Clinic. Or he told Vito Scalia to make the arrangements. It's Vito's ass that's hanging out and he doesn't like the idea of Silento running around loose in the United States. You know, maybe the crazy bastard will get religion if the doctors tell him he's history. So Vito puts some people on him."

"That makes sense," said Moore. "But if Vito has surveillance on Silento, then you might be recognized. Vince, what do you think about using a Bureau agent instead?"

"I don't know. It would mean getting a stranger to the investigation geared up. I'm the only one who has the whole picture. If we're not using Tom, I'd rather do it myself."

"I'm not sure I like that," objected Tom. "Silento's expecting me. He might not talk to anyone else. Then we'd have to start over."

"I'm convinced," Moore relented. "Vince, do you see any problem getting him in and out without stirring up anything?"

"Nope. We have excellent sources at the Mayo. I should know before noon whether Silento is there. If he is, we can have Tom in place by tomorrow, Thursday at the latest."

"O.K. But don't hurry things. This has to be a first-class operation."

"We don't do any other kind."

* * *

An ambulance pulled away from the receiving entrance to the Mayo Clinic and another took its place. The attendants moved quickly. In a few moments, they had the patient in a waiting wheelchair. The admission procedures had been completed in advance. The patient was taken directly to his private room, where a white-coated staff physician was waiting. "Good afternoon, Mr. Ambrose," he greeted, "I'm Doctor Phalen. How are you feeling?"

"A little weak."

"Your medication will do that. When the nurse has you settled, you can take a nap. I'll check in with you later and discuss the tests we'll be running and the treatment you'll be getting. If you need anything, just buzz."

"O.K., Mr. Ambrose," said the nurse, "let's get you comfortable."

When the nurse had left, Miles Ambrose sat on the edge of the bed and observed himself in the full-length mirror on the closet door. The facial flesh not concealed by the unkempt beard was slack. His eyes were sunken behind puffy lids and cheekbones. The wrinkled skin hung in small, sallow folds. He was nearly bald and his scalp area and hands were punctuated with liver spots. As he sat stoop-shouldered, he could see what age and illness had done to him.

Ambrose fell back on the bed with a sigh. The climate-controlled room felt cold. He pulled the bed clothes around himself and closed his eyes, but sleep eluded him. Finally, he left the bed and walked to the closet. He opened the door, reached into his small suitcase, and felt its contents. Satisfied, he returned to the bed and again closed his eyes. The next thing he knew, someone was gently shaking him awake. A smiling Doctor Phalen stood over him.

"Hello again, Mr. Ambrose, it's time for our talk."

* * *

It was 4:30 p.m., Friday, August 28th. A single patient sat in the reception area of the Mayo Clinic's radiology department. He was the day's final patient. His well-muscled body was beginning to show the ravages of illness. He was losing weight. His thick, gray-streaked, black hair was thinning daily from heavy doses of chemo and radiation therapy. The toxic effects were destroying his appetite and making him nauseous. He didn't know which was worse, the cancer eating at his insides or the treatment designed to slow its inexorable march.

The patient ahead of him had just been taken in for treatment, so he faced a twenty to thirty minute wait. Thumbing a magazine, he shifted impatiently in his wheelchair. He looked up to see the double doors from the corridor open and another patient wheeled in.

"All right, Mr. Ambrose," said Dr. Phalen, "here we are. You sit tight; I'll be back."

When Phalen left, the two men nodded and studied each other for a moment. Then Ambrose, still looking at his fellow patient, wheeled his chair within a foot of the other's chair, stopped, and put his right hand inside his robe to touch a metal object taped to his stomach. The other man recoiled in alarm.

"Calm down, Silento; you'll live longer. You are Silento, aren't you?" Ambrose asked, in a low voice. He seized the man's arm to look at the plastic identification bracelet.

"Yeah. Are you one of my guardian angels?"

"Not exactly. I'm Goden."

Silento's eyes narrowed. "How do I know that? You don't look like a cop. You look like shit."

"You called my house at three a.m. Tuesday morning – two a.m. your time. You said you wanted to talk to me about 'the little rabbit with the camera.' I went to a lot of trouble to be here, so start talking and make it fast. We don't have a lot of time."

Silento exhaled in relief. He studied Tom closely, his frown changing to a wary smile. "Nice make-up job. Yours?"

"No. The FBI's."

"Can they protect me?"

"That depends on what you've got to say."

"Are you carrying?"

"No."

"Are you wired?"

"Yes."

Tom checked his watch. "Time's running. Let's have it," he ordered, switching on the tape recorder.

Dominic Silento's words came quickly, precisely, and without trace of emotion.

Tom's face was equally stolid. From all that showed, he could as well have been listening to the details of a family excursion. Once, when Dr. Phalen appeared in the doorway with a questioning look, Tom signaled him away with a flick of his hand. When he appeared a second time, he strode directly to Tom's wheelchair.

"I think you've waited long enough, Mr. Ambrose. We'll reschedule your treatment for tomorrow." As they boarded a waiting elevator, an orderly rounded the corner and entered the radiology department. "That's suddenly become a busy place," Phalen observed.

* * *

At 8:00 p.m., the private line in Page Moore's office rang. He picked up the phone before the second ring. "This is Moore."

"Page, this is Vince. Can you talk?"

"Yeah. What's happened?"

"He's out. We're on our way to the airport. It was a good operation all the way. I've listened to the tape. It's a smoking gun bigger than a howitzer."

"That good, huh?"

"Better! But we have a tricky problem that requires immediate attention."

"Will it hold until tomorrow?"

"Yes. But we should move on it by Monday at the absolute latest."

"O.K., I'll be at your office tomorrow morning."

Moore replaced the phone receiver and began packing his briefcase, his adrenaline gushing. He knew Inserra was not prone to overstatement, and his smoking-gun characterization translated into hard evidence. Moore turned off the lights, locked the door, and crossed the corridor to the men's room. One of the urinals was in use.

"Alex, what're you doing here so late on a Friday night? Not because of that assignment I gave you?"

"Nah," Simone replied. "My office is still a mess after the move. I'm trying to get it in shape. You're here pretty late yourself."

"Force of habit."

"Will you be in tomorrow? Maybe I could fill you in on where I am on that assignment."

"Nope. I'll be in Portland, Maine. Let's try for Monday."

After watching Moore board the elevator, Simone returned to his office. He waited a moment and then picked up the phone.

* * *

It was 10:00 a.m. Saturday, and the same five were again around the table in the FBI conference room – Inserra, Moore, Goden, Hundley, and Borghesani. They had arrived within minutes of each other.

"What time did your flight get in?" Moore asked Hundley.

"Nine-thirty-five."

"That's about the time mine landed. We must've just missed each other at the airport. Anyway, we're all here, so let's get started. Vince, do we hear Tom's tape first or do we discuss that problem you mentioned?"

"I think we run the tape first to put the problem in perspective." Inserra reached to the center of the table and turned on the cassette player. Moore, Hundley, and Borghesani leaned forward in their chairs. Moore knocked over a half cup of coffee. It was ignored.

As the tape was nearing its end, Moore put up a hand. "Hold it. Run that last bit again. It's not clear. And turn up the volume."

"That must be when Phalen stuck his head in the door. Silento turned his head," explained Tom, as the tape was rewound.

"That's a little better," said Moore. "But it seems garbled. Tom, the 'shit' – is he referring to the explosives for the Mintmire job?"

"Yes."

"Where's Revere? Is it around here?"

"No. It's a suburb north of Boston near Logan Airport."

Moore slapped his forehead. "Goddamn! That's fantastic! O.K., Vince, start it going again."

A few minutes later the recording ended abruptly: "All right, Silento, so you're dying. You're lucky I don't kill you where you sit. But that doesn't tell me why you wanna testify."

"That's another story, Goden. You get me out of here and I'll tell you."

"Now look, you – " There was a click and the tape ended.

"That's it?" asked Borghesani.

"That's it," replied Tom. "Phalen came barreling in and the next thing I knew he was wheeling me to the elevator."

"Who's Phalen?" Hundley asked.

"One of the Bureau agents who worked the operation," Inserra responded. "We had Tom made up so his wife wouldn't recognize him, put him in a wheelchair, and got him admitted to a private room at the Mayo on the floor below Silento. When Silento was isolated in the radiology department, Tom made the contact. Phalen and his partners monitored the area. That leads us to our problem."

"Which is?" asked Moore.

"After we talked on Tuesday, we looked at the Mayo's new hires – the people coming on board about the time Silento was admitted. Two caught our eye. They're out of Chicago. If they're who we think they are, they're bad news. Both are orderlies. One's on the day shift and the other's on the night shift. They never let Silento out of their sight. Yesterday is a perfect example. Silento was getting ready to go to radiation therapy and Phalen arranged a distraction. When Ferraro – he's the day-shift orderly – found out Silento wasn't in his room, he tore around the place like a fucking madman looking for him."

"So you figure it's too risky to talk to him again while he's still at the Mayo Clinic?" Borghesani asked.

"That's about it. If we wanna hear the rest of the story, we've got to get Silento out of there. The tape barely scratched the surface."

* * *

The five men left the Federal Building and were walking together toward the parking lot, Tom and Moore bringing up the rear. After they crossed the street and had gone some dozen steps, Tom lengthened his stride to pull alongside the FBI man.

"Vince, did you have a Bureau car down the street while we were meeting?"

"No. Why?"

"There was a navy-blue Grand Am with two men that cruised by when I arrived. I noticed it because it looked like Sarah's car. Don't turn around but I swear the same car is parked at the end of the block."

"Hmm." Inserra thought for a moment. "Interesting. If you're right, and they're watching, we don't wanna spook'em. Maybe they'll follow one of our cars. Let's find out which one."

* * *

Sunday morning, August 30th. Gabriel Buffalino hung up the phone in his Manhattan brownstone, studied his notes of what he had just heard, then dialed the Kennebunkport number of the Scalia residence.

"Vito, we have pictures of Moore and Goden leaving the Federal Building in Portland yesterday, together with three other men. We've identified one of the other men as the agent-in-charge of the FBI's Portland office and another one as the head of the Maine State Police. Looks like they had a three-hour meeting with Moore after he flew in from Washington."

"Who was the fifth man?" Scalia asked.

"We don't know. He's short, and our guys couldn't get a picture of his face."

"Didn't they follow him?"

"No. He split in Goden's car. Borghesani left in his, and Moore and Inserra went to lunch. Their orders were to stay on Moore, so they did. After lunch,

Inserra drove Moore to the airport."

Scalia frowned. "What does Simone think?"

"He says that the publicity after they found Mills's body, on top of your fucking Mintmire deal, forced Goden and the state people to ask for help from the feds. Moore has been assigned to both cases."

"That would explain the meeting," said Scalia, ignoring the barb. "The fifth character sounds like one of Goden's men, a lieutenant name of Tito."

"It would explain the meeting, but I don't like it. I don't like not knowing for sure who the fifth guy was. I don't like the way that SEC investigation is mushrooming. I don't like having Silento here, and I particularly don't like Goden nosing around. The timing of all this is too pat!"

"Gabriel, Goden doesn't suspect shit."

"You don't know that."

Scalia lit a cigar and studied the burning match for a moment before blowing it out. "I do know. It was Goden's wife who told me Justice had pulled my tax returns."

"We already knew that."

"She didn't know we did."

"O.K., O.K., but I still think Silento is a ticking time bomb. It's not enough that those two from Chicago are on him. I don't care how good they are. The don is getting too soft."

Scalia sucked on his Havana, tapping the eraser end of a pencil on his pad as he blew smoke rings. "All right. I can't disagree. Defuse it! I'll handle Grandfather."

But Vito couldn't.

* * *

Don Salvatore was enjoying the balmy air and the view from the villa's balcony when the telephone was brought to him. Eyes twinkling, he acknowledged the caller.

"Vito! How do I have the honor?" The twinkle faded as he listened.

"Yes, I understand, and I have no reason to doubt what you say; but you ask what I cannot give."

Listening again, his initial look of pleasure now fully overtaken by a frown, the don withdrew the telephone from his ear, only to return it with a long-drawn sigh.

"Grandfather, he's dying."

"Then let him die peacefully, in God's own time and in His own way."

Vito fought back his impatience. *Gabriel is right,* he thought, *he is getting soft.* Controlling his voice, he retorted, "Our personal involvement is too great to allow him such luxury."

The don's voice took on a sudden edge. "Vito, Dominic was acting at our direction. He was once your best friend and is still my friend. He would be loyal to you. Have you no loyalty to him?" Vito recognized the ring of finality in his grandfather's voice. But it was an unexpected ring in his own voice, as he ground out his Havana, that caught him by surprise.

"Grandfather, this is a matter of self-preservation. The mind of a sick man can work in strange ways. You are protected by an ocean. Gabriel and I are here – vulnerable and exposed. You must let us decide."

"Basta! Basta! The matter is closed. Act against my wishes and you will answer to me. Is that understood?"

"Yes, Grandfather."

After a pause, Don Salvatore asked, "Why do you distrust Dominic? Is there something you are not telling me?"

Vito, momentarily taken aback, replied, "Grandfather, this is not my request."

"Oh?"

"It is Gabriel's. He blames you for our situation."

"Hmm, perhaps with some justification. He did counsel me against the gathering at your home, quite strongly as I recall. He said Maria agreed with him. So, we lay fault at my door? All the more reason why Dominic should not bear the consequences of an old man's mistake. You may have him watched, but nothing more without my approval."

* * *

Through the remainder of that Sunday, Vito's frustration grew, along with his uncertainty. How would the don respond if Vito went against his clear command? Would he treat his defiance like defiance by one of his *soldati*? Not likely. He was still the don's grandson and he knew the don's affection went beyond any personal disagreement – even a disagreement over life and death. But he also knew that this was not just a business decision for the don; for him, it was a matter of old-fashioned principle – principle for which Vito did not share the same depth of feeling.

Finally, Gabriel's fear of what Dominic might do overcame Vito's fear of the don. So, for now he would do nothing. Having already given the green light to Gabriel, he would let events run their course. If the don learned that Vito had sanctioned what Gabriel was sure to do, he would deal with the don then.

CHAPTER 23

By dinner time Sunday evening, the activity around Silento was building. The two orderlies seemed bored as they watched doctors and nurses with somber expressions hurry in and out his room. Finally, Sam Ferraro walked nonchalantly to the nurse's station.

"What's happening?"

The buxom nurse fingered the top button of her uniform and leaned forward. Three straight bouts in bed with this hairy, muscular orderly and she still tingled just looking at him.

"Silento took a turn for the worse. They have him on oxygen and blood transfusions. I think they're getting ready to move him to intensive care. You gonna be in the mood?"

"I need a rest," the orderly said, grinning. He ambled back to the second orderly.

"What's going on?" asked Angelo Inciso. He was shorter and leaner than his partner, but the hooded eyes were the same.

"Looks like they're getting ready to move him to the ICU. Maybe he'll save us any more trouble. You'd better call. I'll wait here."

Inciso returned within ten minutes and nodded from the end of the corridor. The two men who had ended Samson Smythe's life at O'Hare airport then met by the stairs.

"Well?"

"If he doesn't cash out by midnight, then it's still on," said Inciso.

"Gesu Cristo! What the fuck is their problem? The poor bastard is family. He ain't goin nowhere. Can't they ease off for a few days and let him buy it on his own?"

"You wanna argue, you go call."

"I'll pass on that, Angelo."

* * *

It was 2:00 a.m. Monday, August 31st. Silento lay in his bed in intensive care hooked to an elaborate life-support system. His labored breathing was

139

barely audible over the measured beeps of the cardiac monitor.

The duty nurse was at her station twenty yards down the hall, around the corner from Silento's room. She was chatting with Ferraro when Inciso slipped quickly inside the room, closed the door, and stood quietly while his eyes became accustomed to the dim light. Then he moved toward the bed and reached into his pocket for the syringe loaded with curare, a drug to arrest the action of the motor nerves and heart.

Inciso was lowering the syringe. Suddenly, the monitor's electronic images of the heartbeats were erased by a flat line. The beeps became a steady whine, signifying heart stoppage and the beginning of code-blue procedures. In a blur, Inciso pocketed the syringe and was out the door and into the next room. It was unoccupied.

The nurse raced from her station toward Silento's room, Ferraro following as far as the corner, where he stopped and watched her enter the room. A minute later, a doctor strode past Ferraro and entered the same room. In the next room, Inciso, his ear pressed to the wall, heard the doctor and nurse talking as they worked on the cancer-ridden patient. Their medical jargon was arcane, but the bottom line was not. The massive doses of chemotherapy drugs and radiation therapy had produced shock and heart failure. Dominic Silento was dead.

* * *

Patsy Magaddino's corner office near the top of the Trans America Building gave an unmatched view of San Francisco, the entire Bay Area, and the Pacific Ocean. Modest in size, it reeked of money, from the Persian rugs on the floor to the collectors' art on the walls.

It was early Tuesday evening, September 1st. The sun was a huge red ball as it sank toward the watery horizon. But Patsy wasn't watching the breathtaking sunset; his binoculars focused on Fisherman's Wharf and other parts of the waterfront, which years before his Young Turks had muscled and terrorized to submission. While enjoying the view, Patsy was listening, without interrupting, to Gabriel Buffalino's lengthy account of recent events. He turned from the window and put his binoculars aside.

"Gabriel, what you're telling me is that the only remaining link to you and Vito is Silento's partner, Palazzi, and he's safely in Monreale with Don Salvatore."

"That's right."

Magaddino wiggled the knot of his pearl-gray silk tie. "You didn't come all the way out here to tell me that."

"No, I didn't."

"So?"

Buffalino smiled. "So Vito and I are in your debt for warning us and for delivering Smythe. We're insulated from Inciso and Ferraro, but you're not. They're the last loose end in this whole unfortunate episode. You give the word and we'll see that it's removed."

Magaddino returned the smile, but with a trace of malevolence. "I won't hear of it. Inciso and Ferraro don't know it, but they were following Vito's orders. Since when have generals begun removing loyal soldiers? Anyway, you remove them and you still have a direct link left – a 'loose end,' as you say."

"Who?"

"Me!"

"Patsy, stop joking."

"Gabriel, you know I don't joke. When will the time come that I have to start looking over my shoulder? You hit Inciso and Ferraro and you'll send a message that family doesn't mean shit anymore. Gesu! I can't believe you would actually have done Silento."

Buffalino felt the blood rise to his face. "Chill out! Vito says Don Salvatore cleared it. And stop that crap about looking over your shoulder. What we're talking about is a final precaution. Nothing else. We're simply offering you the option of insulating yourself."

Magaddino reached for his binoculars and again walked to the window. He spoke while he scanned the waterfront. He suddenly regretted the turn the conversation had taken. "All right. Tell Vito I appreciate the offer. But it's not good business. Inciso and Ferraro are two of our best people. We may need them again. We'd be wasting valuable assets." He returned to his desk and put up the binoculars.

"It's your call, Patsy. And I think you're right. But Silento was a special case."

"So be it! Is there anything new on the feds?"

Buffalino studied the diamond cuff links on his white-on-white shirt. "Yeah, there is. Our source at Justice assures us they have absolutely nothing."

"Why are they all over Vito and the business?"

"That turned out to be nothing. The timing was a coincidence. It was only part of that SEC investigation. In fact, Vito's law firm just got word that the

SEC is issuing a no-action letter."

"So as things turn out, the move on Silento was premature."

"That's one way to look at it. But it didn't happen. Let's leave it at that. The matter's closed." Buffalino rose from his chair. "I'm hungry. Some blackened pompano would taste good."

Magaddino thought a moment. "Something was on the tip of my tongue. Oh, well, it couldn't have been important." He rose and placed his hand on Buffalino's shoulder. "Let's go eat."

Thirty minutes later the two were ordering wine. "Now I remember," said Magaddino. "The man you couldn't identify in Portland. The one who left with Goden. Have you found out who he is?"

"No, but we think it was probably one of Goden's men. A Lieutenant Tito."

"Are you going to keep the tail on Moore?"

"No need to," replied Buffalino. "Like I said, the feds have nothing. It's too risky without good reason."

* * *

Moore and Goden, both wise in the ways of court proceedings, knew that a defense lawyer, attacking Silento's credibility, would argue that Silento's knowledge of details was not personal, but was the product of repeated suggestion by the government lawyers in preparing his testimony. It dramatized, the defense would argue, the prosecutors' no-holds-barred determination to obtain convictions. In short, it would prove not guilt but a frame-up.

* * *

The University Club in Washington, D.C. is located on Sixteenth Street next to the former Soviet Embassy. Moore liked early-morning breakfasts in the University Club's large dining room because the room had no ears. On Thursday morning at 7:30 a.m., he was seated at a corner table, the only member in the dining room.

"Coffee, Mr. Moore?"

"Yes, thank you. I'll order later. I'm waiting for a friend."

Five minutes later, Moore rose from his table and signaled to a lanky man in gray flannel and bow tie standing at the entrance. It was Moore's superior,

John Devitt.

The two friends looked briefly at the menu and placed their orders. Moore grew uneasy as Devitt studied him in silence. When Devitt finally spoke, Moore breathed an inward sigh of relief.

"Page, the Attorney General was as pissed as I was that you kept us in the dark so long. He didn't believe me when I told him you were acting on my orders. He knows you too well. He says he'll deal with you when this is over. In the meantime, you have carte blanche to run things your way. He said you'd better get a fucking conviction or start looking for other work."

"I appreciate it, John. And I appreciate the A.G.'s words. I really do."

"No reason to. I agreed with him. Are you absolutely certain those two torpedoes bought it?"

"Positive! Phalen shot up our friend with something that slows down the bodily functions to the point where you'd swear the person is dead. Ferraro got a good look when they wheeled him out. The paperwork is in perfect order. Silento even had a living will which directed that he be cremated. That was a big plus. Still, they came damn close to beating us to him. They might have if Goden hadn't spotted the tail they had on me in Portland. That convinced Inserra and Phalen to plan for the worst."

"Well, Hundley is right," Devitt observed, "those bastards are a government unto themselves. I'm ready to assume they have someone wired in the Department."

"So for lack of a better suspect, we'll continue to watch the lateral, Simone?"

"Yeah. You said he's the only one at the Department who knew you were flying to Portland on Saturday. I know that's thin but the stakes are too high. Keep feeding him fluff, but give him enough on Mills and Mintmire so that he thinks he's in the loop. How long do you figure Silento will be around?"

Moore sipped at his sugar-laden coffee. "It's hard to say. The drugs are working on the cancer but they're beating the shit out of him. The doctor says a year at the outside. But I figure we'd better get a trial and have him on and off the witness stand within six months. That's if Goden doesn't kill him first."

"That bad?"

"Yeah. I might even be tempted. This Silento is something else. A slaughterer in an abattoir. I mean, you talk about ruthless and remorseless! It's beyond anything I've ever heard. We finished interviewing him at nine last night. So we're ready to move."

"Why was Goden there?" Devitt asked.

"Because Silento insisted. For some reason, he trusts him more than us. He says Goden is the one Buffalino kept warning Scalia about."

"Were there any surprises beyond what was on Goden's tape?"

"Uh huh. The tape was only an appetizer."

"Will I be able to follow your notes?"

"Hell no! They're cryptic at best."

"Then you'd better give me a rundown. I have a meeting with the A.G. when we're done here."

Just then, their orders arrived. Devitt poured skim milk over his Special K, while Moore smeared a stack of pancakes with whipped butter and applied enough maple syrup to float the pancakes and sausages. Moore made short work of half the stack and then put his knife and fork down to begin his account of the interview.

Silento had told how he and Carmine Palazzi had worked their way through the Mafia's Sicilian enforcement apparatus until the two cutthroats caught the eye of Salvatore Scalia. They had been the don's personal bodyguards for over ten years. There was very little about the organization's "wet activities" that escaped their attention.

The two accompanied the elder Scalia to Kennebunkport when he attended the wedding of his great-granddaughter. When the guests had left on the evening of the wedding, Silento and Palazzi were sitting in the den with the don, Vito Scalia, and Gabriel Buffalino. The mood was festive. Then came the call from Patsy Magaddino. Silento and Palazzi had sat in on many crisis situations within the Mafia, but this was different. A crime reporter with a national reputation and readership had been able to infiltrate the reception and identify most of the guests. The family was convinced a disaster was in the making.

Vito's mandate to Magaddino had been unmistakably clear. Acting on instructions from Vito, Silento then called a Chicago number and gave orders to Angelo Inciso and Sam Ferraro. They were to intercept Smythe at the O'Hare Airport. Magaddino was to be their contact. Like Magaddino's, their orders were specific. Obtain Smythe's tape recording; interrogate him; then kill him. Don Salvatore, although present, kept silent. Buffalino argued against such drastic action but finally nodded his agreement. He supplied the Chicago number.

The group waited impatiently until Magaddino's second call came. Although Smythe had been taken care of, the family now learned that Smythe had obtained photographs of those attending the reception, but that he did not have the photographs with him. Vito Scalia was near apoplexy until he learned that Smythe's pocket had divulged the name and business address of the photographer. He then gave Silento and Palazzi their marching orders. Find Mills and do whatever necessary to obtain all photographs and negatives. Bring the photos and negatives and eliminate Mills and any others who may have seen or heard of them. This included Mills's wife. Don Salvatore altered the orders. Leave Mills's wife alone. Vito objected, but the don was adamant. Again, Buffalino argued against killing, but ultimately acquiesced.

Moore paused to return to his pancakes and sausage. Devitt, after a bite of dry toast, told him, "Keep going."

Moore wiped syrup from his chin. "At this point, Silento described what they did to Mills in graphics. I've already given you the highlights. Silento seemed proud of their workmanship. He's a very hard case."

"He's more than that. He's a case-study cretin. Keep going."

Moore moved to the highlights of the Mintmire bombing. Buffalino had objected to what he termed "senseless retaliation." At first, Don Salvatore agreed. But Vito assured everyone there would only be property damage, but Buffalino continued to argue against any action. He was fearful it would inspire further involvement by the Kennebunkport police chief. That was not worth sending a message that would not be understood.

Don Salvatore began to waffle. Vito whined and finally prevailed. Buffalino checked with New York and obtained the name of a munitions dealer in Revere, Massachusetts. Silento and Palazzi then received their instructions – level Mintmire's business but make sure no one is injured. When news reached them that Mintmire's wife and daughter had been killed by accident, it was Buffalino who nearly had apoplexy. Vito pooh-poohed Goden. Silento, Palazzi, and the don then returned to Sicily on separate planes, a precaution Buffalino insisted on.

Devitt pushed his chair from the table and crossed his legs. "Correct me if I'm wrong, but I don't recall in Goden's tape that Silento involved Salvatore Scalia. Now he lays it all over him."

Moore speared the last bit of pancake and sausage. "You're right, he didn't. But he's tight with Inciso and Ferraro, and saw them watching him at the Mayo. Now he knows they were about to hit him. He figures only the old man could have approved it. We also got an unbelievable bonus." Moore plopped a piece of cornbread on his plate to soak up the maple syrup.

"O.K., what should I tell the A.G. to expect next?"

Moore's face lit up. He raised his water glass in a mock toast. "Now we start the part that's fun. Writing the indictments."

"Plural?"

"Yeah. I think we want a state of Maine as well as the federal indictment. Silento's physical condition means we need a trial within six months. If we have two indictments, we increase our chances of getting it. Then we go with whichever case gets called first. The other thing is that we'll be charging murder in the state case. That doubles our chance of getting one of the judges to deny bail. If Scalia's and Buffalino's asses are locked up, they'll be screaming for an early trial. I'm hoping the federal case gets called first. That's where we throw the net over everyone. Silento will never last through multiple trials, assuming we don't run into double jeopardy."

"I wouldn't worry about that," said Devitt. "You plainly have separate and distinct offenses. What's the timetable?"

"Well, we've got to get a top state prosecutor involved. Borghesani can handle that. We have to tidy up a few things. Write the indictments. Present the cases to the grand juries. I'm thinking we can make the arrests within the month."

Devitt's expression turned quizzical. "All the pieces seem to fit. Problem is, without Silento we don't have a case. Even with him, we need to corroborate his connection to the other defendants and establish their motive. The photographs are the key, but what if a judge keeps them out of evidence? And another thing, why is he so hot to testify? Sure, he's pissed now, but he called Goden before he knew they were planning to take him out."

"John, I wish I knew. Maybe, he's a mindreader."

CHAPTER 24

Monday, September 21, 1992 was the twenty-fifth wedding anniversary of Maria and Vito Scalia. On the preceding Saturday, the Scalias had hosted a dinner party at the White Barn Inn in Kennebunk for the area's movers and shakers – people like the Godens, Neil Mintmire, Kennebunkport's city fathers, two justices of the Maine Supreme Court, and the State Attorney General, Rudy Briscoe. Now they would hold their family celebration.

Late in the afternoon, Gabriel Buffalino's limousine drove onto the grounds of the Scalia residence and deposited the Saint at the front door. Gabriel embraced his niece, Camilla, pumped her husband's hand, and turned to Vito and Maria. He shadowboxed playfully with his brother-in-law, and then picked up his sister in a bear hug. The three walked toward the house with their arms draped over each other's shoulders. It was a gorgeous, unseasonably warm day. The foliage was turning and the green of the lawn was framed in hues of bright orange and flaming red. Maria is right, Gabriel thought, as he glanced at the pounding surf, Kennebunkport is a jewel.

As the three entered the living room, they were greeted by the mouth-watering aroma of a regal crown roast of veal, just taken from the oven and being garnished in the kitchen. Vito jauntily opened two bottles of chianti waiting on a silver tray with accompanying glasses, poured a glass for each of the party, and asked for attention. After toasting the arrival of his guests, he took a narrow gift box from his jacket pocket and handed it to Maria. Standing proudly by, he watched her remove the wrapping and lift the lid. Maria gasped at the sight of a diamond necklace that could well have graced the neck of a royal princess.

Vito was helping Camilla fasten the necklace about his wife's neck, when the door chimes sounded. The necklace in place, Vito strode jauntily to the door and opened it to four neatly dressed men he had never seen before. He stood, wineglass in hand, wondering who they were and how they could have passed the guard gate unannounced, when one of them displayed credentials of a special agent of the Federal Bureau of Investigation.

"Vito Scalia," the agent began, "we have a warrant for your arrest on an indictment charging you with arson, racketeering, and conspiracy in violation of Title 18 of the United States Code. You have the right to remain silent and — "

Vito listened in stunned disbelief to the recitation of his constitutional rights. He recovered quickly, but was by then in handcuffs.

Two of the agents moved into the living room, and, by the time Vito's volcanic temper erupted in a stream of obscenities, had Gabriel Buffalino also in cuffs.

At nearly the same moment, FBI agents in Chicago and San Francisco were arresting Angelo Inciso, Sam Ferraro, and Patsy Magaddino. In Revere, Massachusetts, the explosives dealer, Paul Bachman, was taken into custody as a material witness.

* * *

In Palermo, Sicily, a high-ranking Italian police official, satisfied that the extradition papers were in order, dispatched two cars to the Monreale villa of Salvatore Natale Scalia. He was expecting them. When ushered into his private office, they found him sitting ramrod straight behind a huge mahogony desk.

"What can I do for you?"

"We have papers from the court. You may look at them, but then we must take you with us to Palermo."

Don Salvatore read the papers with care before replying. "So, a Sicilian may not attend his great-grandchild's wedding in America without being hauled into court, while those who violate the privacy of the celebration are protected?" With no further protest, the don submitted to the arresting officers.

Carmine Palazzi proved a different case. He was nowhere to be found.

Earlier in the day, two Sicilian dock workers in wool caps and black turtlenecks had approached Palazzi. He was in Palermo running an errand for the don. They gave him a copy of the indictment and watched while he carefully read it.

When Palazzi looked up from his reading, one of the dockworkers said, "You've been talking to the wrong people."

"Let's go," said the other. Palazzi, now silent, didn't bat an eye.

The two men, one on either side, propelled Palazzi toward a parked car. As the man on his left dropped his hand to open the car door, Palazzi, in a lightning thrust, jammed his right foot into the solar plexus of the man on his right, sending him to the pavement. As the man opening the door straightened,

Palazzi was already swinging around and brought the calloused edge of his right hand down like an ax on the back of the man's neck. The second man joined his partner on the ground.

Palazzi, now free, tore across the busy street, dodging one car and vaulting over the hood of a second. Reaching the other side, he quickly blended into the crowd.

The two men struggled to their feet. One thumbed his two-way radio. "Are you on him?"

"We have him," came the reply.

* * *

Federal magistrate Brooks Gainsboro was a prickly tempered Portland, Maine liberal, whose rich wife had been a major factor in his elevation to the magisterial bench. He had long ago convinced himself that he deserved to be a full-fledged federal judge.

Magistrate Gainsboro was looking down from his bench at the two defendants who had been arrested in Maine, their attorneys, and the attorneys for the government. "No prior records! Deep business, family, and social ties to their communities! And the government is asking this court to deny bail? I won't hear of it," Gainsboro roared.

"I can only remind the Court of the enormity of the crimes with which they are charged and the need to protect witnesses, the families of the victims, and other potential victims pending a trial," Page Moore responded.

"Alleged victims," the magistrate corrected.

Moore shrugged and closed his file, knowing further argument to be useless.

Magistrate Gainsboro was not rated highly on intelligence, but lawyers who had suffered his ill-temper nonetheless credited him with street sense. And it didn't require a jurist to understand the brutal details of the indictment drafted by Page Moore. The allegations – even granting they were but allegations – told him that this case would soon receive media attention not seen since the days of Al Capone, if then. His liberal scruples were not such that he relished earning a bleeding-heart, soft-on-crime label. So, on studying the tax returns of the defendants that the government provided, he set bail for each of Vito Scalia and Gabriel Buffalino at $10,000,000. It was the highest in Maine's history.

Scalia and Buffalino breathed sighs of relief. Moore's stomach tightened.

Although they were directly implicated in the racketeering counts of the federal indictment, there was no evidence that Magaddino, Inciso, and Ferraro had participated in the capital offense of the Mintmire bombing. For this reason, the government did not oppose the setting of $5,000,000 bail for Magaddino and $1,000,000 each for Inciso and Ferraro.

For tactical reasons, the United States would not oppose bail for Don Salvatore – another $5,000,000, for a grand total of $32,000,000. If this put a dent in the family treasury, it was not serious. Carmine Palazzi, who would later learn that the two men accosting him at the Palermo dock were agents of Interpol, presented the defendants a different problem.

* * *

The team of defense lawyers, having succeeded in obtaining the release of their clients on bail, was now meeting at the offices of Clinton & St. John to plan its first round of delaying tactics. The firm's partners had been unable to resist the whopping retainer Scalia had waved under their noses to recruit them as local counsel. Refusal would also have entailed permanent loss of the firm's biggest client. In any event, they reasoned, every man is entitled to representation. *But*, the new retainer came with a stipulation. Sarah Goden had to go – and go she did.

* * *

By Wednesday, Maria Scalia had tired of her husband's unending fury and had packed and left their Kennebunkport home. Camilla and her husband having already left on Tuesday, Vito and Gabriel had the house to themselves. Vito was in the living room slumped in a wingback chair watching TV. He cracked his knuckles while CNN recounted the allegations of the indictment. Buffalino was at a desk studying the indictment itself and making notes in its margins. Although neither man was a heavy drinker, they had been pouring steadily from a bottle of Stolichnaya, and with each drink their recrimination and blame-shifting intensified a notch.

Buffalino, finally exhausted, spun in his chair toward Vito. "Forget Goden and his wife and concentrate on this indictment. The feds have it wired – It has to be Palazzi. With Silento gone, it can't be anyone else."

"If you're so cocksure, tell me why."

"How would I know? You and that goddamn Mintmire bullshit! Vito, we're looking at life or the chair if we don't find him."

"Stop whining! We'll find him. It's only a matter of time. Besides, without the pictures the jury will never believe him. There's no motive. None of our people flew into Portland. They'll deny they were even here. But it won't come to that. Palazzi is somewhere in Sicily and he'll never leave. I promise. I don't care if they have an army protecting him."

Buffalino had to admit this made sense and began to relax. Scalia had begun to unwind as soon as Magistrate Gainsboro had released them. Neither man had done jail time and neither expected to. The thought was too chilling to contemplate.

Scalia glanced at his watch. "The lawyers are due any minute." A moment later the chimes sounded.

"Must be them," said Buffalino. "I'll get it." He opened the front door – and the other shoe dropped.

"Mr. Buffalino," one of the state troopers began, "we have a warrant for your arrest on an indictment charging you with murder and conspiracy to commit murder in violation of the laws of the state of Maine. You have the right – "

The lawyers arrived as their handcuffed clients were being led from the house. Seeing their clients put into the rear of a state trooper's car, they did not need to be told what was happening. Although the federal government had moved first, the State of Maine was now getting its licks.

* * *

Their handcuffs removed, the two defendants were escorted into the courtroom. Although both carried an air of righteous outrage, they were patently uneasy. The unforeseen state indictment spelled immediate trouble. But Scalia felt somewhat relieved on spotting the State Attorney General, Rudy Briscoe, who had been his guest at the White Barn Inn. "Hello, Vito. Damn shame this had to happen."

"It's outlandish is what it is. Rudy, meet Gabriel Buffalino. He's my brother-in-law." The men shook hands. "Rudy's a good friend," Scalia explained.

"Nice to meet you, Gabriel. Well, this shouldn't take very long."

"Glad to see it's you handling this nonsense," Scalia said. "We're prepared to post any amount of bail you want."

Briscoe put his hand on Scalia's shoulder and gave it a reassuring squeeze.

Then he smiled. "That's good to know. We all have the same interest in seeing justice done."

"Thanks, Rudy, I appreciate that."

The two defendants sat down at counsel table with their lawyers. Scalia winked at Buffalino and furtively flashed a circle with his thumb and forefinger.

Moments later, all stood as Judge James Cotter took the bench to begin the bail hearing. One of Sarah Goden's former partners stepped forward to introduce Marvin Sales, who would be lead counsel for the defendants. They may not have made a wise selection of explosives dealers, but they chose well in picking Sales as their lawyer. He was among the best criminal defense lawyers in New York City.

"Good to have you aboard, Mr. Sales," Cotter graciously welcomed.

"Thank you, Your Honor."

"Mr. Briscoe," the judge said to the Attorney General, "this is a nice surprise having you here. If there are no preliminary matters, let's get started."

"There is one preliminary matter, Your Honor." Briscoe turned and signaled. A man rose from the rear of the spectator section and came forward. "If the Court please, this is Page Moore, the chief of the U.S. Justice Department's Organized Crime and Racketeering Section. I've appointed Mr. Moore a Special Assistant Attorney General to prosecute this case on behalf of the state. His appointment papers and commission are on file in the clerk's office. I have a set here for the Court."

Judge Cotter studied the papers. "You may proceed, Mr. Moore." When Moore had stated the grounds for the state's opposition to the defendants' release on bail, Marvin Sales rose to argue for the defendants.

Sales forcefully argued that pretrial detention would be a form of double jeopardy, inasmuch as Magistrate Gainsboro had already granted bail for essentially the same alleged offenses. But Judge Cotter wasn't biting. The murder of Loring Mills was a separate and greater offense than those charged in the federal indictment. He denied bail and set trial for November 30th, one week after the date set for trial of the federal case. If the federal trial began as scheduled, the state case would be rescheduled.

* * *

Two days after the bail hearing, Sales withdrew as defense counsel. Sarah Goden knew him from her New York City days as an ethical, as well as talented, trial lawyer. "Sales must have heard something he couldn't stomach," she told Tom.

* * *

Meanwhile, Sicily had become a scene from Keystone Cops. The Italian government was chasing Palazzi. The Italian Mafia was chasing Palazzi. Outfit goons and contract hitters imported from the United States were chasing Palazzi. "It's a traffic jam over here," Moore's Interpol contact informed him.

CHAPTER 25

Silento lost ground during the next sixty days. His mind was sharp and the cancer seemed to be in check, but side effects of the powerful medication were killing him. He was a scarecrow. If he lived to testify, the jurors might even empathize with him. Bizarre! But any significant delay in the trial, and they wouldn't get the chance.

Scalia and Buffalino had replaced Marvin Sales with Abe Priest, another highly regarded New York import. Each of the other defendants had his own lawyer, but Priest would call the shots and conduct major cross-examination.

Priest was forty-five. His receding hairline and a few silver streaks at the temples matched his age. One shoulder was a little lower than the other and he walked with a slight stoop. He wasn't a slasher; he spoke softly in measured, precise tones. Overall, he presented a trim, distinguished, and, some thought, handsome appearance. He was a striking physical contrast to Page Moore. Another respected prosecutor had once commented that Priest was the only trial lawyer he knew who was as good as he thought he was. Moore knew this was only ninety-nine percent true. Priest, on the very rarest of occasions, could act impulsively.

The federal case was assigned for trial to U.S. District Judge Jack Smith, a pleasant, slightly rotund workaholic. He was a recent appointee, with no track record on the bench in major criminal cases. But he had a long one in his private practice in Portland. Time was, if you were unfortunate enough to be indicted for a serious felony in Maine, and if you could afford him, you hired Jack Smith. He could pull a very large rabbit from a small hat. "Don't jump to conclusions," Moore told a suspicious Vince Inserra.

Another judge had heard preliminary motions directed at the sufficiency of the indictment and had denied them. "It seems to me if you have any objection, it should be that the indictment is too detailed," the judge had told Priest. He had also denied the motions for severance and separate trials on the arson and racketeering counts.

Moore had only one more meeting scheduled to wood-shed Silento, and then the Sicilian assassin would be as ready to testify as he would ever be. So would the other witnesses. It wasn't necessary to remind them of the need for complete silence. Meanwhile, the furious Mafia manhunt for Carmine Palazzi continued, while Scalia and Buffalino paced their cells at the Portland detention center. When they weren't pacing or cursing, they were meeting with Priest in a conference room at the jail facility.

"You're sure they have no case of any kind without Palazzi?"

"Vito, I've told you that since day one," Priest replied.

"And what happens if the feds walk into court with him?" Buffalino asked once again.

"Same thing. The jury will dismiss Palazzi as a twisted psychopath. Not right away. But when I finish laying the groundwork, the jurors will be sitting on the edge of their seats waiting for the pictures. No pictures, no case."

By November 2nd, Vito's July 4th wedding reception guests had received defense subpoenas to testify. They marked their calendars and began memorizing their scripts. Each was sure he had never attended a wedding reception in Kennebunkport, Maine. Or, at least, he could not remember attending one – and how could he possibly have forgotten such an event?

* * *

On Wednesday, November 18th, Moore was working from an office in the United States Attorney's quarters in the courthouse on Federal Street in Portland. It was three business days before the trial was to begin. He walked from the courthouse to the offices of Clinton & St. John, which had dedicated a suite of offices and two secretaries to Abe Priest's use. A battery of young associates and paralegals was also at his beck and call. Moore, his nose and ears red from the short walk in the ten-degree temperature, went to the reception desk and announced himself. In a moment, he was greeted by a secretary who walked him to the open door of the mock-Chippendale office used by Abe Priest.

"Come in and have a seat, Page. You've come to tell us you're going to dismiss the indictment?" Priest jabbed, smiling broadly. In fact, the apparent dig was not wholly facetious. The conventional wisdom circulating from Sicily during the past week had given the defendants cause for confidence. Sure, Palazzi had talked. But with a trial date staring him in the face, he simply didn't have the stomach to go through with it. So he cut and ran. Mafia intelligence backed this up – they didn't have him yet, but the feds didn't either. This intelligence, however, was incomplete. Interpol had him, and his extradition was underway.

"Not yet, Abe," Moore replied, bending to reach into his briefcase. "Since this is a capital case, I'm here to comply with Section 3432 of Title 18 – you know, the three-day provision. Here's the jury panel." He began to stand. "Oh, I almost forgot," came the return jab, "here's the list of the government's witnesses. Give me a call if you have any questions."

"I will."

Moore was almost out the door and failed to hear the sudden intake of breath when Priest's eyes reached Silento's name at the foot of the list.

Moore left the building and took up a position by the window of a clothing store across the street. He didn't have long to wait. Two minutes later, he saw Priest leave the building and signal for a cab. He wasn't running; he was flying. "Chew on that, you sons of bitches," Moore muttered.

* * *

Buffalino had recovered from his shock. "He's bluffing. Silento's dead." Scalia, gasping like a fish fresh-pulled from the sea, said nothing.

Priest, who had regained his composure in the taxicab, dismissed the possibility that Moore was bluffing. "Moore doesn't play that sort of game. You've been had. Now we have no choice. We must delay the start of the trial. I suggest we move for a six-month continuance. The court would compromise and give us three months. Silento has cancer. He could be dead by then. Even if he isn't, he might be in no shape to testify."

Scalia's face turned crimson. "Not a fucking chance. I'm not staying in here an extra ninety days. You said the jury would write off Palazzi as a psychopath. Silento's no different. You said 'no pictures, no case.' Nothing's changed. We go on Monday."

Buffalino agreed.

Priest persisted in arguing the wisdom of delay until Scalia, tired of words, swept the lawyer's briefcase from the conference table and kicked it across the room. Priest retrieved his briefcase without a word, returned to the table, and extracted a legal pad. "O.K., tell me why you were so certain Silento was dead. It just may be that I can stick this up the government's ass."

CHAPTER 26

In the late afternoon of the day of his jail confrontation with Vito Scalia and Bufallino, Priest was at the podium facing Judge Smith. Moore was at counsel table taking notes.

"So in conclusion, Your Honor, the Defendants' Motion In Limine To Bar Dominic Silento From Testifying should be granted. I submit it is the only appropriate response to the fraud and deceit perpetrated by United States."

"Thank you, Mr. Priest. Mr. Moore, does the government wish to contest the factual allegations? You needn't comment on the characterizations."

Moore walked to the podium. "No, Your Honor."

Smith frowned while consulting his notes. Then he lifted his head and leaned forward. "All right, correct me where I'm wrong. The government admits that the Federal Bureau of Investigation fabricated a death certificate, an autopsy report, related hospital records, notices to civil authorities, notice to heirs, and obituaries, all designed to give the defendants the impression that the witness Silento had died from cancer at the Mayo Clinic. Have I missed anything?"

"Only the burial records."

"Oh yes, Mr. Priest did mention them. The FBI was quite thorough."

"Thank you, Your Honor."

Judge Smith tapped his fingertips together, then leaned back, still frowning. "Mr. Moore, was this charade your idea?"

"In part. I take full responsibility."

"Would you care to inform the Court why the government felt it necessary to deceive the defendants?"

"I will be glad to, Your Honor. May I have just a moment?"

"Certainly."

Moore walked briskly to the corridor outside the courtroom. He returned a moment later. "If the Court pleases, this is FBI Special Agent William Phalen. He has three short video tapes I think Your Honor should see. As they're being run, Mr. Phalen will identify the actors and then answer any questions the Court may have. This procedure will best answer Your Honor's question of why the charade."

"I object, Your Honor, the government has never disclosed these tapes to the defendants."

"Come now, Mr. Priest, there's no jury. This is your motion. The admissibility of the tapes at trial is a separate matter. You may proceed, Mr. Moore."

The first video tape showed the defendants Sam Ferraro and Angelo Inciso as they watched the activity build around Silento's room at the Mayo Clinic. They were still watching when he was wheeled from the room for his trip to intensive care. The second tape showed Ferraro watching Silento's room in the ICU. It showed Ferraro giving the thumbs-up signal and Inciso quickly slipping into the room. Then it showed Inciso leaving the room and ducking into the adjoining one. Finally, it showed the arrival of Phalen and the nurse, while Ferraro watched with his head poking around the bend in the corridor.

Phalen's accompanying commentary was crisp. By the time Moore inserted the third tape, Judge Smith had left the bench to stand within feet of the video screen. Priest didn't know what to expect. Many criminal defendants make the disastrous mistake of not telling their lawyers everything.

The third tape opened with Inciso in Silento's room. There was the syringe descending toward Silento's arm, the flat line on the monitor, the pocketing of the syringe, and Inciso's hurried exit. The tape ended with Phalen and the nurse working on Silento.

Judge Smith asked twice that the tape be rerun. Then he returned to the bench, very slowly and very deliberately. Two newspaper reporters and an Associated Press stringer on the courthouse beat slid from their seats in the spectator section. They stood near the doors, poised for a dash down the corridor to the phones.

"Mr. Priest, do you care to add anything or to cross-examine agent Phalen?"

"No, Your Honor. The defendants' position remains the same. The government has acknowledged its willful deceit and an appropriate sanction should be imposed."

"Motion denied. Mr. Priest, I can't imagine that you knew what those tapes would disclose or anything about the underlying events. If you had, I'm certain you would not have been here this afternoon."

"I didn't, Your Honor, I assure you."

"Mr. Moore," said the judge, "these tapes cannot be used at trial unless you have evidence that the apparent attempt on Mr. Silento's life was an act in furtherance of the same conspiracy alleged in the indictment. Of course, I don't mean to suggest that they would not provide the basis for a separate indictment."

"We hadn't planned to offer them, Your Honor."

"Very well. Then you understand that when Mr. Silento testifies he is not, as in 'not', under any circumstances to mention this episode. If he does, the Court would be forced to declare a mistrial."

"I understand, Your Honor."

* * *

After the hearing, Priest raced to meet with Scalia and Buffalino in the jail. As soon as the guard closed the door on the bare conference room, he was waving his arms and ranting at his two clients. At first, they simply sat and looked at him. Vito was first to respond.

"Fuck off."

"Fuck off?!! Do you guys have any idea what you're doing? You order a hit on the government's star witness and then have your lawyer stand in front of the judge like a complete idiot, bitching because you thought the witness was dead. And if I figure you ordered the hit, do you think a judge like Smith will think anything else?"

Scalia and Buffalino sat down without further response, while keeping their eyes steadily on Priest.

Priest's tone became less strident. "Don't you understand that you have to keep me informed of anything that might bear on the case? I think I may be able to handle this one, but another deal like this and I walk."

* * *

Later that evening, after an intense session with his co-counsel to replot strategy, Abe Priest answered a summons for dinner with Don Salvatore and Patsy Magaddino at the Sonesta Hotel in Portland. After the three had given their orders for wine and dinner, Priest gave his report of the day's events without frills or exaggeration. Like others, he was somewhat in awe of the don and did not repeat the lecture he had given Vito and Gabriel.

"Why can't this Moore use the videotapes at the trial?" Don Salvatore asked.

"Because he has no evidence that Ferraro and Inciso were acting other than on their own. Without such evidence, admission of the tapes as evidence against them alone would be too prejudicial against you and the other defendants – like Patsy here."

The don regarded his wine for a moment, finally taking a sip. "So they are of no immediate concern?"

Priest studied his own wine, glancing at Magaddino, and then returned the don's gaze. "I wouldn't say that."

"What would you say, consigliere?" injected Magaddino. "Get to the point."

Priest put his glass down, looking steadily at first one and then the other until his eyes stayed on Don Salvatore. "I figure that Vito and Gabriel were behind this, and that they wouldn't have acted without clearing it with you. As I see it, Silento will figure the same way. I'd say that's cause for concern because when he testifies he'll put it to you every way he can."

Their food arrived, and the three ate quickly, talking of other subjects. When they were through, Priest excused himself and headed for his room. Eyebrows raised, the don looked at Magaddino.

Magaddino shrugged, palms up. "When Gabriel told me, I went ape. But he said you'd cleared it. Had you?"

"I discussed it with Vito – twice. Both times I told him 'no.' Now, it turns out he was right. If they'd moved on that Judas when Vito wanted to, we wouldn't be in this godforsaken hole now."

Magaddino shook his head. "I'd never have suspected Silento. He must've started spilling his guts as soon as he got to the Mayo Clinic. Otherwise, the feds would've had no call to protect him. They wouldn't run that sweet an operation without reason. But, Gesu, why Dominic? And why didn't Vito trust him? I mean, he grew up with Vito and Maria. To hear you tell it, they were inseparable. Best friends. Some friends!"

Don Salvatore nodded in puzzlement. "I don't know. When we were all in Kennebunkport, it seemed just like the old days – the three played like they were kids. Even kicked a soccer ball around. And when I told Vito that Dominic might be dying, he offered to have him stay in Kennebunkport with them once he came back from the clinic. I know Gabriel didn't trust Dominic, but Gabriel doesn't trust anyone. He finally persuaded Vito, but he could never have persuaded me."

"And now we're all exposed," added Magaddino.

The don gently rested his hand on Magaddino's. "Only for the moment, Patsy. Moore has put Silento in play, but he'll never finish the game."

CHAPTER 27

"Discovery" is the process by which each side in a lawsuit is required to inform the other about what to expect at the trial. In civil cases, the parties have a nearly unlimited right of discovery, so that each side knows well in advance of trial the details of the testimony and documents the other will produce. But such broad-ranging discovery is not allowed in criminal cases, and there is a certain amount of trial by ambush. However, by comparing the witness list to the overt acts alleged in the indictment, Priest and the other defense lawyers had been able to infer the likely subject matters to be covered by most of the government witnesses. This would have to do. The witnesses who could be located – corporate representatives and law-enforcement personnel – weren't talking. The others were in protective custody at unknown locations.

At first, Tom Goden, Cameron Herd, and Dick Hundley had been mystery witnesses. Hundley didn't remain one for long.

"He's a former Chicago cop," reported Buffalino. "Headed the Intelligence Division. He has files on most of our people. He and Smythe were very thick."

"That's it then," said Priest. "They plan to use him to give a lot of unsupported organized-crime crap about the ones Silento will say were at the reception. I'm surprised at Moore. He knows that's inadmissible. What about this Herd?"

"I know him," said Scalia. "He writes editorials for Mills's paper."

"Why would they call him and Goden?" Priest asked.

"I don't know. For Christ's sake, that's what we're paying you for. Figure it out." Scalia banged the table, sending their coffee flying. "I've already told you that Goden probably knows Hundley. I think Goden went fishing with him last summer."

Priest rose to wash the coffee from his tie, then thought better of it. "Have you gone over the jury list?"

"Yeah, we have," replied Buffalino.

"Do either of you know any of the people?"

"No," Scalia answered, handing the list back to Priest. "The names don't ring a bell."

"Are you sure?"

"What is it with you," Buffalino asked, "are you hard of hearing?"

* * *

The Palazzi diversion had bogged down the Mafia's best hitters in Sicily, but when word reached them that Silento was the new target and that he was in the United States, they regrouped and moved quickly. It was traffic jam time again.

The Mafia's highest-placed source in the FBI was not a special agent, nor an agent-in-charge of a field office, nor a deputy director, nor anyone associated with the Bureau's law-enforcement activities, except indirectly. She was a GS-16 supergrade in charge of the Property Section of the FBI's Administrative Division. The section was responsible for, among other things, the myriad of details involved in maintaining the Bureau's network of safehouses. Her name was Annette Baylor. She was a savvy, patient bureaucrat. Within days of Moore's November 18 delivery of the government's witness list to Abe Priest, she was at a pay phone in Union Station in Washington D.C.

"What makes you think he's there?" asked Alex Simone.

"Because of circumstances," replied Baylor. "It went active on August thirty-first, the day you think the Mayo transfer was made. A pass was issued to a hospital-supply company for the delivery of equipment and medical supplies. A doctor from the Bethesda Naval Hospital got a clearance. The level of activity and personnel is consistent with a major op. We don't have anything else in the hopper this big."

"I'll need a layout of the grounds and farmhouse and any change in status."

"You'll have them," Baylor assured.

"We must be absolutely certain he's there."

"I've told you everything I know." Baylor hung up the phone and shivered with fright. Her fate had been sealed the moment she first succumbed to these men. She had no empathy for the faceless people she sometimes served and less for their cause. But the money! It was more than she had ever dreamed of.

* * *

On the Saturday following Thanksgiving, Page Moore took the 6:00 a.m. flight from Portland to Dulles, arriving at 7:36 a.m. At 7:50 a.m., two cars with FBI agents, having picked up Moore at the airport, began a circuitous drive west through Front Royal, south along part of the Skyline Drive to Sperryville, then east to Warrenton, and finally south again. It was after 10:00 a.m. when Moore arrived at the farmhouse for his final session with Silento.

An hour after Moore's arrival at Dulles, Alex Simone, in Washington, was on the phone with Tony Rosato.

"There can't be any question, Tony. He's in the middle of the trial. He wouldn't fly to Washington for any other reason."

"Was he followed from Dulles?"

"Of course not. The Bureau would spot the tail."

"Did an agent meet him?" Rosato asked.

"We think so. He left in a private car."

"Man or woman driving?"

"Woman," Simone replied.

"Jesus Christ! How do you know he's not just shacking up with her?"

"We don't know for certain. In theory, he could be here for twenty different reasons. But I'm telling you, with the trial going on it doesn't figure. There's too much work for him to do to be fucking around in Washington."

"Yeah, you're probably right," said Rosato. "How'll we know when they're ready to move him?"

"Timing. I think Moore will finish calling the foundation witnesses first. My guess is two weeks."

"We need better than that," Rosato growled.

"I'm working on it," Simone replied.

* * *

On Monday, Annette Baylor contacted Simone. "The facility is going to inactive status effective on twelve-three."

"What does that mean?" Simone asked.

"If he's there, he'll be gone by Thursday."

* * *

It was a near record storm for so early in the season. It began to slacken at noon Tuesday, leaving Virginia and the Washington area blanketed under fifteen inches of snow. The man and woman waited until midnight and then were driven from the motel into Culpeper County. They left the car and walked the remaining three miles along the side of the plowed road. When they reached the margin of the farmhouse property, they moved through the woods in single file, the woman first. The man placed his boots in her steps, turning after each stride to cover their tracks. A light snow, swirling in a freshening breeze, added to the cover. Their progress, although painfully slow, put them in position under a makeshift shelter of fallen branches at the edge of the woods just 225 yards from the farmhouse at 4:00 a.m.

The snow provided enormous tactical advantage. Their winter outfits were white from head to foot, and their rifles, silencers, scopes, and tripods were freshly painted white. Even to a trained observer at close range, they were virtually invisible, while any activity at or near the farmhouse was starkly visible. Nonetheless, they could see no sign that the farmhouse was differently used than others nearby. The hours passed tranquilly, the snow's gentle descent undisturbed by sound or movement.

Their patience wearing thin, they saw at 3:00 p.m. a delivery van pull to the front of the farmhouse. "This could be it," the woman hissed.

"Yeah, look! Here come the agents. They're gonna make a sweep."

Assembling at the side of the farmhouse, six special agents formed a skirmish line in which they moved in expanding circles from the house. Two stopped for a moment ten yards from where the couple lay completely covered. "It's clear; let's head in," said one of the agents. "We're out of here in less than an hour."

The couple waited five minutes before stirring. Fifteen minutes later, they slid from shelter and assembled their equipment, then moved twenty-five yards on their stomachs to the edge of the woods. They packed the snow to provide a firm foundation for the tripods and scanned the front door with their scopes. The line of sight to the top of the steps just cleared the roof of the waiting van.

"You want the head shot or the chest?" the man asked.

"Doesn't matter."

"Take the head." Then he thumbed his walkie-talkie. "Route 729 could use another plowing."

The seemingly innocuous message was received, and the Culpeper County Public Works Department truck began to move slowly. A private car followed.

* * *

At 4:10 p.m., the front door of the farmhouse opened and a wheelchair rolled onto the porch. Special agents stood in front and behind the chair, scanning the grounds with binoculars. A pair of eyes came to rest on the couple's position for a moment and moved on. Other agents stood at either side of the wheelchair. An agent in the waiting van was gunning the engine impatiently. There were FBI escort cars in front of and behind the van.

* * *

The couple made a final sweep of the porch, adjusting their scopes until the images were sharp.

The man suddenly broke their mutual silence with an intense whisper. "They're shielding him like he was the president. Forget the head shot. You take out the two agents in front of the wheelchair. On my count of three. O.K.? One! Two!"

The woman interrupted. "Stop! They're moving aside. Steady! Steady! He's coming into line."

* * *

Dominic Silento drew deep breaths of fresh air. The clouds were breaking and the sun's late rays were streaming through, reflecting off snow-shrouded evergreens. With its endless expanse of white blanketing, the rolling countryside began to sparkle. It was a deliciously beautiful winter scene and the sharp bite of the crisp air pushed the cancer from Silento's mind. Two agents were edging his wheelchair to the top of the steps. "Hold it! Wait!"

"What's the problem?" asked one of the agents.

"Get me out of this fucking thing," Silento pled, "I can walk." It was the first time in over three months he had been outside, and he would not let the moment go. The agents looked at each other and shrugged.

The two shielding agents moved to Silento's side, exposing him to the view of the two assassins. As they helped him to stand, two other agents moved the empty chair down the steps. He wobbled a bit, but steadied himself on their shoulders. This momentary lowering of security, it developed, was critical.

* * *

The rifles tracked until Silento's head and heart area were squarely in the cross hairs. Each assassin took a small breath, held it, and increased the trigger pressure until each rifle coughed three times in quick succession. The bullets in flight, they saw Silento's feet fly from under him as he crumpled to the foot of the steps. They rose quickly and trotted, in a half-crouch, toward the road and their waiting car.

* * *

"Jesus Christ!" yelled an agent. "What happened?" Silento was by then lying on his back at the bottom of the steps. Two agents lay next to him. One stirred and rubbed his arm. The other was pushing himself to his knees, gently massaging the back of his head. He looked up. "Those goddamn steps are still icy. Our boy took a flier and took us with him."

"I think I broke my arm," the other agent moaned. He struggled to a sitting position and looked at Silento. "Open your eyes and talk to us, you son of a bitch."

Other agents and a doctor now crowded around the motionless Silento. "Is he all right?" one asked.

"Yeah, he's all right," said the agent with the bad arm. "He let out a yelp when we landed." The agent poked at him with his good arm. "Come on, Silento, stop screwing around."

Silento opened his eyes. "Help me up. I'm getting cold."

* * *

Two FBI agents watched the van and its convoy until it was out of sight. Then they went into the farmhouse for their coats. They would putter around until Silento was safely aboard the FBI plane that would carry him to Maine and another safehouse.

They returned with their coats and walked along the driveway toward the road. One scratched his head. "Walt, how long you been in the field?"

"Ten years."

"Ever hear a bullet go by your head?"

"Only once, why?"

"What did it sound like?"

"You don't hear it. You feel the air. Well, I guess you hear that. It's hard to describe. But, Jim, you'll know when it happens. Pray it doesn't. It'll scare the shit out of you."

"You were standing next to me when Silento took the header. Didn't you hear it?"

"Hear what?"

"What you just described."

"No. Did you?"

"I don't know. I'm thinking I heard something."

"Come off it, Jim." He motioned toward some swaying trees that were shedding their snow cover. "It's the wind."

"Yeah, I guess you're right."

The agents reached the road and stood for a few moments with their hands over their ears. Then they turned to walk back. In three hours, they would close the farmhouse and return home to pack for their flight to Maine.

The bullets that had missed agent Jim Brosnan's head by inches had passed through the open door. They were now deeply imbedded in soft-pine molding at the far end of the farmhouse's front hall.

* * *

Thursday, December 3. "You're saying they missed him?" Rosato roared. "They saw the motherfucker go down."

"Tony, I'm telling you he's alive and he'll be testifying early next week," Simone replied.

"Sonofabitch! This is gonna blow their minds. Where does Moore have him stashed?"

"Don't know. I'm working on it."

"Alex, baby, time's running out!"

CHAPTER 28

On the morning Silento was expected to testify, the lines began forming at 4:00 a.m. It didn't matter that for the past three nights the temperatures had gone as low as twenty-below zero, turning unprotected skin to frostbitten parchment. The word was the government was dropping its hydrogen bomb.

When Moore called the government's twentieth witness, the spectators and media representatives turned toward the set of double doors at the rear of the courtroom for their first look at the bag of bones upon which the United States was pitching its case. A minute passed; then two. People began to murmur. Then the single door to Judge Smith's right swung open, and an FBI special agent pushed a wheelchair around the jury box to the witness stand. Silento rose unsteadily. Moore and the agent helped him climb to the witness chair. With Silento seated, Moore returned to the podium and opened his folder for direct examination. His hands were shaking. His clothes felt tight. There was a hush as everyone looked at the witness.

Silento was now almost bald. All that remained of his thick black hair were some long strands of gray which he had pushed to the side. His close-set eyes seemed to burn from his gaunt face. Although his sallow cheeks were cleanly shaved, his lips were badly cracked, and his reddened gums, visible above crooked teeth, seemed to bleed. His arms were like sticks, and it looked as though his knees would poke through the blue serge of his new suit. Silento appeared no longer as a bird of prey, but like an emaciated rat.

From Silento's perspective, looking from the witness chair, the scene was one of contrast. A single person sat at government counsel table – Moore's assistant, Angela Featherstone, a thirty-five-year-old trial lawyer from the Organized Crime And Racketeering Section. Featherstone had shoulder-length red hair, sparkling alert eyes, an infectious smile, and freckles. She wore a nicely tailored tan gabardine suit and cream blouse over a pert figure. She was fresh and alive and didn't look like a prosecutor. And she was smart and capable. She wasn't Moore, but she was nearly as good. Only a few neatly arranged folders were on the counsel table in front of her. The rest of the case file was hidden from view in two transfer cartons below.

On the defense side, two conference tables had been added since the opening day of trial, and they now formed a three-sided square. Unlike the prosecution table, the three defense tables were weighted with rows of notebooks and expandable folders crammed with documents. The seven defendants and their fourteen lawyers, all outfitted in well-tailored suits, were crowded around the tables -- Vito Scalia, Salvatore Scalia, Buffalino, Magaddino, Inciso, Ferraro, Palazzi, and their legal teams. It didn't look like the full weight of the federal government had been brought to bear on the defendants; rather, it looked the other way around. And there were no Italian silk suits, white-on-white shirts, pearl-gray ties, or diamond cuff links. The conservative pin stripes, gray flannels, and regimental ties were straight from an Ivy League reunion.

"Raise your right hand. Do you solemnly swear the testimony you are about to give will be the truth, the whole truth, and nothing but the truth?" intoned the clerk, unable to take his eyes from Silento's gaunt face.

"I do," said Silento, in a raspy voice. Abe Priest looked at the jurors with slightly arched eyebrows, as if to say, "You just heard the first lie."

But the jurors – seven women and five men – weren't watching Priest or any other of the lawyers. They were watching the defendants and the witness – seeking signs of human reaction between these men who had been so close but were now separated by a gulf as impassable as that between the living and the dead. They saw no reaction on either side. Silento, seemingly oblivious to all else, looked only at Moore. The defendants, staring stonily at the witness, showed no emotion, no recognition.

"Mr. Moore, you may proceed," advised Judge Smith.

"Thank you, Your Honor. State your full name for the record."

Moore's direct examination moved quickly. There were surprisingly few interruptions. Abe Priest had wisely decided that little would be gained with the jury by attempting to disrupt the testimony with objections the court would surely overrule.

In the last row of the spectator section, unobserved by those directly involved in the trial, sat Maria Scalia. One hand tightly clasping the other, she strained for every word. Craning her neck to avoid the obstructing heads in front of her, she tried to pick out the slightest gesture of the actors in the scene before her.

Maria was shocked by Dominic's appearance and the sound of his voice. Her mind would soon be reeling from what he said.

Moore led Silento through his early history and his family's association with the don. He then elicited the development of his close friendship with

Vito, Gabriel, and Maria. Turning his attention to employment by the don, he had Silento describe not only the nature of his own role as one of the don's soldati, but also the general character of the don's business that his role exposed him to. Although Judge Smith severely restricted what Moore could develop concerning the don's multifarious activities, Silento's testimony left the jurors little doubt concerning the basis of the family's wealth.

When Moore came to the details of Loring Mills's torture and death, several women on the jury brought out handkerchiefs, and even some men brought the backs of their hands to their eyes. The appearance of the very pregnant Priscilla Mills on the witness stand was fresh in their minds.

As Silento calmly described his use of the ice pick on Mills's teeth, illustrating its use with his hands, there was a collective gasp through the courtroom. The blood rose to Judge Smith's face, and the woman juror seated closest to Silento sagged forward as though about to faint. Judge Smith declared a fifteen minute recess.

On the jury's return to the courtroom, Moore resumed the podium. "Mr. Silento, why did you do those, those – " Moore started over. "Why did you and Mr. Palazzi inflict such inhuman, horrible pain on Mr. Mills?"

Defense lawyers rose to object to the form of the question, but thought better of it.

"Because he – "

"Who's he?"

"Vito Scalia. He told us to be – I forget the word."

"Thorough?" Moore suggested.

"Yeah. He said it would be our asses if we didn't get all the pictures."

"Did he tell you to kill Mr. Mills?"

"That's right. His wife too. But Don Salvatore told him to leave her alone. So did Buffalino."

"That was thoughtful," Moore observed dryly.

"Objection," interposed Priest.

"Sustained. The jury will disregard Mr. Moore's remark."

"What did you and Mr. Palazzi do after the burial service?"

"Objection," shouted Magaddino's lawyer, "Mr. Moore's sarcasm is unnecessary."

Judge Smith remained impassive. "I don't sense any sarcasm, but I don't recall any testimony about a burial service. Mr. Moore, perhaps you wish to reframe your question."

"I will, Your Honor. Mr. Silento, what did you and Mr. Palazzi do after you stuffed Mr. Mills's body in that metal drum and dumped it overboard?"

"We went back to the house and gave the pictures to them."

"To whom did you give the pictures?"

"Scalia, Don Salvatore, and Buffalino."

"What else?"

"We told them everything."

"Did you tell them what you had done to Mr. Mills?"

"Uh huh. Vito wanted to know so he could be sure we had all the pictures. He told us we did good."

"What did the others say?"

"Not much. They were too busy looking at the pictures."

"Did anyone say anything about the pictures?"

"Yeah. They all said like it would've been a disaster, you know, if the pictures got in the wrong hands. Then Vito called Patsy Magaddino and put him on the squawk box."

"What was said?"

"Vito told him what had gone down and thanked him again for making Smythe on the plane."

"What did Mr. Magaddino say?"

"Not much. I think he was – "

"Objection."

"Sustained. Mr. Silento, confine your answers to what you saw and what you heard; omit what you thought."

"O.K. Magaddino said something like me and Carmine took our work too seriously."

"What did Mr. Vito Scalia say to that?" Moore asked.

"He called him a pussy. Then Vito's wife stuck her head in the den and that was the end of the conversation."

"What happened next?"

"Well, it was getting light out, and Don Salvatore went to bed. Then Vito told Buffalino he wanted to talk to him alone. So they walked out to the yard."

"Did Mr. Scalia take the pictures?"

"Yeah. Don Salvatore had been looking at them – shaking his head – and put 'em back in the envelope and handed them to Vito."

"What did Vito Scalia say, if anything, when he took the pictures?"

"He said 'come to papa'."

Moore moved from the podium to counsel table. He poured a cup of water while Featherstone handed him the examination folder for the July 7th bombing of Neil Mintmire's business. He returned to the podium and took Silento through the entire episode – preparation, placing the charges, setting the detonator.

"What did you and Mr. Palazzi do after you set the explosives?" Moore asked Silento.

"We drove back to Scalia's and went into the den. I told them – "

"Who's them?"

"Vito Scalia, Don Salvatore, and Buffalino."

"O.K., what did you tell them?"

"That the place would blow at eleven-thirty if the detonator worked."

"What did they say?"

"Don Salvatore tapped his cane a coupla times, but didn't say anything. Buffalino, he was yelling at Scalia. I mean, he flipped out!"

"You mean he was mad?" Moore asked

"Mad? Hey, you don't know mad."

Priest began to rise from his chair.

"Mr. Silento," said Judge Smith, "just answer the question."

"Yeah, he was mad," said Silento.

"About what?" Moore asked.

"Well, Buffalino thought Mintmire's place had already gone up and that Palazzi and me had been there to be sure no one got hurt – you know, that the place was deserted. He told Scalia that was their agreement."

"Why weren't you there?"

"Because Scalia, Vito, told us to be at the house when it blew. He said he didn't wanna risk us getting grabbed."

"When did he tell you that?"

"That Tuesday night when we were getting in the car. He pulled us aside and told us," Silento replied.

"Now, getting back to the den, what did Mr. Vito Scalia say when Mr. Buffalino stopped yelling?"

"Nothing. I mean, he said something but not about that."

"What did he say?" Moore asked.

"He looked at his watch and said it was almost eleven-thirty and that he was goin out to the yard to listen."

"Listen to what?"

"The explosion."

"Did Mr. Buffalino say anything to that?"

"Yeah," Silento replied. "He told Scalia he must be joking because that was a good twenty miles away."

"Then what happened next?"

"We all went outside and walked down to the water."

"Did you hear the explosion?" Moore asked.

Priest was on his feet. "Objection, Your Honor, that calls for speculation."

"I'll withdraw the question," said Moore.

"Mr. Silento, at eleven-thirty, did you hear a noise?"

"Uh huh, it sounded like thunder in the distance. Lasted maybe half a minute."

"What, if anything, did Mr. Vito Scalia say when you heard the noise?" Moore asked.

Silento regarded the group at the defendants' counsel table for a moment. Then he looked directly at Vito Scalia.

"Mr. Silento, do you understand the question?" Judge Smith asked.

"Yeah, I understand it. But Scalia spoke in Italian – not English."

"What did he say?"

"He said, 'messaggio recapitato.'"

"And what does that mean in English?"

"It means 'message delivered'."

CHAPTER 29

Moore completed his direct examination of Silento in two hours, so the court broke for lunch at 11:30 a.m. At 1:00 p.m. Priest began cross-examination. It was both savage and deft. He built minor failures of recollection into sinister concealment. He carved at Silento with a scalpel until irrelevant inconsistencies assumed gigantic proportions. He used Silento's lack of remorse like a bludgeon to pound his credibility. But always the pictures. Priest led Silento down that path as if he had him on a leash. Then came the coup de grace.

"Mr. Silento, I've handed you a document that has been marked as Defendants' Exhibit 1 for identification. Do you know what that is?"

"Yeah."

"What is it?"

"It's a list of names."

Moore studied the copy Priest had given him. He started to rise, but then sat back.

"Who are those people?" Priest asked.

"They're business associates of the Scalias' who were at the reception."

"Are these the same people you say you met over the years at Salvatore Scalia's villa?"

"That's right."

"These are the same people you also say were in the pictures no one seems able to locate, isn't that correct?"

"Listen up. There were pictures. I told you I gave them to – " Silento began to cough deep, wracking, and liquid.

Priest waited patiently until he was quiet. "No, you listen up. We have only your word for that."

Moore rose and just as quickly sat down.

"Would it surprise you to know," Priest began, "that each of these people is under subpoena to testify, and that they will – "

Now Moore was on his feet. "Objection, Your Honor. It's a double question. The first part I have no objection to. It's what's coming after 'they will'."

"Overruled. Let him complete the question."

"And that they will testify they were nowhere near the wedding reception?" Priest finished.

"Objection," Moore repeated. "The question is based on unsupported and speculative assumptions, first that they will so testify, and second that it will be truthful testimony."

"I'll overrule the objection. Mr. Silento, do you have the question in mind?"

"Yeah. I wouldn't be surprised because – "

Priest interrupted and rolled his eyes. "Because they'd be lying, right?"

"Right."

"Now, Mr. Silento, see if you can find it in yourself to answer at least one question truthfully."

"Objection."

"Sustained. Mr. Priest, I'm allowing you a lot of latitude, given the importance of this witness to the government's case. Don't abuse it."

"I'm sorry, Your Honor. I just find it difficult to – "

"– control yourself," Smith completed.

Several jurors laughed.

"Now, Mr. Silento, if you were one of the jurors and you heard all this testimony, the thing you'd want most to see would be those pictures, isn't that right?"

"Objection. This is a plain invasion of the jury function."

"Overruled. Answer the question, Mr. Silento."

"I suppose you could say that," Silento answered, in his raspy monotone. It was apparent he was tired of lawyer games and wanted to follow the course of least resistance.

"And if the government didn't come up with those pictures, you'd have a reasonable doubt about the whole government case, wouldn't you?"

Moore popped to his feet. "Objection, Your Honor. That calls for an even bigger invasion of the jury function, not that Mr. Priest has left much to be invaded."

"I'll allow it. I'm sure the jurors understand that they are the sole judges of the facts and the credibility of the witnesses, and what weight to give to the evidence."

"You'd have a reasonable doubt, wouldn't you?" Priest repeated.

"Yeah, but I'm telling you – "

"You've answered the question, Mr. Silento. Your Honor, I have nothing further at this time."

Moore slumped in his chair. There they were. The pictures! He had committed the defendants. They had taken the bait. But had he outsmarted himself?

"I see it's past time for our normal afternoon break," said Judge Smith. "We'll take thirty minutes."

"All rise," called the bailiff.

After the judge and jury left the courtroom, the defendants and their lawyers huddled. "That went better than I expected," said Priest. "My recommendation is to leave it at that."

But the other lawyers wouldn't hear of it. Priest had softened up Silento. Now they all wanted a piece of him. Besides, this trial was playing nationally and they had their reputations to nourish. After all, they weren't wallflowers. Priest became adamant. "Leave well enough alone. Get him off the stand now, while the reasonable-doubt business is fresh in the jury's mind. We have nothing more to gain."

"Bullshit," Magaddino responded. "Keep working him over. He's not going to get off that easy."

"Gabriel, what do you think?" Vito Scalia finally asked.

The expandable file folders on the tables had long cloth strings to secure the flaps. As each day of trial began, Salvatore Scalia would cut off one of the strings. Then he would spend the day winding the string into a tight ball, unwinding it, and rewinding it. Before Buffalino could answer, Don Salvatore put down the cloth ball. "Make the whore bleed some more."

* * *

Cross-examination resumed at 4:30 p.m. and continued until 6:00 p.m. It resumed at 9:30 a.m. the next morning. By 2:30 p.m., it was apparent that the judge and jury were tired of hearing the same ground replowed. The spectators were bored and almost no one in the courtroom was paying much attention.

Maury Clinton, one of the lawyers for Don Salvatore, was at the podium. He had insisted on going last. In raw intelligence, he was the brightest of the defense team, but he was a corporate-law expert and had not tried a criminal case in over five years. Clinton had been brought into the trial because he was a close friend of Judge Smith. He was also the managing partner in Clinton & St. John, Sarah Goden's old firm. Short and chubby, with a round face, a thin upper lip, fuzzy eyebrows, and curly white locks, he looked like a fat elf. But he used a booming baritone and facility with words to full effect.

Priest and Moore were doodling when Clinton began to plow some new ground.

"Mr. Silento, you testified that you went to work for Salvatore Scalia in 1980?"

"That's right."

"And that you grew up with Vito Scalia?"

"That's what I said."

"He was your best friend, wasn't he?"

"He was."

"And you were his best friend, weren't you?"

"He's the one who'd know that. I figured I was."

Clinton studied his notes. His line of attack required that he carefully skirt the Mayo Clinic incident in order to give the government and Silento no excuse to bring it in the back door. But instinct told him the prosecutors were hiding something unrelated to the attempted Mayo assassination and that whatever they were hiding could seriously undermine this scrawny raven's credibility. He meant to expose it.

"Mr. Silento, when did you decide to testify against your best friend? Just give us the time. It was before you became a patient at the Mayo Clinic wasn't it?"

"Yeah, it was right after the Kennebunkport deal, when the doctor in Sicily told me I was in bad shape."

"By then, you and Mr. Scalia had had a falling out, hadn't you?"

"You might call it that."

"Mr. Silento, it's not a question of what I would call it. What would you call it?"

"A falling out."

"Had you done something Mr. Scalia disapproved of?"

"You could say that."

"Would you like to tell us a bit more about it?"

"Not if I don't have to."

"Tell me this, did you talk to Mr. Moore about this 'falling out' before you took the stand today?"

"I told him about it."

"And he told you, didn't he, that it would be just as well not to mention it in court?"

"Something like that. He said it didn't have anything to do with the case."

"In fact, he said it would hurt the case. Isn't that right?"

"He said it wouldn't do it any good."

"And you don't want to hurt the case, do you?"

Silento raised himself in the witness chair and shot back, "Why would I want to hurt the case?"

"Don't be cute, Mr. Silento," Clinton warned, as he poked holes in the air with a stubby finger, "I'm the one asking the questions."

Priest suddenly became attentive. He leaned over and whispered to Vito Scalia, "What's this 'falling out' he's talking about?"

"Beats the shit out of me," Scalia whispered back, "but it can't be much."

"That's right," Buffalino agreed from Priest's other side. "If it meant anything, Moore would have brought it out."

Priest wrote quickly on his legal pad.

Clinton waddled in front of the jury box. Then he bounced back to the podium. A note from Priest was waiting: *"Leave it alone! You don't know where it will lead!"*

Clinton turned, smiled at Priest, and gave him an imperious wave-off. He was on a roll. He could feel it. Why else would Moore fidget in his chair that way? And his assistant was trying much too hard to appear unconcerned. Now, it was time to change course ever so slightly.

"Mr. Silento, you've testified that the reason you're here is because you're dying of cancer, is that right?"

"That's what I said."

"You don't really expect the jurors to believe you suddenly got religion, do you?"

"That's up to them."

Clinton feigned a look of exasperation. "You'd be here even if you weren't dying, isn't that right?"

"It's hard to say. Right now I don't have anything to lose. Let's leave it at that."

"No," roared Clinton, "we won't leave it at that." He pointed an accusing finger. "You talked to Mr. Moore about your testimony, didn't you?"

"Yeah."

"And didn't he ask you why you were willing to testify?"

"That's right. I told him and Goden the same thing."

"And they told you they didn't believe you, didn't they?"

"Uh huh."

"I would think so. They said you must have another reason, didn't they?"

"That sounds right."

"And you gave them that reason, didn't you?"

"No. I told them there was no other reason."

"What did they say?"

"They said bullshit, we don't believe you."

"How often did they tell you that?"

"Every time I talked to them. After the first coupla times, it was just Moore who talked to me."

"Didn't he tell you that you must be trying to get revenge, that you hated the defendants?"

"Yeah, something like that."

"What did you say?"

"I told him he was wrong."

"Did he believe you."

Moore rose. "Objection, Your Honor."

"Sustained."

"What did Mr. Moore say?"

"He said the jury would never swallow that."

Priest was on his feet. "Your Honor, may I have a moment with counsel?"

"Certainly. Would you like a short break?"

"That won't be necessary." Priest walked to Clinton's side. They smiled at each other. "Maury, don't ask anything more. That was beautiful! You made your point. Moore thinks Silento lied to him. Don't get greedy. It can't get any better."

"Don't worry," Clinton replied. "I just have a few questions more to wrap things up."

"Goddamn it, Maury, this isn't a corporate merger. It's a criminal trial. Lay off, now!"

Priest sat down as Clinton approached the podium. He picked up his cross-examination folder. "Your Honor, I have just one more question of the witness."

Judge Smith concealed his surprise, while Priest gritted his teeth. "Very well, counsel, but sometimes the last question is one too many."

"And so, Mr. Silento," Clinton began, "the government's own prosecutor, Mr. Moore, put you on the witness stand well-knowing that you were lying to him about your real reason for testifying, isn't that correct?"

Moore rose. "Objection. That's a mis-characterization of his testimony."

"It's close enough. I'll allow it. You may answer, Mr. Silento."

"That's not correct. Moore said he couldn't believe that I didn't have another reason, and that he wouldn't put me on until I told him what it was. So I finally told him."

"And what did he say."

"He said it wasn't – I forget the word."

"Relevant?"

"Yeah, it wasn't relevant so he wouldn't be asking me about it, and I wasn't supposed to give it. No matter what. He said it could fu – screw up his case."

"It involved the 'falling out' you said you didn't want to tell us about, didn't it?"

"Yeah, it did."

Clinton drew himself to his full height. Then he turned toward the jurors for effect. "And, Mr. Silento, what was it that Mr. Moore didn't want you to tell the Court and jury?"

The sharp crack of Priest breaking his pencil could be heard throughout the hushed courtroom. He rose to his feet, trying to appear casual. "Your Honor."

"Sit down, Mr. Priest," the judge ordered. "A question is pending to which no objection has been made. Mr. Clinton, perhaps you would like to withdraw the question."

Clinton paused for only a fleeting second. He was not going to back off, nor would he let the government hide something that would hurt its case against his client.

"No, Your Honor, I would like an answer."

Judge Smith tried again. "Mr. Clinton, you might find yourself trying to get toothpaste back in a tube."

Priest half rose, but resumed his seat. The jurors were motionless, straining not to miss any gesture, any inflection. Maria, in the back of the courtroom, had her eyes tightly shut.

Priest leaned over to Scalia and Buffalino. "I could object, but the judge would overrule it. Clinton is out of his mind. Are you sure you never fucked over Silento? I'm not talking about the Mayo Clinic. Some other time?"

"Positive," Vito replied.

Clinton turned to the court reporter. "Please read back the last question."

"Question: And, Mr. Silento, what was it that Mr. Moore didn't want you to tell the Court and jury?"

Silento drew a deep breath and then spoke very rapidly. "It goes back a

180

long time. I caught Vito Scalia and Buffalino's sister – she's his wife now – in the woods bare-ass. When they finished doing it, I put a flashlight on'em and had myself a good laugh. A few days later, a coupla men showed up at my apartment in ski masks. I thought they were just hustling my money, but when I saw them lay out the tools and start the burner I knew what they'd come for. Anyway, they did me like Vito and me used to do the sheep – took my balls. And they did it old style, by cutting them out. They left 'em on my dresser and took off. Said they didn't need 'em and anyway didn't want to take anything that wasn't theirs. Mr. Moore asked me what that had to do with my testifying, and I told him that I knew as sure as I sit here that Vito sent those guys. It couldn't have been anyone else."

Clinton kept smashing the podium with his fist. "Stop! Stop! Stop!"

The other defense lawyers were on their feet shouting at once. The courtroom was a bedlam.

Smith gaveled for silence. Finally, a semblance of order was restored. "Let the witness finish, then I'll hear you."

"But, Your Honor – "

"Gentlemen, I've ruled. Continue, Mr. Silento."

"That's about it. I never told anyone. There was no point telling the don, and I didn't want my family to know. Or anyone else, for that matter. And I knew Vito wouldn't tell anyone. Sure, I'm getting back at Vito. But my testimony has been straight."

Priest, who had remained standing and whose face had now become crimson, declared in a near shout, "This entire line of testimony has been outrageously prejudicial. The defendants move for a mistrial."

"It's quitting time," Judge Smith responded. "We'll dismiss the jury for the day and take a short break. Then I'll hear you."

Fifteen minutes later, Judge Smith addressed Priest. "Let's save ourselves some time. The testimony was knowingly elicited by defense counsel. Unless I miss my guess, you, Mr. Priest, probably advised Mr. Clinton to steer clear. You'll recall the Court even tried to suggest this. A fair characterization is that it was dragged from Mr. Silento. So I don't see how you could show that he was programmed by the government to blurt it out at the first opportunity."

"Your Honor, that's not the point. For starters, the government knew Silento had been castrated and learned long before the trial that he attributed his castration, without the slightest evidence, to Vito Scalia. Under Brady versus – "

"Not so," interrupted Moore.

"Get Mr. Silento back in here," ordered Smith.

In less than a minute, Silento was back in the courtroom.

"You can stay in the wheelchair, Mr. Silento," said Smith. "I have a few questions. I'll remind you you're still under oath. Do you understand that?"

"Yes."

"Did you tell Mr. Moore or anyone connected with the government that you were willing to testify because you wanted to get back at the defendant Vito Scalia?"

"Sort of. I told him I sure didn't owe Vito anything."

"Is that when you told him about the castration?"

"No, sir. I didn't tell him that until a few days ago – the last time we talked about my testimony."

"And did you ever suggest to Mr. Moore, or anyone else with the government, that you wanted the jury to know what you thought Vito Scalia had done to you?"

There was no hesitation in Silento's response. "No, sir. I didn't want the jury or anyone else to know."

"Do you have anything, Mr. Priest?"

"Not at the moment."

"Anyone else? All right, the witness is excused until nine-thirty a.m. tomorrow. Mr. Priest, I'll allow you or any defense counsel to probe that tomorrow before the jury, if you dare. Do you have anything else?"

"Yes, I most certainly do. Revenge as a motive for testifying is highly relevant to a witness's credibility. Under the rule announced by the United States Supreme Court in Brady v. State Of Maryland, the government had the absolute obligation to disclose that information to the defendants the moment it learned of it. Instead of doing that, Mr. Moore even told Silento *not* to disclose it."

"Not to disclose it on the government direct," said Smith. "There's quite a difference. If that had come out through Mr. Moore's direct examination, tell me you wouldn't have asked for a mistrial."

"That's beside the point. The government failed in its Brady obligation to inform the defendants. As a result, the jury has been given the highly prejudicial, inflammatory, and wholly unsupported allegations of a depraved mind."

"Mr. Priest," Smith replied, "the Brady rule only requires the government to disclose exculpatory or helpful material – material which does or could lead to information or evidence tending to show the defendant's innocence of the charges in the indictment. I'll give you until tomorrow morning to demonstrate how the material which the government did not disclose is exculpatory. Otherwise, I'll deny the motion for a mistrial."

"Your Honor is still missing the point," pleaded Clinton. "If that material had been disclosed, then – "

"You wouldn't have put your foot in it," Smith finished. "You've made the point better than I. See you all at nine-thirty a.m. tomorrow."

* * *

Moore, his trial assistant, Angela Featherstone, and Vince Inserra were eating lobster at the wharf in Portland. Moore was on his fourth mug of dark beer. He was in his version of sport clothes – no tie and the coat from one suit with the pants to another. Since the beginning of the trial, he'd eaten late dinners in his hotel room while he brushed up for the next day's events. There was still a mine-laden road ahead, but it was time to unwind a little. He was feeling the incredible high that comes after a courtroom coup.

"I'll tell you," said the FBI man, "until today I thought I'd seen everything. Silento deserves an Oscar. I even felt a little sorry for the bastard. Talk about sympathetic twinges!"

Featherstone laughed and put down her wineglass. "When Silento pointed to himself I watched the jurors. The women covered their mouths and the men covered the family jewels."

Moore cracked a lobster claw and then wiped drawn butter from his chin. "I'd about given up hope after Smith pulled that toothpaste bit on Clinton. Warned him twice, in fact."

"I counted three times," said Inserra. "That Clinton, what a guy! What a guy!"

"Not anymore," Featherstone tossed in. "He'll be lucky if they don't get his balls."

By their second round of after-dinner coffee, Inserra noted that Moore's elation had subsided. "So, what are you thinking about now?"

"Oh, just about how lucky we've been so far, and asking myself how long our luck can hold," Moore replied.

* * *

While the prosecution team was dining, Vito Scalia was facing his grandfather in the conference room of the Portland jail. At their request, and so they might meet alone, a guard had brought Vito from his cell a bit early for what was to have been a scheduled evening conference with the defense attorneys.

Save for a conference table, several straight-back wooden chairs, and a wastebasket on the linoleum floor, the long, high-ceiling room was bare. The two regarded each other across the table, their complexions strangely waxen in the eerie light of a single blue-white fluorescent tube above them. It was another bitter night, and the frigid arctic air seeped through the double-barred, but uninsulated, windows.

Don Salvatore pulled his heavy winter coat more tightly about his body, and then reached across the table to grasp his grandson's wrist.

"So, Vito, we now know why you defied me – and why you feared Dominic."

Despite the chill of the room, Vito began to perspire. Pulling his wrist free, he leaned forward in his chair.

"Grandfather, on my mother's grave, I swear I did not – "

The don shot from his chair, pinning Vito with the point of his cane. For half a minute, each stared wordlessly at the other, neither flinching. Slowly, the don withdrew his cane and resumed his seat.

"Don't lie to me," he hissed. "You couldn't control your temper any better than you could control your cock. Gesu Cristo! You had your friend's balls cut off for the sort of prank you would have pulled yourself if the table had been turned. Stupido! You thought Dominic would get your message and stay silent? So? You stopped playing the fool when you learned he was dying and would soon be beyond anyone's reach. You knew what you would do in his shoes, and now he's done it! And would you have gone on deceiving me until the day I died – covering your disobedience with one stupidity after another? Even today, why didn't you warn that idiot Clinton? Was it your pride or your stupidity?"

Vito exploded to his feet, yanked the cane from his grandfather's grasp, and banged it flatwise on the table. Startled, the don pulled back as two guards burst through the door, weapons drawn. "There's no problem," Vito assured the guards, tossing them the cane. "He'll pick it up when he leaves." Satisfied, they withdrew.

Vito turned back to his grandfather. Leaning forward across the table, his body quivering but his voice steady, he snarled his response to the old man's question.

"You want to know why I didn't warn that asshole? You want to know why?! I'll tell you why! Because I knew nothing about the job done on Silento."

CHAPTER 30

While Vito and the don were in the jail conference room, their lawyers were commencing what would be the all-night task of researching and writing a legal brief in support of the defendants' motion for a mistrial. The brief was on Judge Smith's desk at 7:00 o'clock the next morning.

Court resumed promptly at 9:30 a.m. Wednesday. "Mr. Clinton," the judge opened, "I've studied your brief very carefully. Let me say it's the most impressive and articulate analysis of the Brady rule I've read."

"Thank you, Your Honor. We submit the Court has no alternative but to grant the defendants' motion for a mistrial."

Moore and Featherstone were suddenly uneasy. Now they wished they had foregone the lobster in favor of a few more hours on the government brief.

"Mr. Clinton, if the government had disclosed to the defense Mr. Silento's revenge motive, would you have disclosed it to the jury?"

"That's not the point, Your Honor."

"That's precisely the point," Smith pressed. "If your answer is 'yes', then you have not been prejudiced because the jury has in fact received the so-called exculpatory information through your cross-examination. If your answer is 'no', then we can assume you do not believe it is exculpatory. The real issue is whether the prosecutor had the duty to advise you that the witness was in possession of incredibly inflammatory information of dubious relevance, so that, forewarned, you could have avoided its disclosure to the jury."

"Well put, Your Honor. And the answer must be a resounding 'yes'! As you know, in Berger v. United States the Supreme Court held that the duty of the government in a criminal case is not to obtain a conviction but to see that justice is done."

"Yes, that prime directive must control here," agreed Smith.

Moore felt light-headed. Then a wave of heat rose from his collar to his face. Featherstone gripped his arm. Was the case about to go down the drain?

"But, Mr. Clinton, the Supreme Court also said that the government could strike hard blows so long as they were not unfair ones. I do not find that Mr.

Moore acted unfairly, although I must say that the issue is close. Mr. Moore, I advise you to exercise extreme caution in withholding anything else from defense counsel. The Motion For Mistrial is denied. When it comes time to instruct the jurors, should that time arrive, I shall instruct them that they are not to consider Mr. Silento's testimony about his castration as evidence of the guilt of any defendant; and that they are to consider that testimony – should they choose to do so – only to the extent it may bear upon Mr. Silento's credibility. Mr. Clinton, are you done with cross-examining Mr. Silento?"

"Yes, Judge," responded Clinton, his voice barely audible.

"Mr. Moore, any redirect?"

"No, Your Honor."

"All right, bring in the jury."

Angela Featherstone now sat at the government's table in the chair closest to the witness box, Moore behind her. Moore did not believe in hogging the show. He had divided the number of witnesses evenly between them, a fact not lost on the seven female jurors. They spontaneously returned Featherstone's friendly nod.

"The government calls Thomas Goden," announced Featherstone.

Tom took the witness stand looking very handsome in his chief's uniform. Feathersone moved him quickly through the preliminaries, and then handed him Government Exhibit 25. He recognized it as the scrap of paper found in the seat cushion of Loring Mills's car bearing the letters and number "R L 160H."

Prior to trial, Moore, as required by the Federal Rules of Criminal Procedure, had given the defense copies of all documents in the government's possession upon which he would rely in proving the government's case. Priest pulled his copy of Exhibit 25 from an exhibit folder, together with rental car information corresponding to New York license plate R L 160H that Mafia investigators had assembled. Tom and Inserra weren't the only ones Exhibit 25 had fooled. Vito Scalia leaned over to Priest. "The plate number is a dead end. Where's the bitch headed?"

"Listen, and you'll find out," Priest replied acidly.

"Now, Chief Goden, did your subsequent investigation disclose whether those letters and number matched anything other than a license plate?"

"Yes, it did. They matched the post office box number of a Richard Hundley in Rice Lake, Wisconsin."

"Did you know Mr. Hundley?"

"Yes, I'd known him for years. He's a retired captain of the Chicago police department."

"What did you do next in your investigation?"

"I phoned Mr. Hundley, and then flew to Rice Lake and met with him at his home."

"I have nothing else," said Featherstone.

The abrupt end of her direct examination caught the defense by surprise. It was now clear that Tom's appearance was only as a foundation witness, just as the chain of government witnesses preceding Silento had prepared the ground and provided the corroborating details supporting his damning accusations. Priest knew instinctively that another bomb was being fused, but he had no idea what it was. The after-buzz in the spectator section suggested that Priest wasn't alone.

"If there is no cross-examination, the government may call its next witness," said Judge Smith.

"The government calls Cameron Herd," Featherstone announced.

The editorial writer for the *York County Coast Star* took the stand. He looked like this was the last place in the world he wanted to be. He pulled nervously at his beard and then at the stem of a briar pipe protruding from the breast pocket of his rumpled sport coat. The defendants and their counsel, no less than the jurors, sensed another crucial juncture in the trial.

Featherstone eased Herd through warm-up questions and moved quickly to substance. He was the newspaper's chief editorial writer. Had been for over ten years. He knew Loring Mills quite well. On the evening of July 4, 1992, Herd went to the newspaper to pick up some work. He was going to Nantucket Island the next morning for a vacation and needed it for editorials he would write while away. He was getting ready to leave the newspaper – it was about 10:15 p.m. – when he ran into Mr. Mills. Mills appeared to be on edge about something. Jumpy you might say.

"Did you and Mr. Mills talk?" Featherstone asked.

"Yes, he asked me to – "

"Objection to what Mr. Mills asked," challenged Priest, "on grounds it's hearsay."

"Sustained."

"And Mr. Mills seemed jumpy?"

"Asked and answered," Priest objected.

"It has been," ruled Smith. "Move along, Ms. Featherstone."

"Excuse me a moment, Your Honor."

Featherstone made some check marks on her examination outline, and then left the podium to confer with Moore for a moment. The defendants watched as Moore nodded his head in agreement. "Looks like she's done," Buffalino observed to Priest. "That didn't hurt."

"Seems that way," Priest replied.

Featherstone returned to the podium. "I have just a few more questions, Your Honor." Abe Priest rested the point of a pencil on his legal pad.

"Mr. Herd, when you met Mr. Mills at the newspaper, did he give you anything?"

The point of Priest's pencil broke from the sudden pressure. Sonofabitch! He looked at the defendants and the other defense lawyers. They were light years away from comprehending what was coming.

"Yes, he did."

"Would you please describe what it was."

"Well, it was one of those large manila envelopes with a 'Don't Bend' label. It was very bulky."

"And what did you do?"

"Well, he asked – "

"No," interrupted Featherstone, "don't tell us what Mr. Mills said; just what you did."

"I took the envelope, meaning to mail it on my way home. But I forgot. So I mailed it from Nantucket the next day. No, not the next day – that would have been Sunday. I mailed it on Monday."

"Do you recall the name and address on the envelope?"

"Objection," said Priest, "the envelope is the best evidence."

"Your Honor, the government does not have the envelope," said Featherstone.

"The witness may answer," Smith ruled.

"I don't recall the name. The address was a post office box in Rice Lake."

"Rice Lake, Wisconsin?"

"Yeah, Rice Lake, Wisconsin. Box one something."

"One sixty H?"

"It could have been."

"Object and move to strike," interposed Priest.

"Mr. Herd, are you guessing?" Judge Smith asked.

"Well, I think it was one sixty. I don't remember the letter."

"That answer may stand."

"Have you exhausted your recollection as to the name?" Featherstone asked.

"I had it on the tip of my tongue – Hinkley, Hartley, something like that."

"Hundley?"

"That's it, Richard Hundley."

"No further questions."

"Cross-examination?" Smith asked.

"None," replied Priest.

"The witness is dismissed."

"Your Honor, before the government calls its next witness, I'd like a side bar," Priest requested.

The judge nodded his assent, and the lawyers, with the court reporter in tow, took positions at the end of the bench away from the jury. The clerk activated the "hsss" of a background noisemaker that would prevent the jurors from overhearing what was said between the judge and the attorneys.

"Your Honor," Priest began, "unless I miss my guess, the government is about to call Mr. Hundley."

"That's right," Moore agreed.

"I thought so," Priest continued. "Now, I don't know for certain what counsel intends to elicit from Mr. Hundley, but I do know this. Well prior to trial, the defense made a Rule 16 request for all documents and tangible objects that the government intended to use as evidence or were material to the preparation of the defendants' defense. We received neither the envelope Mr. Herd testified he mailed nor whatever was in that envelope. Under the circumstances, it would be plain error to allow Mr. Hundley to give any testimony concerning the envelope or its contents. I suspect that is where this is headed, and I wanted the Court advised in advance as to the defendants' position."

"Well, this seems premature. You make your specific objections and I'll rule."

"But, Your Honor, the damage could be done by a leading or suggestive question, or by the witness blurting out an answer before I can interpose an objection. The whole area should be off limits."

"That sensitive, is it?"

"That's the point, Your Honor. I don't know because the government withheld the materials required by Rule 16 to be produced."

"Mr. Moore, who's handling Mr. Hundley?"

"I am, Judge."

"O.K. You examine him by the book. No leading or suggestive questions. Do not – and I underscore *not* – allow the witness to tell what was in the envelope unless and until it is admitted in evidence. Is that understood?"

"Yes, Your Honor."

"Perhaps it would speed things along if Mr. Moore were to tell us all what was in the envelope, assuming he knows," Smith suggested, with just the smallest twinkle in his eye.

"That isn't necessary," said Priest. "This transcript is public, and it would be most inappropriate to read in the paper about highly improper evidence after the Court has excluded it."

"I can understand that. Mr. Moore, call your next witness."

Moore walked Hundley carefully through his background and his close friendship with the *Tribune* crime reporter, Samson Smythe.

"Would you say that you and Mr. Smythe had the same professional interests?"

"Yes."

"Which were?"

"Objection."

"I'll withdraw the question. While you were head of the Intelligence Division at the Chicago Police Department, did you have any particular area of specialty?"

"Yes."

"Describe that area."

Priest shot to his feet. "Objection. May we approach the bench?"

"Certainly."

Priest addressed Judge Smith in a low voice. "Your Honor, Mr. Hundley is considered somewhat of an expert on organized crime and the Mafia. Unfortunately and unfairly, I might add, these inflammatory buzzwords are often applied indiscriminately to anyone with an Italian name. In the circumstances of this case, the question calls for a highly prejudicial answer of no relevance to the issues."

"I disagree," said Judge Smith. "We're not trying this case in a vacuum. A certain amount of detail about a witness's prior employment is permissible. Your objection is overruled."

Moore was back at the podium. "Do you have the question in mind, Mr. Hundley?"

"Yes. My area of specialty was the investigation of the Mafia and organized crime in this country."

"Was this the professional interest which you shared with Mr. Smythe?"

"Yes. We often exchanged information on the subject."

WILLIAM A. CAREY AND ST. JOHN BARRETT

"Tell the Court and jury what the terms 'Mafia' and 'organized crime' mean."

"Objection."

"Sustained. Mr. Moore, don't insult our intelligence by asking the witness to define household terms. Move along to something else."

"Now, Mr. Hundley, did you take a trip on July 1st of this year?"

"Yes."

"Where?"

"To Atlanta to visit my daughter."

"When did you return to Rice Lake?"

"Not until early Monday, July 27th."

"Did you then go to the post office for your mail?"

"Yes."

"What was your box number?"

"One sixty H."

"Was there mail in the box?"

"Yes, quite a bit."

"Was there a large manila envelope with a Nantucket postmark?"

"Yes there was."

"Did you bring it with you today?"

"Yes."

"Since the time you picked it up at the post office on Monday, July 27th, have this envelope and its contents ever been out of your possession?"

"No, they have not."

"Have they ever been within the possession, custody, or control of the United States Government?"

Priest was on his feet before the question was finished. "Objection. Those are words taken straight from Rule 16. The question is both leading and calls for a legal conclusion."

"I see it's time for our normal morning break," said Judge Smith.

After the jury left the courtroom, Judge Smith turned to the witness. "Mr. Hundley, please wait in the witness room. Mr. Moore, is it your intention to offer the envelope and its contents in evidence at this time."

"Yes, Your Honor, once the contents have been identified."

"All right. Is it your position that they were never in the government's possession, custody, or control, and that is why they were not given to the defense for its inspection and copying as required by Rule 16?"

"That's the government's position."

"Mr. Priest?"

"Your Honor, this is a blatant ruse designed to avoid the government's responsibilities. Mr. Hundley is a friendly government witness, a former high-ranking law-enforcement official."

"Let's take our break," said Smith. "Before we recall the jury, I'll allow you to cross-examine Mr. Hundley on this issue. If this was a ruse, the contents of that envelope will never see the light of day."

Twenty minutes later, Priest was tearing into Hundley with zest – not loudly, but with the rapid fire of an automatic weapon. He'd known Tom Goden, Vince Inserra, and Page Moore for years. They were friends. Moore was a close friend. Jerry Borghesani he'd met this summer. The Kennebunkport police chief, the FBI agent-in-charge, the government prosecutor, and the Maine State Police commandant had all seen the envelope's contents on more than one occasion. He'd shown the contents to them in the course of the investigation. Sure, he wanted the government to win this case. Sure, he'd do everything in his power to help the government. Yes, Moore had told him the envelope and its contents would be an exhibit at the trial. No, he didn't want the defendants to have them prior to trial. Yes, they discussed the tactical advantage of a delayed disclosure. Yes, the delayed disclosure was for the purpose of locking the defendants into an unprovable defense.

"Mr. Moore, do you have any questions of the witness?"

"Just a few, Your Honor."

"Proceed."

"Mr. Hundley, do you recall that on September 7th of this year, there was a meeting at your home in Rice Lake?"

"Yes."

"And I was present, together with Chief Goden, Mr. Inserra, and Commandant Borghesani?"

"That's right."

"Do you recall that I asked you – "

"Objection. It's leading."

"Sustained."

"Did I make a request of you at that time?"

"Yes you did."

"And what was that request?"

"You asked if I would turn over to you – you used the term 'the government' – would I turn over to the government the – the things we're talking about."

"The envelope and its contents?"

"That's right."

"What did you say."

"I said I wouldn't because too many people had already – "

Priest was on his feet with his hand up. "Objection. He's already said they didn't want the defendants to have them prior to trial. Any other reason is irrelevant to the Rule 16 issue."

"Well, maybe he was afraid the government would lose them," Smith observed, as he looked at the witness, expecting an answer to the unasked question.

"That wasn't the reason," said Hundley.

The judge narrowed his eyes a bit and studied Moore for a long moment. Then he turned to the witness. "Did Mr. Moore coach you in any way? I mean, when he asked you if you would turn over those materials, did he in any way suggest that you should give a 'no' answer?"

Hundley wrestled with himself. *Tell the truth! Tell the truth! You're under oath*, he thought. *If you lie, you're no better than they are*. The inner turmoil flickered across his face.

Moore felt a pain in his chest like the first twinge of a heart attack. His legs were rubbery and a sheen of perspiration began to form on his forehead. He grasped the podium with both hands and the courtroom spun. If Smith excluded the pictures, he'd outsmarted himself. The defense would parade the whole lot before the jury. They'd flatly deny being at the reception, and Silento would be made out a perjurer. He shouldn't have been so cute. In attempting to commit the defendants to an unprovable defense in front of the jury, he had brought the government's case to the brink of ruin. He'd committed the cardinal offense. He'd over-tried the case. He'd been greedy. Shit! He'd been dumb.

"Mr. Hundley, I asked you a question," Judge Smith reminded.

"Mr. Moore didn't coach me. And he didn't suggest I give a 'no' answer. But in all honesty, I must say he put the question to me in a way that wasn't in keeping with the informality of the occasion. The question was very deliberate, very precise. Like he was taking his words from a legal decision."

"You mean he used terms like possession, custody, and control?"

"Yes, Your Honor. It made me think real hard before I answered. Then I decided there was no way I was going to let him have what he asked for. He could have asked until hell froze over, and the answer would have still been 'no.' If he had said the defendants wouldn't be shown the materials or told about them, I still wouldn't have let him have the stuff. It's my property, and it stays that way until it's an exhibit in this case."

"Your Honor," said Priest, "the government could have used a subpoena inasmuch as it knew who had the materials and already intended to use them as evidence at trial. It's clear from this witness's testimony that Mr. Moore has played word games with the clear mandate of Rule 16. Not only that, he enlisted the aid of a close friend to work a fraud on this court. I realize that's a harsh characterization of Mr. Moore's conduct, but one can reach no other conclusion from Mr. Hundley's testimony. The government has forfeited whatever right it might have had to use this evidence."

Judge Smith frowned. His frown deepened. He pursed his lips, and his jaw tightened. He placed his steepled fingers over his mouth, leaned back, and surveyed the ornate ceiling. Finally, he broke the hush that had fallen over the courtroom – attorneys, defendants, jurors, and spectators alike.

"Since it's near our regular time to adjourn, I'm going to hold this until tomorrow. Counsel will report a half-hour before the jurors, in case I need oral argument."

CHAPTER 31

When the attorneys appeared in court Thursday morning at 8:30, as directed by Judge Smith, the judge did not ask oral argument on the defense objection to admission of the photographs. Rather, he moved directly to addressing Page Moore.

"Mr. Moore, you've been skating on some very thin ice. Whether you've broken through depends upon the contents of that envelope. If the prior testimony in this case has shown, or if you will represent that the government is prepared to show, that some or all of the defendants had, prior to trial, actually seen the contents, then I shall overrule the objection and admit the evidence. Failing such a representation, it will be excluded."

The pain in Moore's chest subsided slightly by the end of Judge Smith's statement, but he felt weak, and his mouth was dry. He thought of walking to counsel table for a swallow of water but didn't trust his legs.

"Your Honor, what if the defendants have seen duplicates?"

"That's what I meant, Mr. Moore. Obviously, they haven't seen what Mr. Hundley has held so tightly."

"Then I so represent."

Priest rose slowly as he weighed his response. Then, in a measured voice, filled with challenge, he addressed the court. "Your Honor, your ruling mocks both the letter and spirit of Rule 16. Indeed, it is outrageous. Mr. Moore has used his abundant skills to completely circumvent the obligation imposed by Rule 16. You have not only failed to impose a sanction on the government for Mr. Moore's misconduct, you have, by your ruling, encouraged other prosecutors to emulate it."

"Mr. Priest, approach the bench please. Come around here. Mr. Moore, you may join us. We won't need the court reporter." Smith and Moore stood up and walked to the far side of the bench. The clerk again activated the noise curtain.

Judge Smith and Abe Priest stood staring at each other. Neither flinched. "Abe, we've known each other for years. Do you want my response to be on or off the record?"

"Jack, I appreciate your asking. Off the record. I already have enough on the record to get your ass reversed."

The judge's howl of laughter boomed through the hsss of the noise machine. Despite the puzzlement of the spectators, the tension in the courtroom was broken.

"Abe, you always had a delicate touch. But my ruling is reversal-proof. Now hear me. You know and I know what's in that envelope. Loring Mills probably saved Hundley's life. Those hitters screwed up real bad. They tortured and butchered that young man for nothing. Nothing! Then they massacred a man's family and destroyed his business to send him a meaningless message. I don't know if your clients gave Silento and Palazzi their marching orders, but I'm not about to deprive the jury of the corroborating evidence it needs to make that determination. Another thing. Those pictures just gave your defense a lobotomy. You acted impulsively. You should never have committed yourself in front of the jury. You let the government set you up."

"Tell that to my clients. You know they're calling the shots."

"Abe, be careful. You're too good a lawyer to let yourself be led by your client."

Judge Smith returned to the bench, the jury was summoned, and the proceedings continued on the record. Hundley identified the pictures and they were admitted in evidence over a barrage of defense objections. Then Moore had him run through the names of the people in the pictures – Joe Zicari, Bartolo LaDuca, the Falcones, Thomas Riccobono, Patsy Magaddino, Tony Rosato, Frank Scozzari, Gabriel Buffalino, Santo Lombardozzi, and the rest. Loring Mills had been right. It sounded like the Palermo phone book.

The pictures were passed to the jurors. They arranged them in neat stacks along the rail of the jury box, then crowded around like children getting their first glimpse of the sex act. "The government has no further questions," Moore announced.

On cross-examination, Abe Priest tried again to extract from Hundley an admission that he had been coached to withhold the photos from the government in order to deprive the defendants of their Rule 16 rights. But his examination was desultory.

Finally, Moore objected. "Your Honor, this line of questioning has already been exhausted. The pictures have been admitted into evidence, and the question now before the witness has already been asked and answered."

"What took you so long?" Judge Smith snapped. "Objection sustained." That was the end of cross-examination.

Dominic Silento was then recalled to the witness stand.

"Mr. Moore, I needn't remind you that I've allowed the government to recall Mr. Silento for the sole purpose of identifying – if he can – Government Exhibits 26(1) through 26(75)."

"I understand, Your Honor. Mr. Silento, I've handed you seventy-five photographs marked Government's Group Exhibit 26. Take your time and look at each one carefully. Then I'll have some questions."

Silento turned the pictures, slowly at first, and then more quickly. He scratched his head and kept scratching. He looked bewildered. Halfway through, he looked up at the defendants. Vito Scalia's knuckles were white. Buffalino and Priest, sitting on either side of Vito, each had a restraining hand on his nearest arm. Then it dawned on Silento. His face took on a strange expression – a seeming mixture of sadness and pain. Although some jurors took it as an expression of remorse, Moore knew better. It reflected injury to Silento's professional pride. Silento now realized that he and Palazzi had let a second set of prints slip through their hands without knowing. Turning his attention again to the prints, his expression gradually changed. On turning the last of them, and using his right hand to shield the jury's view of his mouth, he looked straight at Scalia and silently mouthed two words: "Fuck you!"

"Mr. Silento, are you done?" Moore asked.

"Yes, sir."

"Do you recognize those pictures?"

"I recognize them. It's what I've kept telling you. These are the pictures I gave to Vito Scalia, Gabriel Buffalino, and Salvatore Scalia." Then, taking his eyes from Moore, he suddenly pulled himself to his feet. Almost toppling over the rail of the witness stand, he managed to steady himself and looked directly at the three principal defendants. Gripping the witness rail with his left hand, he slowly raised his right. The jurors pulled back in alarm. Then he suddenly brought his arm down and jabbed his right forefinger three times in cadence at Gabriel Buffalino, Vito Scalia, and Salvatore Scalia. "Him, . . . and him, . . . and him!" Now shouting, he plunged on. "Hey, Vito, who's lost his balls now?"

The first reporter through the courtroom doors stumbled and fell, upending the two following on his heels. Inside, Judge Smith tried vainly to control the pandemonium. Outside the courthouse, the sky was gray and street lights were coming on. Maria Scalia slipped from the courtroom, removed her sunglasses, and signaled a taxi.

CHAPTER 32

Dominic Silento was the last government witness, and through him the last government exhibit had been admitted in evidence. Page Moore addressed Judge Smith. "The government rests, Your Honor."

The judge, after excusing the jury for the day, made short work of the defendants' motions for acquittal and directed that the defense case begin promptly at 9:30 the next morning.

* * *

Really good trial lawyers live for the challenge of cross-examination. It is both their reputation-builder and the ultimate test of mastery of their profession. But Moore and Featherstone didn't get the chance to display their wares.

Friday morning Abe Priest made an eloquent presentation to Judge Smith, one he would expand upon in his closing argument to the jury. The government, he explained, had the heavy burden of establishing every essential element of the alleged offenses beyond a reasonable doubt. But it had not and never could meet this heavy burden. The case should never have been brought. Why? Because every essential element of the government case rested upon the wild hallucinations of a remorseless savage who, years before, had sworn vengeance against the defendant Vito Scalia, whom he wrongly blamed for his castration, and was now seeking, through his own perjured testimony, to bring down both Scalia and his codefendants. He went on for five minutes, building steam with every sentence. Finally, Judge Smith interrupted.

"Mr. Priest, are you about to tell the Court that the defense will offer no witnesses or exhibits?"

"Yes, Your Honor, none are required in view of the government's failure to meet its burden of proof."

"Well, we'll let the jury decide that. Mr. Moore, is the government prepared to give its closing argument? I realize this is abrupt. Maybe you expected it, but I certainly didn't."

"May I have a few moments?"

"Certainly. Let's take ten." When the judge left, Moore and Featherstone huddled.

"Jesus Christ, what's going on?" Moore asked.

"Beats me. All I can figure is that they've sold themselves on the idea the jury won't believe Silento. Face it, he is an animal. I wouldn't need an excuse not to believe him if I were on that jury. Smith is fair. He'll give a very strong reasonable doubt instruction. Remember, there's no evidence that anyone at the wedding reception, including the Scalias and Buffalino, is other than a law-abiding citizen. Priest will play to the jury's conscience. He'll harp on how un-American it is for the government to penalize people because of their names. We have to be damn careful there. And Priest has probably convinced them that one slipup in putting on a perjured defense and they'll all sink."

"You're probably right, Angela. Every one of the defendants is Mafia down to his shoes. They usually won't subject themselves to government cross-examination for any reason. But all this is beside the point. You're the one starting our closing argument. How close are you to ready? We could ask until tomorrow."

Featherstone opened a folder and thumbed through the typed sheets summarizing the evidence supporting each allegation of the indictment. Satisfied, she closed it. She was a bundle of nervous tension waiting to be released. "Not necessary. An hour to get the exhibits in line, some touching up, and I'm ready. You'll have the tough part with the rebuttal."

The two prosecutors then rose and walked to the side of the courtroom to chat with reporters. When Judge Smith reentered, Moore moved to the podium with Featherstone, where they were joined by Abe Priest.

"Your Honor, Ms. Featherstone will be prepared to begin the government's closing argument at eleven-thirty this morning. We'd like two and a half hours for argument."

"That includes rebuttal?"

"Yes, your honor."

"Have defense counsel decided how much time they need for their closings? Not per defendant but total to be divided among yourselves."

"Seven hours, Your Honor," Priest replied.

"My! You're not going to leave any words wasted. All right. We'll start with Ms. Featherstone at eleven-thirty. When she's done, we'll break for lunch and go until six. Then we'll have a short meeting on jury instructions. I've already informed you of my action on each side's requests. We'll begin the balance of the closing arguments tomorrow morning at nine. I estimate that by four tomorrow afternoon the jury will have this case. Any questions? If not, we'll break until eleven-thirty."

* * *

At 1:00 p.m., Angela Featherstone pushed aside her outline of closing argument. She was nearly finished. She walked from the podium to within feet of the jury box, where she stood silently for several seconds. The jurors watched her closely. The fire which had flashed through much of her argument was largely gone. But her eyes still smoldered, and there was some anger in her tone as she anticipated Priest's closing argument. She meant to blunt it.

"You are a very important part of America," she began, "the most important part, I think. You are an American jury. You hold in your hands justice for all our people. You protect us from abuses and the wrongs of our own government; you protect us against trumped-up charges of crimes never committed; you protect us from perjured testimony; you protect us if prosecutors like myself and Mr. Moore were to pursue weak cases that should never have been brought, because government prosecutors are just as likely to be wrong, or negligent, or ambitious as anybody else; and you protect us from the animals running loose in our country who take orders from other animals."

Featherstone paused for a moment and then concluded. "You protect us from torture, ice picks, metal drums, and watery graves; from the bombing of our businesses; from being stabbed to death in broad daylight; and most of all, you protect us from people who say 'come to papa' and who direct other people to do their dirty work." Then Featherstone turned and pointed her finger at each of the defendants. "You protect us from them!"

CHAPTER 33

Sergeant Mike Magruder lived alone in a tiny rented house on Pier Road in Cape Porpoise, a house that commanded a breathtaking view of the harbor. He had Friday off and slept until nearly noon. Still in his pajamas, he wolfed down a platter of eggs and bacon. Then he played the game: What do you do to avoid cabin fever on a weekday in Maine when the temperature is below zero? Tonight was no problem. He was having dinner with a leggy blond in Portland. He glanced at the calendar on the kitchen wall. Fourteen days until Christmas. That's it. He'd drive to Freeport, begin his Christmas shopping, kill a little more time, and drive to Portland for his date.

* * *

For at least fifty years, Freeport, a small town north of Portland, had had but one business of any note. But what a business! L.L. Bean's retail-clothing and sporting-goods store was open 24 hours a day, 365 days a year, and the doors had no locks. You didn't explore Maine without paying a visit. Its huge crowds of shoppers eventually convinced others that L.L. Bean needed competition. Today, Freeport is a maze of discount outlets and factory stores.

Mike Magruder drove into one of the municipal parking lots. He locked his Jeep Cherokee and walked up a steep incline to the center of town. Freeport was bustling despite the frigid weather and a forecast of snow. He meandered through six or seven stores, finally found a wild sweater he thought his teen-aged sister would like, and then decided he'd try L.L. Bean.

Magruder was on the second floor holding a winter sport shirt at arms length when he saw the two men. An alarm bell went off in his head. No, it couldn't be, he thought. Then he looked again from behind the shirt. Sonofabitch! It is them. Carlo Lumbardino and Carmine Gambini were standing less than twenty feet away. The happiness twins. Tony Rosato's goons. The men Goden had spotted in Dock Square last January. What are those apes doing in Freeport? Not Christmas shopping, he decided. He put the shirt down and wandered casually until he was at a safer distance. He picked out a sport jacket and began modeling it in front of a mirror. He could see their reflection over his shoulder. They were watching someone, apparently indifferent to whether they were themselves seen.

He rehung the sport jacket and pulled another from the rack. Lumbardino and Gambini were staring at two other shoppers, a man and a woman. The couple, seemingly uneasy, moved to another counter. Lumbardino and Gambini moved with them, staring for a few minutes longer, and then walked to the stairs.

Magruder tossed the jacket aside and followed the men from the store. They crossed the main street and walked down a side street toward one of the municipal parking lots, four blocks from where he had parked. Now what? He'd never get to his car and back in time to follow them. The two men passed a restaurant and stopped. Gambini said something, and they turned back and went inside. Magruder ducked into a book store, waited for a minute, and then walked slowly past the restaurant. The men were seated at the bar ordering a drink.

He raced the four blocks to his car. A fine snow began to fall. He glanced at his watch and thought about the leggy blond. It was 4:15 p.m. He drove to the bottom of the side street where he had left the happiness twins, pulled into a private driveway, and waited.

At 5:00 p.m., the men left the restaurant and retrieved their car. By 5:15, they were driving south on Interstate 95 toward Portland. It was snowing harder. By 5:30, traffic was at a crawl. Magruder was five cars behind them while he talked to Tom Goden on his car phone.

* * *

Lumbardino and Gambini were staying at a large motel on Western Avenue near the Portland airport. When they went into the motel's restaurant for dinner at 7:00 p.m., Magruder was in his car in the motel parking lot. At 7:15, another car pulled into a space near him. Two men stepped out and approached his car.

"Sergeant Magruder?"

"Yes." He slid out and pulled up his coat collar.

"Sergeant, I'm Special Agent Roberts of the FBI. This is Special Agent Timothy."

The three men shook hands and flashed their shields.

"They're in the restaurant having dinner. You can't miss 'em. Look like they escaped from a zoo. That's their Thunderbird over there," Magruder said, pointing. "I figure it's snowing too hard for them to go anywhere tonight."

"Good work, Sergeant," complimented Roberts. "We can handle it from here."

"Thanks. I've got a better place than this to get snowbound."

CHAPTER 34

The case of United States v. Vito Scalia, et al. was submitted to the jury by Judge Smith on Saturday at 3:45 p.m. Veteran observers, courtroom buffs, the media, the court reporter, the marshals and bailiffs, Judge Smith's law clerk, the court clerk, and the newsstand operator in the courthouse lobby all predicted the jury would be out only long enough to select a foreman and take one vote, a vote of guilty on all counts. The jurors should be home in time for dinner. They were wrong.

On Tuesday, December 15, at 11:00 a.m., the jurors filed into the courtroom and took their seats under Judge Smith's fixed gaze. He addressed them:

"Ladies and gentlemen, the verdict to which a juror agrees must be his or her own verdict. Nonetheless, to bring your twelve minds to a unanimous result, each of you must examine the questions submitted to you with candor, and with a proper regard and deference to the opinions of your fellow jurors. You should consider that this case must at some time be decided, that you are selected in the same manner and from the same source from which any future jury must come, and there is no reason to believe that this case will ever be submitted to twelve men and women more intelligent, more impartial, or more competent to decide it, nor that more or clearer evidence will be produced on one side or the other. With this in mind, it is your duty to decide the case if you can conscientiously do so.

"The burden of proof is upon the government to establish the guilt of each defendant beyond a reasonable doubt, and if you are left in doubt as to the guilt of a defendant, he is entitled to the benefit of that doubt and must be acquitted. But in conferring together you should pay proper respect to each other's opinions and reasons, and have a disposition to be convinced by each other's arguments. If the larger number of you are for a conviction, the dissenting jurors should consider whether the doubt in their own minds is a reasonable one since it makes no impression upon the minds of so many men and women equally honest, and equally intelligent, who have heard the same evidence, with the same attention, with an equal desire to arrive at the truth, and under the sanction of the same oath. On the other hand, if the majority of you are for acquittal, the minority should equally ask themselves whether they should not reasonably doubt the correctness of their judgment, which is not concurred in by a number of those with whom they are associated."

The jury was hopelessly deadlocked eleven to one. The so-called "blockbuster" instruction, just given by the judge, was the only hope for avoiding a mistrial.

* * *

Anna D'Amico was pushing her grocery cart toward the checkout counter when she again saw the two swarthy, heavyset men. They stood motionless by the counter, staring at her. She had seen them off and on for two weeks. At first, she had dismissed their presence as a coincidence. But their appraisal of her had become increasingly open and bold. This was now the fifth time in five days she had seen them. She was trembling when she wrote the check for her purchases and penned in the wrong amount.

As she drove from the parking lot, a car pulled in front of her so sharply that she had to brake hard. The same two men turned in their seats for a moment to look at her, and then the car turned and sped away.

* * *

Anna was in the kitchen preparing dinner two hours later when her teenaged daughter burst through the back door. "Mom, that was scary!"

"What was scary, dear?"

"This car kept following me down the street. There were two men in it and they were looking at me with funny smiles. You should tell Dad when he calls tonight."

* * *

At 7:00 p.m., Tuesday, Page Moore and Angela Featherstone were meeting with Vince Inserra in the FBI office at his request. They were already frazzled and depressed, with little hope of a conviction, and his briefing was doing nothing to lift their spirits.

He was explaining a new group of pictures, recently taken by zoom lens, that were spread on a long table. Each print bore a notation of date, time, and location.

"O.K.," Inserra continued, fingering the American flag in his lapel, "we start with Saturday morning, December 12th. That's the day after Sergeant Magruder spotted Lumbardino and Gambini in Freeport. Now follow me through these. Here they are outside Montgomery Ward at the Maine Mall in Portland. Here they're outside the supermarket in Biddeford. Now they're walking next to a busy service station. Here they are again at the Maine Mall outside the movie theaters. There are always people around. But this woman we've circled shows up in nearly all the pictures. Magruder recognizes her from L.L. Bean."

Inserra pointed at another group of pictures. "Until today, we couldn't identify her. The happiness twins, as Goden calls them, would park at a heavily traveled intersection near her street. We wouldn't know which car the twins were following. But today they got greedy. Here they are back at the same supermarket. Then she leaves and they cut in front of her car. Agents Roberts and Timothy got her license plate. Now look here. The bastards followed the woman's daughter right to her house."

Moore chewed thoughtfully on an Almond Joy. "So, what are we talking about? You've done a first-rate surveillance. But I didn't know there was a federal anti-stalking statute. Was this woman a witness in the case? I don't recognize her."

"No," Inserra replied, "her name is Anna D'Amico. She's the wife of the number-twelve juror, Paul D'Amico."

Featherstone broke the ensuing silence. "Well, at least we know why they didn't put on a defense."

"Angela, I should've followed your woman's intuition on D'Amico. You wanted to strike him. But he's the best law-and-order type we have. Shit! His brother's with the State's Attorney's office in Rhode Island. Vince, what's with this D'Amico guy?"

"We figure they hit on him early, made the contact, and they're sending him reminder messages by stalking his family. The Bureau will take some blame for this."

"Why," Featherstone asked, "did you miss something in his background data?" Her pleasant freckled face suddenly became challenging.

"We did. He has a slew of aunts and uncles. We missed Tony Rosato. You can thank Goden for picking it up. He has a New York City P.D. file on him."

"And the Bureau doesn't?" Featherstone asked coldly. Moore turned to her.

"Angela, knock it off. That won't solve anything. Vince, one thing I don't understand. Magruder spots Lumbardino and Gambini, tails them, and calls

Goden. He calls you, and you commit all these Bureau resources."

"So did Goden. He and his men did some shifts."

"Whatever. Did he think there might be jury tampering? The jury hadn't even gone out."

"Yes, he did. It was a hunch. Goden is a good cop. Remember, he's the one who had this case figured out before Silento even surfaced. When he told me he smelled a jury fix, I wasn't gonna argue. I worked cases with him when he was with the New York P.D. He has incredible instincts."

"I can't argue either. But a sense of smell can only take you so far."

"Page, are you suggesting Goden knows something he isn't telling us?" Featherstone asked. She still looked like she was ready to throw something at Inserra.

"No. I was just curious. The important thing is he was on the money. Now what can we do about it? The alternate jurors have been dismissed. The law requires a unanimous verdict from a jury of twelve. The jurors are deadlocked, and Judge Smith won't keep them out indefinitely. My guess is he'll declare a mistrial by no later than Thursday, if there's no verdict. Any ideas?"

CHAPTER 35

Wednesday, December 16th. At 7:00 a.m., Lumbardino was outside banging on the door of the motel room. After three salvos, the door opened a few inches, and Lumbardino could glimpse the beefy head, bloodshot eyes, and black stubble of Gambini. Assaulted through the crack by Gambini's heavy breath, laden with garlic and alcohol, Lumbardino turned his head.

"I was wondering why you didn't answer the phone. Now I smell why. Carmine, you drink too fucking much. Get dressed and meet me in the coffee shop."

"Why? I thought we were sleeping in and then heading back to New York."

"They want us to make the mother and daughter piss in their pants once more for good measure."

"Don't they know when's enough?"

* * *

The jury sent Judge Smith a note at noon Wednesday. Despite the judge's supplemental instruction of the day before, the jurors were still hopelessly deadlocked. The judge summoned the lawyers to the courtroom and read them the note.

Clinton looked as cocky as a bridegroom on his wedding night, but not Abe Priest. Priest looked like the all-pro quarterback who had been benched for the championship game. Moore and Featherstone were stone-faced.

"Your Honor," began the corporate-merger lawyer in his sonorous baritone, "I submit the court has no alternative but to discharge the jury and declare a mistrial. It is obvious that your most recent instruction has had no effect. These conscientious jurors have now been deliberating four full days, and no purpose is served by keeping them from their families a minute longer."

"What is the government's position?" Smith asked. "The jurors clearly feel their deadlock is hopeless."

"The government position is that four days is not unduly long, given the number of defendants, the seriousness of the charges, the length of the trial, and the complexity of the case," Moore replied. "The government suggests that the jury be required to deliberate another twenty-four hours."

"Your Honor, the defendants object most strenuously. That's simply unconscionable. It smacks of – "

"Mr. Clinton," snapped Smith, "no lectures on what's unconscionable. It's now twelve-thirty. If the jury has not reached a verdict by seven this evening, then I shall declare a mistrial. The Court stands in recess."

* * *

A half-hour after the Court adjourned, Anna D'Amico saw the two men on the sidewalk watching through the window as she picked up her dry cleaning. She was now almost as bothered by her husband's persistence that she not notify the police as she was by the men's obvious efforts to intimidate her. But her husband could be a hard man, and she was not about to disobey him. With the clothes over her arm, she walked firmly from the shop without glancing at the men.

When she reached her home in Biddeford, the town just north of Kennebunkport, the men were not in sight. At 4:00 p.m., Anna bundled herself against the cold, stepped from her front door, and walked the half-block to Route 1. She crossed the highway, turned right, and walked another fifty yards to a school bus stop, where she would be able to see the school bus come down Route 1 to drop her daughter, Rosita. Within five minutes, she saw the stubby, yellow bus round the bend some one hundred yards to the south and come toward her, its yellow caution lights blinking and its signal arm flopping up for the coming stop.

Then she saw the two men. Their faces already etched in her mind, she recognized them at once through the windshield of an oncoming Ford Thunderbird that was gradually gaining on the rear of the bus as it slowed. When the bus reached a full stop, the driver hit the lever to open the door in the right front of the bus for Anna's daughter to alight. Anna, with the Thunderbird – now stopped several car lengths behind the bus – still in her vision, stepped forward and took Rosita's hand as the girl stepped down.

Anna and Rosita, walking hand in hand and looking neither right nor left, retraced the steps Anna had taken in coming to the bus stop. Recrossing Route 1, Anna could see to her left that the car was still stopped on the northbound shoulder of the highway, the men standing by their open car doors, apparently talking across the car. She saw the men reenter the car and the car start. Quickening her pace, she held fast to Rosita's hand.

Fumbling with her keys, Anna unlocked and opened her front door as she saw the car come around the corner from Route 1. She pushed Rosita ahead of her, closed the door, quickly turned the deadbolt, and leaned her forehead against the inside of the door.

"Mom, what's the matter?"

"Nothing. I came up the steps too fast. I'm just a little dizzy."

Anna went to the front window and looked out. She saw the Thunderbird pull past the house and stop a car length beyond their driveway. The car doors opened and the men got out. Anna felt her knees buckle.

Across the street, a camera recorded the scene from the second floor of a vacant house. The agent thumbed a walkie-talkie. "I have it. Move in." On the next street, an agent acknowledged the message.

As soon as Lumbardino saw the curtain in the front window fall back in place, he gestured Gambini into the car and they slowly drove to the end of the block and took a left. Another car was coming toward them. Suddenly, Lumbardino hit the brakes as he saw the other car make a half U-turn, blocking the street. He shifted to reverse and slammed the accelerator to the floor. The tires screeched and smoked. "Sonofabitch!" Gambini yelled.

Before Lumbardino could reach the intersection he had just come from, he could see in his rear view mirror a second FBI car turning left from Anna D'Amico's street to block any escape in that direction. The doors of the second bureau car opened, spilling out special agents with riot guns at the ready. FBI special agents from the first car were now walking toward Lumbardino and Gambini with drawn machine pistols.

By time the agents from the second car reached the men, Lumbardino and Gambini had their legs spread and their hands on the roof of their car. Vince Inserra watched as they were patted down, disarmed, and handcuffed. The tension now eased, he allowed himself a rare smile.

"Well, well, look what the cat dragged in. Carlo and Carmine, as I live and breathe. Leaning on women and kids no less. You should've quit last January when you were ahead. Hey, Carlo, tell Carmine he smells like a piece of shit."

* * *

Anna was still trembling. But her fear was now crowded by growing anger. These men were not going to terrorize her again! She no longer cared what her husband thought. She would call the police. As she reached for the phone, there was a knock on the front door. Looking out the side window, she breathed a sigh of relief. It wasn't the two men. She opened the door.

"Mrs. D'Amico, we're special agents of the Federal Bureau of Investigation. We'd like to talk to you and your daughter."

* * *

At the same time the agents were displaying their credentials to Anna, Judge Smith, at his desk in chambers, was reading another message from the jurors. They had given up even the pretense of deliberating. He frowned and shuffled the papers on his desk, got up, paced, looked at his watch. *No sense prolonging this,* he decided. Returning to his desk, he buzzed his law clerk. "Round up the lawyers and the defendants. I'm going to discharge the jury."

The news spread. By the time the lawyers and defendants were assembled, the courtroom was packed to overflowing. The corridor outside was crammed with special lighting and TV camera crews. In a matter of minutes, the United States Government, having won all the legal battles in the case, would lose the war.

Patsy Magaddino was the last defendant to take his seat. He had been on the phone with Tony Rosato. Rosato had been trying to reach Lumbardino and Gambini to tell them to pack it in and go back to New York.

Judge Smith took his place on the bench and looked at Angela Featherstone. "Where is Mr. Moore?"

"He should be here in moment, Your Honor."

A minute later, Moore, visibly exhausted, entered the courtroom and walked to the bench, motioning defense counsel to join him. The trial and the long wait on the jury had taken its toll on Moore, and Smith noticed.

"Mr. Moore, you don't look well."

"Just bushed, Your Honor. Nothing a good night's sleep won't cure."

"Well, this won't take long. I've received another message from the jury telling me it's hopeless. I see no reason to hold them until seven. Does the government wish to be heard?"

"Yes, Judge, but the matter we would raise is better heard in chambers."

"Very well."

"Your Honor, I don't know what might better be heard in chambers at this point," Clinton objected. Abe Priest seized Clinton's elbow and tried to whisper that there was nothing to lose, but Clinton ignored him. It was obvious to Clinton that Moore must have something he didn't want the media to hear. "I think we all have a distaste for star-chamber proceedings."

Smith shot an irritated look in Clinton's direction. "Mr. Moore, it seems counsel thinks you're trying to hide something again."

"Far from it, Your Honor. We'll do it in open court, if that's what Mr. Clinton wants." Moore nodded to Featherstone as he returned to the counsel table. She walked briskly to the corridor and returned with Vince Inserra, Tom Goden, and Mike Magruder.

"Judge," Moore began, "you know Mr. Inserra and Chief Goden. The third gentleman is Sergeant Magruder of the Kennebunkport Police Department. A little over an hour ago, special agents of the Federal Bureau of Investigation arrested Carlo Lumbardino and Carmine Gambini. The reason for these arrests and the events leading up to them are matters which the government believes are appropriate for the Court to hear."

Judge Smith sat back quietly until the howls of objection had subsided. Priest leaned over to Clinton. "Who are those guys?"

Vito Scalia stuck his face in Priest's and hissed, "Forget it, counselor, they're too late. The jury is deadlocked and there's nothing anyone can do about it."

Smith leaned forward in his high-backed chair. "You may proceed, Mr. Moore, on your assurance this is relevant to these proceedings."

"We believe it is, Your Honor." An expectant hush fell over the courtroom.

Tom described his first encounter with Lumbardino and Gambini in Dock Square and their known association with Tony Rosato, one of the guests at the wedding reception. Magruder followed with a description of the L.L. Bean incident. Then Inserra spread the recently taken photographs along the rail of the vacant jury box. Smith left the bench to look. Inserra explained the pictures, pointing in some to the circled woman and her daughter. "These last ones were taken just before the arrests," Inserra concluded.

Moore knew how to build story and suspense. Not once did the judge ask for the woman's name. Nor did anyone else. After the blood returned to his face, Clinton had adopted a we-couldn't-care-less-because-it-doesn't-involve-the-defendants demeanor. Priest, now cut out of the loop, was again the only defense attorney who sensed what was coming.

The judge returned to the bench. Moore rose from his chair and approached the podium. "Your Honor, I would now ask that we adjourn to chambers."

"Yes," Smith replied, "I think it's time we did." The court reporter, the lawyers, and the defendants followed the judge from the courtroom. His law clerk scurried for extra chairs.

* * *

"All right," Smith said to Moore, "what's this all about? Who is the woman, and how does all this relate to these proceedings?"

"One moment." Moore went to the door to the judge's chambers and opened it. Special agents Roberts and Timothy were standing with an attractive, slender brunette. Despite the warmth of the small reception area, the woman had her heavy winter coat buttoned and was shivering. She clutched her handbag under her arm and held her daughter's hand tightly.

Moore spoke a few words of encouragement and led the two into chambers. "Your Honor," he said in a low voice, "this is Anna D'Amico and her daughter, Rosita. Mrs. D'Amico is the wife of Paul D'Amico, the number-twelve juror. She has something to tell you."

Anna was halting at first, but Judge Smith had a special way with frightened witnesses. Soon, she was pouring out her story, telling of her intimidation at the hands of Lumbardino and Gambini, how they had accosted her daughter, her nightly reports to her husband, and his instructions to say nothing.

When Anna was done, Patsy Magaddino's lawyer jumped to his feet, flashing his plastic smile. George Nickerson was a broad-shouldered, slightly florid, middle-aged slasher, handsome enough to fool an occasional female juror. He had no Italian blood, but loved the food. He loved the rich monthly retainers even more. Nickerson was a former Assistant United States Attorney who early on in private practice had allowed himself to be corrupted by mob money and women.

"Judge," he began, "I don't know what Mr. Moore is trying to do, but one thing is clear. If the jury wasn't about to be discharged, Mrs. D'Amico would have told her husband when he called that she had been questioned by FBI agents. Regardless of the government's good intentions, such activity constitutes official intrusion into the privacy of the jury. This entire proceeding is tainted."

"Mr. Moore, what charges have been brought against Lumbardino and Gambini?" Judge Smith asked.

"Your Honor, they have been charged with attempting to corruptly influence and intimidate a juror in violation of Section 1503 of Title 18, and of conspiring to do so."

"Does the government have any information implicating the defendants?"

"No, Your Honor. Of course, they stand to benefit – not that that is relevant in and of itself."

"You know it isn't. Does Mr. D'Amico know Lumbardino and Gambini?"

"We don't know. However, he is a nephew of Mr. Rosato, their employer."

Nickerson's face turned crimson. "Your Honor, it's time to bring this farce to an end. We were summoned here because the jury was to be discharged. Nothing has changed. This is simply a grandstand play by Mr. Moore. Other than buying time and getting himself a lot of publicity, I can't imagine what else he thinks he can accomplish. But whatever it is, it can wait until the jury is discharged and a mistrial declared."

"I was about to ask him that," said Smith. "Mr. Moore, would you care to enlighten us?"

Moore steeled himself against a growing feeling of desperation. It was time to play his trump card, but it was a low one because there was nothing to implicate the defendants in what everyone must now guess to be a clear case of jury tampering. "Yes, Your Honor," Moore began, "the government requests . . ."

CHAPTER 36

By 6:45 p.m., many of the spectators had decided that the fireworks were over and had left. The hard-core afficeonados and media stayed for the anticlimactic dismissal of the jury. They were milling around the courtroom, impatiently awaiting Judge Smith's appearance. Lawyers from both sides made aimless small talk. Scalia, Buffalino, and Magaddino were attending Don Salvatore. Like good soldiers, Inciso, Ferraro, and Palazzi formed their own group.

Suddenly, there was commotion in the corridor. Vito Scalia nodded to Maury Clinton to investigate. He returned promptly, beaming like he'd won the lottery. "The hospital has released a bulletin that Silento died an hour ago. This time it's for real."

Mafia protocol was forgotten for the moment as the defendants embraced each other indiscriminately. Featherstone turned to her boss. "Hang tough," was all she could think to say.

In the corridor outside the courtroom, the "veteran observers" were being interviewed by the media. "Does this mean the government won't be able to retry the case?"

"Absolutely! In fifteen minutes, the defendants walk for good."

$$* * *$$

Judge Jack Smith was at bottom a pragmatist. He had grown up in a mill town outside Lewiston, Maine. He had three brothers and a sister. His father was a skilled cabinet maker who could always put food on the table, but not much more. Jack clawed his way to college and law degrees by working two different jobs six nights a week. When he passed the state bar, he was looking for one thing. Money!

Jack spent months and what little cash he had sending resumes around the country, but the big law firms weren't interested. He was a quick study, but his grades didn't show it. He was moderately handsome, but slightly roly-poly. He certainly didn't cut the urbane figure the power partners in the corner offices associated with a potential rainmaker. Forget the big firms; even the small ones weren't interested. So he hung out his own shingle, and began frequenting the state and federal courthouses hustling criminal defendants. Unlike personal injury work, criminal defense meant cash on the barrel-head, up-front money.

He might have gone the way of George Nickerson, mob in-house counsel, but he never had the opportunity, at least not until his practice was booming. By then he could afford to pick and choose his cases, winning or losing – but mostly winning – on ability and nothing else. He had accepted appointment to the federal bench for two reasons. He could afford it, and seeing good trial lawyers at work from a different perspective promised an interesting and relaxed change of pace.

So much for the pragmatist. Jack Smith had not become so hardened that he wasn't deeply bothered by what had unfolded in his courtroom over the past weeks. The defendants were animals. He had relished watching the government lawyers skillfully herd them toward their waiting cages.

He first sensed trouble when the defendants rested without a defense. Now he knew why. He could smell their jury tampering. Hell, the stench made Abe Priest ready to run and hide. But as judge he felt powerless to do anything. In the absence of hard, court-worthy evidence to the contrary, his judicial conscience dictated that the defendants were presumed innocent of the tampering. He didn't believe they were, but what other choice did he have? And no words had ever passed between the goons and Anna D'Amico or her daughter. The pressure had been highly professional – it could be viewed as much a product of the D'Amicos' imaginings as anything their two tormentors had said or done. Now Silento was dead and in five minutes he would declare a mistrial, the functional equivalent of setting the animals free.

He gave up his pacing and sat again in his high-backed chair at the old desk from his former office. He opened a Supreme Court reporter to the Berger case and began fashioning its words to fit the case at hand. He acutely felt the weight of his judicial role. He would not deviate from what he perceived to be the letter of the law, however the result might offend his personal sense of justice. It was as much his duty to refrain from an improper ruling calculated to produce a conviction as it was to allow every legitimate means to obtain one.

He looked at his watch. It was almost 7:00 p.m. With a sigh, he rose from his desk and walked to the coat rack for his black robe. Then the phone rang.

It was the marshal. He listened for a moment. "Yes, it's O.K. Use the judges' elevator."

Two minutes later there was a soft knock on the door. Judge Smith opened it, and Sarah Goden stepped into his chambers. Her smile was hesitant, but she extended a tentative hand. Smith smiled warmly. "Sarah, it's so good to see you."

She ran a hand over her hair, adjusted her glasses a fraction, and then squared her shoulders. "Hello, Your Honor, sorry to bother you. I have no choice."

"Can this hold for a few minutes? I have an unpleasant job waiting in the courtroom. I'm about to discharge the jury in the Scalia case and declare a mistrial." His smile was gone.

"I heard that. It's why I'm here. There's something I need to tell you."

* * *

"All rise," the clerk intoned. "The United States District Court for the District of Maine is now in session, the Honorable Jack Smith presiding. United States v. Vito Scalia et al., for further proceedings." It was 7:30 p.m.

Smith stood for a moment at the bench, surveying the courtroom. It was packed again. Holding a statute book he had brought from chambers, he carefully arranged his robe as he took his seat. He opened the book and placed it at his elbow. For a full minute, there was dead silence. People began to squirm. Finally, Maury Clinton rose.

"May I respectfully remind Your Honor that we are now thirty minutes past the designated time for discharging the jury."

"You have just done so."

Clinton sat down, frowning, and the silence continued. In a moment, Priest passed him a note: "I think you'd better get ready to strap on the asphalt, assuming there's enough in Portland to cover your ass."

Clinton shot to his feet. "Surely, Your Honor is not seriously considering Mr. Moore's outlandish motion."

"I have considered it." Judge Smith removed a single sheet of paper from his notebook. Glancing at the hurried reminder notes he had scribbled, he continued.

"The jury has had the case for five days. Despite having received a supplemental instruction that it has the duty to decide this case if it can conscientiously do so, the jury has repeatedly advised the Court that it is hopelessly deadlocked. Indeed, it has ceased its deliberations because they have become fruitless. Accordingly, it would seem that the Court has no alternative but to discharge the jury and declare a mistrial."

Newspaper reporters eased toward the courtroom doors for the dash to the phones. Clinton crunched Priest's note into a ball and tossed it toward him. Moore and Featherstone began collecting their loose papers.

"However – "

The single adverb hung in the air, freezing all motion.

"– the government has directed my attention to a little-known and rarely used provision of law. Insofar as applicable here, Rule 23(b) of the Federal Rules of Criminal Procedure provides, and I quote:

"Juries shall be of 12 but at any time before verdict the parties may stipulate in writing with the approval of the court that the jury shall consist of any number less than 12 or that a valid verdict may be returned by a jury of less than 12 should the court find it necessary to excuse one or more jurors for any just cause after trial commences. Even absent such stipulation, if the court finds it necessary to excuse a juror for just cause after the jury has retired to consider its verdict, in the discretion of the court a valid verdict may be returned by the remaining 11 jurors.

"The government contends that just cause now exists to excuse one of the jurors in this case. It also contends that I should exercise my discretion and direct the remaining eleven jurors to resume their deliberations and to allow them, if they can, to return a unanimous verdict."

"Judge," George Nickerson bellowed, "this is a sterile exercise. It's worse than that. For this court to accede to the government's request would make a mockery of my client's right to a trial by a jury of twelve. You heard Mr. Moore admit there's not a scintilla of evidence connecting the defendants to the unfortunate improprieties involving Mrs. D'Amico. That's point one. Point two is that the juror is not incapacitated or ill. That is the only cause that would justify excusing him."

"Mr. Nickerson, lower your voice and stop waiving your arms," Smith ordered. "This is a courtroom, not a saloon. Now – "

Clinton was on his feet, cutting the judge short. As he carried on the argument, Vito Scalia seized Priest by the arm. "Get up and say something, for Christ's sake."

Priest shook him off and leaned into his face. "Be quiet! You probably already had D'Amico wired. The pressure on his wife was unnecessary. I warned you from the start to lay off the jurors. Vito, you've sent your last message and smoked your last victim."

Judge Smith allowed Clinton's interruption and let him finish. Then he glanced again at his notes. "Now, as I was about to say, Mr. Nickerson's second point is misplaced. The incapacity of a juror need not be physical. It can result from the imposition of outside forces which could reasonably be expected to interfere with his ability to render a just verdict. I am persuaded that this has happened here."

The judge fixed on Magaddino's lawyer. "The first point raised by Mr. Nickerson is more bothersome. On the record before me, I must find that the defendants, and each of them, lack knowledge and bear no responsibility for the so-called improprieties which have occurred. But again, this is not determinative of the motion. In a criminal case, the United States, no less than the defendants, is entitled to have each juror give fair and impartial consideration to the evidence free of the taint of corruption. When the government has been deprived of this right – as I find it has been here – the issue is not one of blame. The issue is whether Congress has provided a remedy short of a mistrial. Plainly, it has in Rule 23(b).

"Judge Smith drew another breath and concluded. "I do not know whether the number-twelve juror has in fact been influenced in his deliberations by the attempted intimidation of his wife and daughter. Nor do I know whether he is responsible for the deadlock. In my view, these are extraneous questions. The only issue remaining is whether I should exercise my discretion in the manner requested by the government. I have decided to do so. The number-twelve juror will be excused, and the jury will be instructed to resume its deliberations."

* * *

At 9:00 p.m., December 16, 1992, the remaining eleven jurors filed into the courtroom and took their seats in the jury box.

"Have you reached a verdict?" Judge Smith asked.

The jury foreman rose. "We have, your honor."

"Please pass it to the clerk." The clerk took the verdict and handed it to Smith. He studied it impassively and handed it back. "The clerk will read the verdicts."

"On count one of the indictment – the Anti-Arson Act – we the jury find the defendants Vito Scalia, Gabriel Buffalino, Salvatore Natale Scalia, and Carmine Palazzi guilty as charged.

"On count two of the indictment – the Racketeer Influenced And Corrupt Organizations Act – we the jury find Vito Scalia, Gabriel Buffalino, Salvatore Natale Scalia, Carmine Palazzi, Angelo Inciso, and Sam Ferraro guilty as charged."

Patsy Magaddino breathed a mighty sigh of relief. The clerk, noticing, paused for a moment as if all the verdicts had been read. He then continued.

"On count three of the indictment – conspiracy – we the jury find Vito Scalia, Gabriel Buffalino, Salvatore Natale Scalia, Patrick Magaddino, Carmine Palazzi, Angelo Inciso, and Sam Ferraro guilty as charged."

Moore and Featherstone exchanged nods of relief. Then they turned toward the jurors to smile their thanks.

The TV crews were powering up. Their scoop lights bathed the back of the courtroom as the reporters tore through the swinging doors for their final dash to the phones.

Judge Smith watched the defendants' faces as they jawed at their lawyers. His face remained impassive while his mind's eye conjured the scene that would have followed had he granted a mistrial. For the rest of his life, he would probably regret that his decision to deny a mistrial had been prompted by the secret and extra-legal communication from Sarah Goden. Then he snapped from his reverie and savored the scene before him. He locked eyes with Vito Scalia and Gabriel Buffalino until they finally looked away. They were hearing what he was hearing – the clang of jail doors closing and the hiss of gas capsules in the center of an airtight chamber.

CHAPTER 37

Even before the defendants' sentencing, Justice Department appellate lawyers in Washington, D.C. picked apart the cold trial record. It was ivory-tower time. In this rarefied atmosphere, no one's name ended in a vowel, the Mafia made for good movies but nothing else, swarthy people with black hooded eyes lost their menace, and fair play was the order of the day. Common sense didn't disappear, but it wasn't allowed to interfere with twenty-twenty hindsight. These lawyers saw big trouble brewing in Appeal City.

The defendants had already jettisoned their trial lawyers in favor of the best appeal experts and brief writers money could buy. The Justice Department hierarchy decided that anything that would intensify appellate scrutiny should be avoided. For this reason, Page Moore was instructed not to seek the death penalty for the Scalias, Buffalino, or Palazzi on the Anti-Arson Act conviction. He was agreeable. They'd come so close to losing that he would be satisfied with any substantial prison time if the probability of affirmance on appeal would be enhanced.

On December 30th, Judge Smith sentenced the Scalias, Buffalino, and Palazzi to life imprisonment and a $20,000 fine for the bombing deaths of Neil Mintmire's wife and daughter. He sentenced all the defendants to twenty years and a $25,000 fine on each of the racketeering and conspiracy convictions – the maximum penalties. The sentences were to be served consecutively, rather than concurrently. He did not order property forfeiture because there was no evidence that any property had been obtained as the result of the murders which were the predicate acts of the racketeering activity.

Neil Mintmire and his daughter, Nancy, sat in the rear of the courtroom to witness the sentencing. With them was Priscilla Mills, holding her infant son, Loring. She hadn't lost her house because Mintmire's business was back up and running, and he had employed her at a generous salary. In front of them sat Tom Goden, Vince Inserra, Dick Hundley, Jerry Borghesani, Carl Tito, and Mike Magruder. It had been a good team. Sarah Goden was missing because she was in the middle of a trial. She would learn about the sentencing from Tom. Tricia Smythe and her daughter, Jan, would read about it in the *Chicago Tribune*.

Following the verdict, Rudy Briscoe dismissed the State of Maine indictment. The Attorney General advised the state judge that the death of Dominic Silento left no alternative. Vito Scalia and Gabriel Buffalino were again each free, pending a final decision on their appeals, on the $10,000,000 bail previously set.

On June 14, 1993, a divided panel of the United States Court of Appeals for the First Circuit, by a 2-1 vote, reversed all the convictions in United States v. Vito Scalia et al and ordered a new trial. The court's majority opinion borrowed freely from affidavits of news representatives who had interviewed jurors after their verdicts. A number of jurors said there had been two turning points in the trial. First, Silento's castration testimony had left them feeling he could be believed. Second, and even more decisive, was the government's dramatic production of the pictures and the recall of Silento to identify them. The pictures sank the defense Abe Priest had promised and confirmed Silento's credibility. They were the visible glue that held an otherwise weak case together. The prosecutors had outsmarted the defense. They had offered the bait and the defendants had grabbed it.

The majority opinion then found that the government, in its zeal to obtain a conviction, had deceived the defendants and interfered with their preparation of a defense in three fundamental ways. It had fabricated Silento's death; it had failed to disclose Silento's motive for testifying; and it had concealed the existence of the pictures. While no one of these factors, standing alone, would justify reversing the convictions, the opinion reasoned, in combination they displayed prosecutorial misconduct designed to obtain a conviction in a way unworthy of the government. This misconduct was aggravated by the brief but pointed reference during Hundley's testimony to the Mafia and organized crime.

The two-judge majority did not find that excusing the number-twelve juror, Paul D'Amico, was error. But the two judges were influenced in their decision to reverse the convictions by a startling disclosure made by two of the jurors. During most of the jury deliberations, the vote had been 10-2 for conviction. Then D'Amico suddenly changed his mind and voted to convict. Something his wife told him had apparently made him mad. When D'Amico was excused, the lone holdout had been a woman. Intense pressure from the other ten jurors finally persuaded her that, although the government might be engaged in a vendetta against Italians, these defendants were guilty as charged. At least that's what she said, but other of the jurors felt she was afraid that if she continued to hold out she too would be excused.

The third judge on the panel wrote a blistering dissent. He accused the majority of improperly making the rule of full pre-trial disclosure in civil cases applicable to criminal cases, of wrongly penalizing the prosecutors for simply outwitting their opponents, and for naively turning criminal trials into a game in which the accused held all the high cards. This played very well in the press.

The Justice Department petitioned for a rehearing before the full Court of Appeals, and the petition was granted on July 1st. On September 13th, the full court voted 4-3 to reverse the panel decision and to reinstate the convictions, other than the conviction of Salvatore Scalia. The court found that evidence of his statement at the time of his arrest in Sicily had been improperly admitted because the arresting officers had failed to read him his rights under the Constitution of the United States.

On December 16, 1993, the United States Supreme Court, in another split decision, declined to review the case. The judgments of conviction, by the margin of a single vote, became final one year to the day after Dominic Silento's death.

* * *

The day after the jury verdict, Mafia lawyers had begun identifying those countries that had no extradition treaties with the United States or, if they did, ignored them. Numbered bank accounts were opened, huge sums of money transferred, false passports and identities prepared, escape plans laid, and the right people bribed. No detail was left to chance.

Because the defendants were all free on bail, delicate timing was required. There was a better than even chance that the Supreme Court would review and overturn the convictions. That was the preliminary sounding and the most desired result. And if the defendants won, they didn't want to be on the run. If they were, they would lose the fruits of their victory and face the alternatives of either going to jail for jumping bail or remaining fugitives. On the other hand, if the Supreme Court denied review, and they wanted to flee, it was vital that all defendants slip their traces at precisely the same time. If one defendant jumped early, bail for the other defendants would be revoked.

Vito Scalia, Gabriel Buffalino, and Patsy Magaddino were each assigned a separate Mafia team. A fourth team would handle Inciso, Ferraro, and Palazzi. Spouses had the option of following at their leisure.

* * *

No one learns in advance how the United States Supreme Court will decide a case. Until they are publicly released, the decisions are guarded like nuclear secrets. On Friday, December 10th, a law clerk to one of the Supreme Court justices made the telephone call for which she had been paid $100,000. The justices planned to announce their decision in the Scalia case on Thursday, December 16, at 10:00 a.m. It would not be favorable to the defendants.

The final countdown began. The word was passed among the defendants that they would violate the conditions of their bonds and become fugitives on Tuesday, December 14th, at 8:00 p.m. Eastern time, two days prior to announcement of the decision.

* * *

The conditions of Vito Scalia's bail virtually confined him to his home. He was allowed to travel only within Kennebunkport under the supervision of the U.S. Marshall Service and the FBI. Similar restrictions were imposed on Buffalino, Magaddino, Inciso, and Ferraro. Palazzi was confined to the Sonesta Hotel in Portland.

Since December 1991, the UPS truck serving Kennebunkport had made regular stops at the Scalia residence. The stops were a daily occurrence during the Christmas season. The Scalias were big at gift-giving, and the same UPS driver had been on their route since they moved in. Bobby McGarrity liked the Scalias. Maria, or Vito when he was home, always had a cup of coffee and a big tip waiting. Things didn't change after the convictions, except now only Vito was around. Vito was affable and unpretentious, and Bobby began to wonder if he could believe everything he'd read in the papers.

The jovial Irishman didn't smoke, cheat on his wife, or drink heavily. But he gambled on everything from the horses to local elections. Around Thanksgiving, he was reminded by his South Portland bookie that he owed over $25,000 in accumulated losses. It was pay up within a week or get fitted for a new pair of kneecaps. It seemed the most natural thing in the world to confide in Vito. The deadline came and went and Bobby wasn't limping. A miracle!

* * *

On Monday, December 13, 1993, the day before the defendants' scheduled jump, Bobby made the Scalia house his first stop. He had four packages, one of them a priority from Vito's office. As he turned into the Scalia driveway, he slowed to be sure that the two FBI agents – one in the guardhouse and one in a parked car – recognized him. Getting their wave of recognition, he drove through and up the winding driveway to the house. To his left he could see the blue of the ocean with a lone patrol boat lying at anchor offshore from the Scalia estate. It had been lying there since Vito Scalia's return on bail. Bobby pulled up at the front entrance, jumped from his truck, and sounded the chimes. Vito opened the door.

Five minutes later, he pulled to a stop at the guardhouse on his way out. "Mind if I have a look in back, Bobby?" the special agent asked.

"Help yourself." He stepped from the truck and walked to the FBI car to shoot the breeze with the other agent.

The first agent entered the truck and slid back the door next to the driver's seat. He entered the cargo area, moved some parcels around, and hesitated. Then he moved more parcels. Satisfied, he left the truck and motioned to Bobby.

"You're early today."

"Yeah, there was a priority overnight package for Mr. Scalia. I usually try to deliver those first thing. See you tomorrow."

Bobby edged from the driveway and turned right onto Ocean Avenue. Ten minutes later he was at his first stop in Dock Square. He slid open the cargo door and began rearranging three rows of parcels stacked floor to ceiling. Vito Scalia was curled in a ball inside a large empty cardboard carton in the back corner of the truck.

"There you go, Mr. Scalia, thanks for everything."

"You stay cool, Bobby. Here's your bonus."

Bobby took the envelope containing fifty $1,000 bills and put it inside a larger one addressed to him at his new post office box. He walked across the street and dropped it in the mail box. Vito was gone when he returned. He broke down the empty carton and put it in a nearby dumpster.

* * *

While Bobby was mailing his bonus, the special agent with whom he had been shooting the breeze back at the Scalia estate left his car and walked to the guardhouse.

"Did Bobby seem nervous to you?" he asked his partner.

"No, why?"

"I don't know. Something doesn't feel right. Call the house."

* * *

When Vito stepped from the UPS truck, a car pulled up behind it. He jumped inside and the car drove slowly across the tiny bridge over the Kennebunk River into Kennebunk. As it did, Tom Goden parked in his police space in front of the UPS truck and walked across the street to Allison's Restaurant for his usual coffee and an English muffin. He was inside looking out the window when an FBI car sped into the square, two agents spilled out, and the two accosted the UPS driver. Bobby shrugged, his palms extended. "Beats the shit out of me," he said, "Mr. Scalia was sure there when I left."

* * *

By 1:00 p.m., the other defendants were being taken into custody, and bail-forfeiture proceedings were underway. Vito's unlawful flight to avoid imprisonment had triggered a conclusive legal presumption that his co-defendants would do the same.

Maria Scalia was with her brother at his Manhattan brownstone when the FBI special agents arrived. This was now the second time she had watched Gabriel being handcuffed. She took a cab to the federal courthouse in Foley Square to attend the bail-forfeiture hearing.

The hearing was brief. The marshals replaced Gabriel Buffalino's handcuffs and began escorting him from the courtroom. In the past fourteen months, his black hair had picked up more silver. His face was drawn, but still movie-star handsome like Vito's.

Maria knew Gabriel would have no special privileges in a maximum-security federal penitentiary. There was no class system favoring Mafia chieftains. He could even be raped and sodomized by the stronger animals – inmates like Palazzi, Inciso, and Ferraro.

As he walked between two deputy marshals toward the side door from the courtroom, Gabriel saw his sister standing in the spectator section. He squared his shoulders, held up his manacled hands, and fashioned a smile. Maria wiped her eyes and ran to him. Embracing her brother, she felt the cold steel of the manacles press into her stomach. Before the deputy marshals could separate them she was able to whisper, "Gabriel, you will be back, and I will be waiting." The officers pulled the two apart and pushed Gabriel through the door and into the prisoner elevator.

His sister's words, intended to console, served but to sharpen Gabriel's sense of separation from his family, from past pleasure, from all that he had hoped for his future. Come back? Could he come back to scrounge for fragments of a happy past and hope to weld them into new life? Dominic Silento had not come back. Vito, for all his flash and flare, would not come back to what he'd lost. Even the don, though free, would lack the strength. And he, Gabriel, carried far more than they. He knew what they did not. As the elevator slowly descended, Gabriel's mind was propelled back to Monreale and Don Salvatore's summer-ending festa years ago. Why had he let his temper overwhelm his judgment? Why had he let stupid pride submerge compassion?

Scenes flashed through his mind as from a rapidly turning kaleidoscope. There was Maria – dancing, twirling, mocking, enticing – using every guile to arouse and lead Vito on. His own sister playing the role of a vulgar tavern wench! And her conquest? Gabriel's own best friend. Even now, Gabriel's face flushed as he envisioned the two slipping out the door hand-in-hand.

Now, as then, he tried to tell himself that what Vito and Maria did was their business, not his. Now, as then, he told himself it was not really a matter of family honor. But now, as then, he remained torn and uncertain.

And now, as then, his hands clenched in anger at the scene – the searing, painful scene – of Dominic returning to the ballroom and joking – laughing – with his loutish friends while lewdly stroking his private parts.

Even after all these years, Gabriel felt the burning shame and anger that drove him to search out his sister in the villa that night. He found her alone in the guest room that the don had set aside for her, sitting on the bed, her feet tucked beneath her, tears streaming down her face.

"So there you are, hiding! No twirling and laughing now? And where's lover boy? He's got what he wanted and back dancing with some other slut! And our friends are laughing! Everyone's laughing!"

Gabriel could feel even now his own exhaustion as, his fury spent, he sank to a seat on the edge of the bed. Through it all, Maria had sat motionless, her eyes on his, tears streaming. Finally, she spoke.

"Gabriel, it is not what you think. I love Vito."

Now, as then, tears came to Gabriel's own eyes, and he would now, as then, have embraced his sister were he able. But his fury now did not turn, as then, to Dominic. It turned on himself.

It consoled Gabriel little that he had never intended to visit upon Dominic the injury and shame that had been inflicted. He did not tell Vito, just as he had not told Maria, of what he knew to have been Dominic's role. The retribution was solely his, and he told no one. But, until Dominic testified in open court, he did not know the horrible form it had taken.

To keep it from the family, he had hired two mercenarii from the mainland to carry his message to Dominic. When they had asked what it should be, his rage had seized him.

"You should know what to do! Why am I paying you? Do you not understand a family's honor?" And so he had left it in their hands. Or had he? Had he said something about testicali? But if he said it, they knew he couldn't mean that! They knew Dominic was his friend.

The elevator door opened to a grey wall.

"O.K., to your right and through that door," said the marshal. The door clanged behind him.

CHAPTER 38

When Vito walked into the Cayman Islands Savings and Trust, he looked like a typical American tourist – thong sandals, Bermuda shorts, gaudy sport shirt, dark glasses, straw hat with a headband proclaiming "Bermuda Triangle."

Vito strode directly to the window of the chief teller.

"I wish to make a withdrawal from my account. Victor Sullivan." Vito handed his account card to the teller.

"Of course, Mr. Sullivan. Please fill out this form and I'll give it to the vice president for his approval."

Vito filled out the form for a $500,000 withdrawal. The teller accepted the form, took it to the vice president, and returned to the window.

"It will take an hour to process your application. Would you like to wait or would you prefer coming back?"

"I'll wait."

Vito sat down in one of several deep leather chairs in the public section of the bank. As customers came in and out, he became increasingly uneasy. After twenty minutes he left.

Ten minutes later, a limousine pulled in front of the bank and discharged four men. The driver stayed behind the wheel, motor running. Two of the men entered the bank while the other two waited outside, one on either side of the door. The two men inside spoke briefly to the teller who had served Vito and then rejoined the two outside. All four re-entered the limousine, which slowly drove off.

* * *

It was the second harvest season since Don Salvatore had escaped the criminal charges that returned his co-defendants to custody for sentencing. Again, he sat on his balcony in Monreale watching preparations below for the fall festa. Guido, the old gardener, father of Silento, had died, his duties now assumed by a nephew, Donatello.

The don seemed shrunken from his former self. A woolen scarf around

231

his shoulders despite the warmth of the high sun on a crystal day, he rarely spoke out or acknowledged the occasional waive directed to him by those bustling about below. Donatello came in and out of the garden, carrying fresh flowers — roses, chrysanthenums, hibiscus, gladioli — into the house.

Donatello appeared at the glass door to the balcony.

"Don Salvatore, I have an envelope for you that a visitor has left. He is waiting to see if you have a response." Don Salvatore took the envelope, opened it, and slowly read the handwriting on a single sheet.

Honored Don:

I must see you. No one will recognize me.

V.

"I will see him. Bring him to me."

Donatello returned leading a heavily bearded man, unkempt hair potruding from a black peasant's cap, clothed as though for work in the fields. The don waived Donatello away.

"Sit down, my son."

"You know me?"

"I have been waiting for you."

"How are Maria and Camilla?"

"They are well. Maria is here for the festa. Camilla is expecting her first child, your first grandchild. She is home."

"I ache to see them. But it is impossible. You know that both the police and the family are looking for me?"

"I know. The police may never find you, but I expect the family will."

"You will not betray me?"

"Betray my only grandson? No. But someday you will betray yourself. You will finally despair of a life without money, without family, without friends, without work that means anything to you. And you will start taking more risks, like the one you are taking today. That is what will betray you."

"Grandfather, will you call the family off?"

"I cannot. I no longer control the family. They defer to me from respect and affection, but I no longer control any part of their lives they do not want controlled. No one can turn them from pursuing you. But even if I could, I would not turn them now. You chose your path. I should have seen how you were going and stopped you while I could. Now it is too late."

The don beckoned Donatello to return to the balcony, and he quickly appeared behind the glass door.

"Goodby, my son. No one will know that you have been here."

When Donatello and Vito reached the front gate of the estate, Donatello asked if Vito was being picked up.

"No, I'm walking."

"Where are you headed?"

"Palermo."

Three days later, the *Palermo Il Giorno* reported that the body of an unidentified man had been found in a ditch along the highway about three kilometers east of Monreale. The man, middle-aged, was dressed as a common laborer. A small amount of currency was found in his clothing, but no identification. He had been garroted. The report of the police pathologist noted that his testicles had been removed before he died.

* * *

Tom Goden looked up from the Sunday paper. "Hey, Doll, there's an article about Jack Smith. Did you know he's considering quitting the bench and going back to private practice?"

"Yes, he told me over a drink last week."

"That's bad news for prosecutors. Do you think he'll do it?"

"I know he will. He said so."

"Since when did you become so tight with the judge?"

"Years ago, honey. I met Jack in New York. We were both representing defendants in the same trial. We got to dating and he asked me to marry him. I would have, if you hadn't come along."

"Why didn't you ever tell me?" Tom asked.

"Oh, I don't know, I guess it never seemed like something that would interest you."